. . . in a strange land

CH00606272

With best wishes.
Mary Bolster

Mary Bolster

**Foreword by
Baroness Caroline Cox
of Queensbury**

Pymme's Publications

. . . in a strange land
First published in the United Kingdom in 2005 by Pymmes
Publications.

ISBN 978 0 955 113604

Written by Mary Bolster

A catalogue record of this book is available from the British
Library.

Cover Photograph by James Laurie

Map: The Karenni Provisional Government

Printed by The Alpha Xperience, Newbury, Berkshire.
RG14 5RG

Pymme's Publications, 2, Windmill Road, Edmonton,
London N18 1PA

Acknowledgements

I would like to express my sincere gratitude to Jenny Kyriacou for her thorough and accurate work in editing the text of this novel. Her support and encouragement have meant a great deal to me and I could not have completed the preparation of the text without her.

Dr Sandra Dudley has carried out an extensive and in-depth anthropological research on the Karenni Refugees in Thailand for her D Phil Thesis. I want to thank her for allowing me to use the information she has gleaned in the sections on the *dicu* and *ka thow bow* festivals.

I have drawn inspiration from Caroline Cox and her tireless work for many suffering minorities in the world including those from Burma. She has taken a personal interest in the Karenni and has visited them many times. I want to thank her for her encouragement to me in writing a foreword.

In any of my visits to the Karen and Karenni people they have treated me with the utmost kindness and unbounded hospitality. I want them to know that I am forever grateful to them all.

Thank you to my former colleagues at the Luton and Dunstable Hospital for their advice on surgery, anaesthesia and the use of certain therapeutic drugs. Also a big thank you to my friends and family who have helped and encouraged and generally stood by me during the creation of the story. I especially want to mention Yeh Htoo, Mike Lowe, my daughter Suzie, my daughter-in-law Lucy and most important of all, my husband David.

Foreword

As a general rule, I can skim texts and distil the essence of a story quickly. But, as I started to read this one, I found myself increasingly unable to flick quickly through the pages. I became gripped by the story and was drawn deeper into this powerful, moving and evocative account of the suffering of the Karenni people.

Mary Bolster writes with such authoritative accuracy and compelling detail that I could not put the book down. Reading late into the night, I was drawn into the lives of the people whose experiences she depicts as their situation changes catastrophically. The early pages describe the relative tranquillity of traditional Karenni village life in a rural community. Then fear enters the scene, as soldiers of the ruling military junta, with the Orwellian name 'The State Law and Order Restoration Council', invade the area.

The author takes us alongside her characters as they endure the tribulations inflicted on them by soldiers: the killings of the villagers, the afflictions of those forced to serve as porters - and, for the girls, the additional sexual abuse. We then accompany those who felt they had to flee to Thailand in order to survive, being given glimpses into the ordeals of their journeys and the deprivations of life in the camps in a strange land, separated from their families back home.

We also meet some of the British volunteers who go to try to help the displaced Karenni people in the camps, sharing the challenges they experience in what is 'a strange land' for them and as they encounter the suffering of those around them.

Maybe it was because I was already aware of the enormity of this tragedy that I could appreciate the author's superbly authentic account of the anguish of the people, for I have visited them many times. We have the privilege of helping to support an orphanage for Karenni children and I have frequently wept as they describe what happened to them, their families and their villages back in their homeland. Sometimes they draw pictures of their memories of their earlier life in Karenni State, telling us in detail how soldiers attacked their villages, raped, tortured, killed their families, slaughtered their livestock, plundered their homes and destroyed their crops.

Some of the pictures painted by 'our' children are seared onto my heart: one shows soldiers beating her elderly grandparents and pregnant aunt as they struggle to carry impossibly heavy loads, another shows them attacking a school and shooting the children as they try to flee.

The catalogue of brutality seems endless and breaks our hearts every time we meet our Karenni friends, for the situation continues to deteriorate as more and more innocent civilians are being captured, and abused.

But that is not the whole picture. Despite the destruction of their homes, villages and traditional way of life; despite all the brutality inflicted upon them; despite the loss, in so many cases, of those nearest and dearest to them – sometimes murdered in cold blood in front of them – the Karenni people maintain great dignity, amazing resilience and generous hospitality. We always return humbled and inspired beyond words by their refusal to allow suffering to brutalise them and by their indomitable spirit of graciousness.

I can vouch for the authenticity of the kinds of situations described in this fictional account. By writing this book, Mary Bolster has brought to our attention in a powerfully readable form, the plight of so many of the people of Burma. I hope that the book will be widely read and that it will move each and every reader to do something to help to change this horrendous situation – before it is too late and the SPDC's genocidal policies have wrought irreversible destruction of a brave, gracious people and their historic, rich culture. We can no longer plead ignorance.

There is enough evidence now for the SPDC, to be brought to account for crimes against humanity. One problem is that many of those crimes have been perpetrated behind closed borders, out of sight.

Anyone who reads this book must feel profoundly moved. There is a saying: "Pity weeps and turns away; compassion weeps - and puts out a hand to help". I hope and pray that all readers who weep with and for the Karenni people described in this book will not turn away.

Caroline Cox,
House of Lords,
London.

MAP OF KARENNI STATE

1

Katie braced herself against the side of the truck as the driver negotiated the vehicle down the steepest incline she had ever seen used as a road. She heard some of the others laughing quietly behind and turned round to see Richard winking at her. "Wooow . . .Katie. What would this be like in the rain?" He said playfully.

"Oh don't." She smiled at him ruefully. "This is bad enough."

"It gets a lot worse than this, believe me," said David, "sometimes it's completely impassable."

Ever since the truck had left the road they had crouched down between the luggage so as to stop themselves being continually buffeted against the sides and the floor, and Katie herself was relatively comfortable. Of course the word relatively was an important one in this case. There were four of them in the back of the small pick up truck with the luggage and various gifts and supplies and the jungle track was generously pitted with ruts and potholes. It was far from comfortable, but Katie was so excited: she thought nothing of the discomfort and loved every minute of it.

When they had climbed down the airplane steps she had found the stifling midday heat almost overpowering but once they had left the town behind and were onto the open road the breeze had refreshed her.

Then they had turned off the main road and almost immediately their way had deteriorated to a rough track. The trees encroached on both sides, at times their leaves brushed along the sides of the truck. Sometimes long thick creepers hung right across the path and reached down between the passengers as they lurched along. Then the trees would part for a while revealing what she guessed to be paddy fields of an almost iridescent green with low, scrubby hills in the middle distance. Several times she spotted farm labourers in their pointed hats just like the ones she had seen in childhood books long ago and was reminded again of the strangeness of the whole adventure.

In many ways Katie felt that she was the one in the group who had the least to give. She had decided she wasn't clever enough to be a doctor. She could never hold the floor the way Richard obviously could. It was no surprise to her that he was planning to be a teacher. She was a nurse, just a nurse, she was inclined to say, but Sarah would have none of it. She had wanted her to come with them. "It's always fun to travel in a group," she had said "and you'll get such a lot out of it."

"But I'll have nothing to give. I don't think I can teach. What will you want me with you for?"

"They need people to help them with their English, you don't have to be a teacher, just let them talk with you so that they can practise. You might surprise yourself. And I would really like you to come with us."

So Katie had allowed herself to be persuaded into joining them and now here she was in the back of a truck being driven through the remote mountainous jungles of

Northern Thailand heading towards a refugee camp on the Burmese border. She turned again to look out of the front of the truck and her eyes widened in horror. They were heading straight for the river at the bottom of the steep slope and there seemed to be no way of avoiding it. Richard saw her consternation. "All right?" He asked as he put his arm around her shoulders just as the wheels of the truck entered the water. She nodded and laughed with relief as the vehicle continued across, making its way through the shallowest parts of the river and out onto the far bank. The engine revved hard and then they were off again, climbing the steep slope on the other side. This was to be repeated so many times that soon Katie took it all in her stride as, indeed, all the rest of the passengers seemed to be doing.

She was aware of Richard's hand and arm still resting on her shoulders and wondered briefly what it meant, but then decided he was just being kind. Or did he find her attractive? She couldn't imagine that he did. There was certainly nothing special about her as far as she could see with her plain dark hair cut short and her almost pure white skin. She had never imagined herself to be 'sexy' or even remotely attractive. Martine had been sexy, dancing on her own like that with the black blouse that showed off her figure to the best possible advantage. Declan hadn't been able to take his eyes off her. He hadn't just watched her the way all men will look at a pretty girl. No, there had been an intensity there that had signified pursuit, real pursuit. She still remembered how she had felt then even though months had passed. Suddenly she had seen, in that clarifying moment, that he would no longer be satisfied with her, that he was only using her to keep house for him until someone better came along. She had felt like a child and realised that that was how he had treated her.

When she had come home early from work a couple of weeks later and had found them together she hadn't been surprised. Shocked, yes, but not surprised. Deep down inside her she had known that the relationship was far from healthy. When she had first met him she had still been almost numb with grief after the death of her mother, even though it had happened a few years before and once he had shown an interest in her she had clung to him and come to depend on him for everything. She had moved in with him too easily and had been too willing to lie to her father. Declan had lied to his own parents too. Such had been her insecurity and need for human comfort that she had mistaken his attentions for love and had agreed to whatever he suggested. She still shuddered at the way she had trusted him and how he had betrayed that trust.

But that was the evening when she had recognised Sarah in Mac's bar and had first spoken to her. And that had been the evening that had set in motion the train of events that had brought her to this place. They worked together in the same department in the hospital and over the months that had followed Katie come to appreciate Sarah as a real friend in spite of the difference in their ages.

She realised that the truck was slowing down. The driver stopped to pick up some women who had been walking along the track. The women all climbed into the back of the truck, so having all moved around to accommodate them, the vehicle was now more crowded than ever. One of the women gave a wide smile that showed blackened teeth. Another had something inside her mouth that made her cheek bulge out hugely on one side while a drop of red-stained moisture oozed out between her lips. Katie felt her stomach churning with revulsion. David caught the expression on her face. "Betel nut. A lot of them chew it here." Katie forced a smile at the woman and was rewarded by another open mouth full of thick red matter. David put his hand out to the women and it was shaken by all three of them.

"Hello."

They all took their cue from him and so began a session of handshaking and laughter. "They're great hand shakers here," he told them. " So if you don't know what to do just shake hands and smile." His face crinkled with laughter. There was so much going on in the back of the truck now that Katie had failed to notice that they were in the river once again and that this time there were children playing in it.

"That means we're almost there," said David.

The truck climbed up on the far bank and drove between two wooden houses. The forest opened out and Katie could see that they were now surrounded by an assortment of wooden buildings. They had finally reached their destination.

Hauling themselves out of their cramped positions in the back of the truck they all clambered over the side and jumped down, glad to be motionless at last. It was now late afternoon and the dusty heat of midday

13

had begun to give way to slightly cooler air. Here in the village, that was in reality only a wide clearing in the forest, the air seemed somehow fresher and greener than that in the city, so although she was tired from the journey Katie already felt relief. In every direction she could see the tops of the surrounding hills still low enough to be entirely covered with trees, while nearer there were banana trees with their gigantic leaves seemingly growing beside most of the wooden houses. For a few moments she watched a groups of small boys playing on the trunk of an old tree just beside the path.

"We're staying here," said Sarah, indicating what looked to be the most substantial house in this part of the village, with intricate latticework woven into the bamboo at the front. "You're all going to stay with some of the students. They'll take you there and we'll all meet at supper."

Katie and the others all turned their attention to unloading the luggage, strong young arms reached out to help them and then they were on their way along the dusty path to what was to be their home for the next three weeks.

"How are you feeling Katie?" She felt the gentle touch of fingers on her hand and turned round to see Vicki, the other girl of the group beside her.

"Excited . . .afraid . . .I don't know."

"Tired?"

"Yes, but . . "

An astonishingly beautiful girl of about Katie's age came alongside her and Vicki and broke into their conversation.

"You two are to come this way. You're going to share with me," and she led them down a side turning across a small dry ditch, up some steps and onto a small wooden veranda. "Here's our bedroom, and my name is La Meh."

"And we're Katie and Vicki," Vicki said.

"What about the others?" Katie had come to rely on Richard in particular. She enjoyed his gentle humour and good nature and she wanted to know that he wasn't far away. He and the others in the group had been part of the recovery process for her. "You'll see them all at supper; so once you've put your bags in here and unpacked a bit, we can all go and eat."

Night fell quickly in the jungle camp, the speed of it's coming intensified by the lack of electric light. True, some of the houses had strip lights that were powered by a diesel generator but these were in the minority. Now Katie knew why they needed torches.

Supper was taken with a family who had no tables or chairs and no electricity. They ate sitting on the floor by candlelight. Katie was awed and amazed that here were people who had so few possessions, yet radiated peace and contentment such as she had never experienced before. In the midst of this stark simplicity there was a welcome as rich as she had ever known. The six visitors crowded into the small square room. In fact to call it a room was something of an exaggeration, as it was more like a platform set on posts about four feet above the ground. Two women and a teenage boy appeared in the space between the two walls with dishes of food and placed them on the floor between their feet. Each visitor was handed a dish and a spoon, while the members of the household seated themselves on the floor around the edge of the room.

"It looks like we have an audience," Richard muttered under his breath. Katie let out a small, suppressed laugh.

An old man, who was dressed in the grubbiest old *longyi* that Katie had seen so far that day, stood up and launched into a speech, which, once she had seen Sarah respectfully bowing her head, she realised must be some sort of prayer. The words had a surprisingly musical quality about them that she found quite easy to listen to. She jumped as soft fur brushed against her leg. Opening her eyes she saw a scrawny kitten advancing on the food dishes so she quickly scooped it up into her lap. As she listened to the sound of the man's words she became aware of another sound, a muffled grunting and snorting that seemed to be coming from directly below them.

"What's that noise?" she whispered as the prayer came to an end.

"Pigs," said Richard. "Come on, tuck in Katie."

Katie deposited the kitten behind her and set herself to trying to understand the food. One of the women was helping her by spooning rice into her dish. Now she helped herself to an unrecognisable green vegetable and to some lumps of something that she assumed was a sort of curry. There was a large dish of vegetable soup that she saw Sarah help herself from, a small dish of a red substance, and what looked like a large amorphous omelette. Katie picked nervously at each of the dishes; the red substance looked as if it needed particularly careful handling. "What do you think this is going to be like?" she asked.

"Mummm. . . your mouth will recover after about three weeks," Richard laughed.

She gingerly took a tiny amount; her instincts were correct, it was fearfully hot while the small lumps of meat were so tough that they were virtually inedible. Meanwhile the family sat and watched them. "Have they already eaten or will they eat later?" Katie asked.

"They'll eat later," was Sarah's reply. "That's why we mustn't eat everything. But that won't be difficult will it?" she muttered as she struggled with an unchewable piece of gristle.

Katie wanted to laugh. If only the girls at the hospital could see me now, she thought. What would they think of me eating my dinner in a place like this, with pigs scratching around underneath the floor? More to the point, what would Declan think? Even now, nine months after the break up, she often felt a stab of pain at the hurt he had caused her. She felt that she wanted to show him how much stronger she was now, show him that she didn't need him anymore and that he couldn't hurt her like that again.

The church was dark; it consisted of just a roof and four walls that reached up to waist height. There were a couple of strip lights in the centre lightening the gloom a little. The building was packed with people of all ages sitting on crude benches or standing several deep around the sides. The visitors were all given chairs to sit on, while someone began to play on the electric keyboard. A few young boys quickly joined in with their guitars.

It was when they began to sing that Katie felt a thrill rush though her body and goose bumps appeared on her arms. She could not believe that these people who lived so simply and apparently in such poverty could sing with such a deep and rich harmony. Tears flowed down her face. Then she felt an arm resting on her shaking shoulders.

"It's beautiful isn't it?" she heard Richard whisper in her ear.

"It's just so moving," Katie answered, trying to hold back the tears. "I didn't realise . . ." she paused, looking for the words." I didn't know it would be like this."

"Yes," Richard agreed. "I thought these people would all be miserable but they seem so, well, happy. In spite of everything."

"There's something about this place but I can't think what it is." She looked at him

"Dignity?" Richard suggested taking hold of Katie's hand.

"Yes," Katie nodded. "I'm so . . . ." she said, with a gentle sigh, "so glad I came. I want to know what this is all about. I want to understand why they're here. I mean really know. And I'm going to find out."

2

Thaw Reh began to be aware of the chill of the night. For some time he had been drifting between sleep and wakefulness. Then, for a brief interlude of confusion, he had forgotten where he was until his mind had slowly cleared.

As it did so he realised that the fever had reduced and he was feeling a little better. In recent weeks he had become all too familiar with malaria, its ebb and flow of fevers and periods of debilitating weakness. As he stared into the blackness he wondered if Pee Reh was still near him. They had escaped together, with the help of Aung Gyi, deciding that to run away was their only choice. Pee Reh wanted to try to get to Thailand because his uncle was there in a refugee camp and they knew that if they could reach the border they would be safe.

At first they had made good progress, as they were strong, in spite of the meagre rations that the soldiers had kept them on. They had passed through villages where people had given them food, although, God knows, they were poor enough themselves. Pee Reh had said he knew the way, and they had put a considerable distance between themselves and the unit they had escaped from. Later, the terrain had become more mountainous, and the settlements were fewer and further between but according to Pee Reh this was a good sign as the fact that they were in mountains meant that they were getting nearer to the border.

Then Pee Reh had fallen ill, and their progress had become painfully slow. Eventually they had simply stopped in the forest and slept, with no shelter at all. Then Thaw Reh himself had succumbed, and they were both helpless. Sometimes he had heard the voices of his friends as he had drifted in and out of a feverish sleep, but at night the only sounds were those of the forest

Now that he was feeling just a little better, he began to wonder if they could move again at daybreak. He turned over to try to get back to sleep and find some relief from the long nightmare.

Thaw Reh had only known a happy family life. He didn't think about it in those terms of course, it was only when he had lost everything that he realised how precious were his childhood memories. With a mother and father, brothers and sister and grandmother to share his life he knew nothing of the pain of loss.

As a builder his father took a pride in his work. He had heard the words 'hill tribe people' spoken with disdain by travellers from the plains, who occasionally passed their way, but he took no notice of their tone. Why should he? He knew his craft, he knew the forests, he provided well for his family and his wife held her head high among the women of the village. The business was going well, even expanding, and there was plenty to occupy him and Thaw Reh and his other two sons if they had the mind to follow him, which of course he believed they would. There were enough contracts coming his way now in the neighbouring villages.

That was not to say that Nga Reh and his family were unaware of the needs of others. They had seen men killed or maimed while working in the forest, they knew of families where the mother had died in childbirth and they had seen the poverty that followed, so Nga Reh was humble too, his pride not being of the sort that considered itself better than others, just fortunate.

There was a school in the village that had originally been established by Catholic missionaries in simple wooden classrooms. Old Khaw Htoo, himself a Catholic, was the schoolmaster. He had a real love for learning, and managed to instil into the children that same love, in spite of there being so few books and desperately few teachers.

"I remember old Khaw Htoo's father," Thaw Reh's mother had told him. "He used to work for a British family. He was very old then, and I was just a small child, but I used to see the white people. I was so afraid of them. We all were. They looked so strange to us children." She laughed. " My mother told me that Khaw Htoo often used to go missing, but they would always know where to find him. He would hide in the library, amongst the books. That's how he came to know English so well."

So, the children of the village were fortunate in their schooling. In spite of that, most were only ever destined for the life of a small rice farmer, or labourer. Some would earn a little more, working in the forests as loggers, or perhaps in the nearby mines.

The family home, typical of village houses found all over this part of Burma, was built on large wooden posts, with the main living area raised above the ground so that it was necessary to climb steps to enter. At the top of the steps at the front of the house there was a veranda, which was underneath the overhanging roof but still out in the open. Here Khaw Htoo would often sit with Nga Reh. "You are always welcome," he would say, as they quietly smoked together, in easy companionship, in the warm tropical evenings.

One day Thaw Reh remembered clearly how he had listened to Khaw Htoo talking. "I have heard that the army is closing schools in parts of Burma. The older children have nowhere to go, in some places even the little schools are closing. They don't want us to teach our ways, tell our stories . . . " the old man's voice faltered and broke. He saw his father reach out a hand to comfort Khaw Htoo. Thaw Reh knew about poverty, he had seen suffering, but what did this mean? He had a sense that whatever was upsetting the old man so much was something new and he wondered how serious it really was.

As Thaw Reh grew older, he began to join his father in the workshop. That was what he had wanted to do since as a tiny child he had sat under the bench playing with the wood shavings and sawdust, watching his father at work. It was as if he had taken in the skills of a woodworker and builder with his mother's milk and after school each day he had loved to help his father. Now, as a boy entering manhood he was fully able to take part in the business.

While at work one morning they saw soldiers approaching the house. Nga Reh put down his tools and made to welcome them. He recognised them as soldiers of the KNPP, the local army. Thaw Reh often saw soldiers in the village, he knew some of them, especially those he had been at school with. He found some of their talk loud and ribald, but what did that really matter? They were friendly and this was their country. One glance at the captain's face told Nga Reh that this was a serious visit. "*Poquow,* go to your mother. Ask her to bring tea for the captain." Turning to the captain he pointed to the bench on the veranda, "Sit down sir, won't you?" The captain sat down, pulled one of the homespun cigarettes out of his pocket and lit it with a bright plastic lighter. He drew the smoke deeply into his lungs. Nga Reh waited. Thaw Reh glanced around the cluster of soldiers. An aura of uncomfortable expectancy hung around the small gathering.

At last the captain spoke. "We are getting some worrying reports. The Tatmadaw have reached as far as the River Salween in Karen State. Many Karens have had to cross into Thailand. We must recruit, so as to strengthen our defences. We need someone from every family in the district for our unit." Nga Reh knew what was to come. "You have three good sons, Nga Reh. We ask that you provide at least one of them."

Thaw Reh just hoped that his father would not insist that he go to join the unit. He knew his brother Sah Reh would much rather be a soldier, and this confirmed by the nudge that he felt in his ribs from his younger brother, who had quietly joined Thaw Reh as the captain had been talking.

And so, a few days later, it was Sah Reh who marched proudly out of the village square with the other recruits, watched by their families. Boys becoming men, proud fathers standing by, mothers, wives, and sisters holding back tears, fearing what the future held.

The spaces left by the departing recruits soon closed over, and village life returned to what it had been before, with the weekly market, the school, the church, the small businesses.

The square boasted mains electricity, and Hay Reh, who owned the teashop, had installed a refrigerator, filling it with ice cream, beer and soft drinks, creating a meeting place for the younger members of the community. "That's what they all want," he would say. "They've seen the American films, so they all want Coca Cola now." He always had an eye for business.

Thaw Reh went to the square each week and it was there that he had first seen Suu Meh. Now, each week he would walk across to her side of the market and watch her from a distance for a few minutes. The vivid blue of her blouse stood out in stark contrast to the greens and yellows of the vegetables on her stall, lighting up that particular corner of the market. She would tie her black *sarong* tightly around her waist, so emphasising her figure. In a moment of fantasy he wondered if she had done that just for him, and he imagined how he would encircle her with his arms and kiss her. As she smiled and talked to her customers, she seemed to be taking a real interest in them. She seemed to invest even the humble act of selling goods in the market with a certain grace.

He wondered whether she noticed him, as her eyes alighted on him once or twice, when he passed by with his brother. At last, gathering his courage he leaned across the boxes on the counter and spoke to her. "I'd like to buy you an ice cream, can you get away later?" He could feel his heart performing a noisy, riotous dance inside his chest as he spoke. To him it seemed so loud that he wondered if she could hear it too. She glanced sideways towards her mother who stood at the other end of the stall, then leaned forward to answer him, her eyes flitting between Thaw Reh and his youngest brother Ree Reh. As she did so he noticed two tiny scars on her forehead just above her right eyebrow. "I will ask my mother, perhaps after lunch when it's quieter, and my niece can come with me." She caught sight of her mother looking at her then and bowed her head before him, feigning concentration on her work. Thaw Reh liked that. As she looked down he saw her profile, her fine features perfectly enhanced by her upswept hair and his heart seemed to melt. He was woken from his reverie as his brother nudged him in the ribs.

"Pineapple," Ree Reh hissed.

"What?" Thaw Reh turned towards his brother with a frown.

"A pineapple, ask her for a pineapple."

"You want a pineapple?" she asked. They nodded in reply and Thaw Reh was forever grateful to his brother for making the suggestion. This was her party piece; they had watched her before.

"Well, sit down here," and she cleared two boxes for them at the side of the stall then seized a sharp knife and skilfully set to work. They watched mesmerised as the peel slid onto the table before them. Then slicing with lightening speed she pared the fruit into small pieces and proudly presented them on a banana leaf. There was no need for words, the pineapple cutting display was enough to fill the space between them.

After that she began to join him in the teashop each week on market day, for a break from her work. The little group would talk together, and entertain her young niece as they did so.

"What is your work?" Suu Meh asked

"I'm a builder, I work with my father. We have a good business. My father is a good teacher, he's sometimes impatient because he wants everything just right, but when things go well he is full of praise. Then I feel better. What about you? I don't remember you from the school."

"We used to live near the mines. My father used to work there, but now he's too sick: the dust has damaged his chest, so he can't breathe properly. We moved here to be near my grandparents. Now my mother works with them in the gardens, and we sell our fruit and vegetables at the markets in some of the villages around here "

"Hard work for them?"

"Yes, and I help them too. The worst part is carrying the water from the river up to the garden. That's my job. My father told me about the pumps they use to take water out of the mines and I want to try to use one of them to bring water out of the river for us. I'm sure it would work, but we have no spare money and no electricity, so we must wait, and I must still carry the water."

He listened intently as she spoke, admiring everything about her, her intelligence, her capability, the light that shone in her eyes. "Suu Meh," he asked her, "do you read English?"

"No, our teacher didn't know English. Why do you ask me?"

"I have borrowed a book from Khaw Htoo's library, and I am trying to read it, but it is very difficult."

"What's it about?"

"It's about England. It's a very beautiful country, but very different from Karenni."

"What happens in the story?"

"Well, it's about a beautiful girl from a very poor family. She tries to make a better life for herself but it is so difficult for her."

"It's like my family. I want to make life better for us, but it's so hard. Who wrote the book?" she asked him.

"Someone called Thomas Hardy. I like his writing because he seems to care about poor people. I just wish I didn't find the words so hard to understand."

"I would like to see this book: will you show it to me?"

"Next market day?"

"Next market day." He went home with a light heart. Life was good and he had everything to look forward to.

When the time for the *Dicu* festival came round the new army recruits were given leave, so most came home to spend time with their families. This was an opportunity to kill a pig or a chicken, and mothers and wives brought out all their best recipes. The new soldiers sitting in Hay's bar for hours attracted the attention of the local girls, who, just a few weeks earlier, had not even been interested in them.

Suu Meh was one of the dancers. It was a festival that went back further than anyone could think of, to the days when the spirits of the ancestors were remembered and honoured. The young people danced through the village stopping at many of the houses, eating and drinking with the families. It was a time of great joy for everyone. Rice wine and whisky flowed, and a gentle merriment spread through the whole village.

As the dancers reached their house, Thaw Reh's mother brought out all her best food. Once she had finished serving she sat down and looked on with pleasure as the young people ate. Suu Meh sat with the other girls on the floor of the house while Thaw Reh watched her, willing her to move away from her friends and join him, even for a moment. At last, as the time came for the merriment to move on to the next house she came close to him and he saw his chance.

"Mother," he said as she came close to him" this is Suu Meh, I want you to meet her." He saw a look of approval pass across his mother's face, as she gave the girl the traditional handshake of greeting.

"You are always welcome in my home," she said.

Later, as the crowd of young people walked home through the village he spoke to her again. "I'll take you home."

And as she fell into step beside him he moderated his pace until the crowd had left them behind then he slipped his arm around her waist. As they slowed to a stop, he wrapped his arms around her and drew her close to his body, so that he could feel her soft breasts against his chest. She melted into his embrace, as he kissed her, gently at first, and then more firmly. "No, Thaw Reh," she gasped as she fought to free herself from him a little. He had known she would do that. That was the way for good Karenni girls. Then she looked up to him and in the darkness he saw the unashamed happiness in her eyes and he knew that this was the girl that he wanted for his wife and to be the mother of his children. They walked on, unhurriedly, holding hands, treasuring the moment and enjoying being alone together for the first time. He delivered her to her home, his mind teeming with thoughts of their first embrace.

3

Thaw Reh saw more and more of Suu Meh as the weeks went by. They had talked of marriage and Thaw Reh worked harder than ever, spurred on by thoughts of their future together. Suu Meh responded to his embraces with warmth and promise, a woman in love, she had opened out and blossomed, much to Thaw Reh's delight. As he worked, his father often saw a smile pass across his son's lips. "*Poquow*," he would say, "don't leave that wood like that, it's still too rough." And Thaw Reh would realise that he had indeed been allowing his attention to wander away from his work.

Alas, Nga Reh's thoughts were not so happy. Since the recruitment there had been more visits from the KNPP soldiers in the village. They brought with them reports of whole villages in Karenni State having to move to new townships. If the people offered any resistance they were rewarded with rapes and killings and their houses were burnt to the ground. The men of the village often talked these things over among themselves and they tried to comfort each other with brave talk.

"Those villages are in the west . . . here in the east we are better able to defend ourselves."

"Look at all the men that were recruited, they are all strong, all good Karennis."

"We know this country so well. Our enemies just get lost in the forest, they are no match for our soldiers."

But each one knew in his heart that the reality was serious for Karenni State and as the dry season wore on they saw more and more soldiers passing through the village. Once the target of the men had merely been Hay's bar and the village girls, with nothing more than home comforts on their minds. Now they were armed and moving in columns up to the front line to defend their homes. The noise of war moved ever closer.

It was late in the afternoon and they had been working hard all day in the shop. Nga Reh had a contract to build offices and outbuildings for the nearby mines and they had been sawing and planing the wood in readiness for when they would load their truck and drive up to the site in a day or two. Thaw Reh thought that he saw a movement outside behind the shop. He walked slowly through and out to the yard outside where his mother kept her cooking pots under the kitchen lean-to. He stood for a moment his eyes ranging across the courtyard with its latrine and washroom and then over the vegetables and pineapples and his grandmother's fruit trees growing behind the low fence. There was nothing unusual there. Turning his back to the yard he returned to the workshop and reached out for his saw but never picked it up. He was stopped in his tracks by the sound of someone banging and shouting at the front of the shop. Father and son froze. The shouting was Burmese; could this be the Tatmadaw?

Thaw Reh's heart pounded in his chest; he felt that he couldn't get enough air into his lungs. At a glance from his father he took a deep breath and with a supreme effort tried to bring his body under control. He wanted to run, but slowed himself down and walked quietly through to the back of the workshop again. Once there he turned left and went up the steps into the house which was next to the workshop. As he entered it everything seemed so normal. He could hear his grandmother telling his young sister a story, just as he remembered her doing when he had been a young child. His mother was bent over the vegetables she was preparing. One look at his face, and she knew immediately that something was very wrong.

"I think it's the Tatmadaw! At the front of the shop!"

"Stay in here *Poquow*. Where's Ree Reh?"

" I don't know, Mother."

His mother's face drained of all colour while a look of terror passed between them. They knew from what they had heard from other villages that once the Tatmadaw were in an area the villagers never had any peace. They were regularly expected to provide workers to act as porters for the troops and labourers to work on the roads. It did not matter whether it was harvest time; they still had to work for the army without pay while the rice waited to be cut in the fields.

Meanwhile his father forced himself to walk slowly to the front of the shop. He was not going to let the soldiers see that he was afraid of them. The officer in charge spoke. "You! Headman!" They had made a mistake. The house was one of the largest in the village and they had assumed that it was the headman's. Nga

Reh relaxed a little, he felt his shoulders drop down again and he began to breathe more easily.

"I will take you, " he said. "Follow me." Law La Htoo lived at the corner of the market square. He, too, was an old friend of Nga Reh. As the soldiers approached his house, Law La Htoo could be seen looking out over the front of the veranda. He was a thickset man with a broad heavily lined face that had a smile for everyone. He even managed to welcome the officer and his men with a greeting that seemed almost warm.

"Good day to you, Nga Reh," he said to his friend. He extended his hand to the officer. "I am Law La Htoo." He invited them up the steps, but they did not come right into the house, his welcome did not extend that far.

"We are looking for soldiers of the KNPP," said the officer. "We want to rid this district of all resistance and rebellion."

Law La Htoo's face remained unmoving, inscrutable, giving nothing away. Nga Reh's heart thumped in his chest, as he thought of his second son. "There are no soldiers here," said Law La Htoo with authority.

"Our objective is to bring peace to the district," the officer went on, as if he had not heard Law La Htoo. "In due course, you will be hearing from the District Law and Order Restoration council. They will inform you, in writing, of your tax and labour obligations. Meanwhile, we have a duty to uncover all subversive military activity. We shall expect you to comply fully with our requirements, then all shall go well for you and your village." Law La Htoo extended his hand as if to say goodbye to the officer and his men. He had a strong physical presence about him; at that moment it was stronger than that of the soldiers, in spite of their numbers and their firearms.

The soldiers backed down the steps. "I shall look forward to working with you Law La Htoo," said the officer." Good bye." The two men watched them leave, and then turned to one another.

"What does this mean for us?" Nga Reh asked of his friend.

"We must hold on, we must be strong, and we must stand together." Law La Htoo sounded braver than he felt. "Now, you must go home to your family".

The order came two days later

> ORDER
> Company 2
> Date : 4.3.97
> To : Village Head
> Daw Klaw Leh Village

You are ordered to attend the 231 Infantry Battalion Headquarters on 6.3.97 at 0700am.
You are to provide 12 male labourers and 5 female. Bring spades and machetes and food
for 3 days.
Your taxation requirements are:
3,000 roofing shingles.
Ten sacks of rice.

> Company Commander

Company 2
No 231 Infantry Battalion.

Law La Htoo showed the letter to the members of the village council. "My suggestion is this. Some of us should go as a delegation to the headquarters. We should ask for a reduction in the requirements"

Ka Law, one of the council members spoke up, "I suggest that we ask to keep women back from the forced labour. My cousin tells me that he did not like the way that the women from his village were treated by the soldiers."

"What do others think," Law La Htoo asked.

All nodded in agreement with Ka Law's idea. Suggestions as to how they would ask for a reduction were batted around the group until finally they decided to send three men to the Battalion Headquarters with their ideas.

Major Khin Maung the company commander was anxious. His home was in Rangoon and that seemed a very long way away. Inwardly he felt isolated and vulnerable. The soldiers in his company were a restive bunch, but that was because they, too, were a long way from home up here on the frontier, in this godforsaken place. Wages were low, and they sometimes went hungry. That was why he had had the idea of ordering some women with the labour detachments. He had concluded that to have a few of the local girls, who were reputed to be very beautiful, around the camp would help to bring a little contentment to the troops, and generally keep the men happier. As he congratulated himself on this good idea a slight smile spread across his face and for a few moments, he felt a little better.

This district was known to be a KNPP stronghold and they were all aware that they were in dangerous territory. Khin Maung knew these locals were in sympathy with the guerrillas, supplying them with food, hiding them in their houses and fighting alongside them. The answer was to bring the whole situation under tighter control. This was the Law and Order Restoration Council, the generals had between them decided on the name. His job now was to restore law and order, he told himself; so he would do it to the best of his capabilities. The villages were due to bring their *corvee* labour detachments today; he wondered what sort of unruly rabble they would have to work with this time.

Law la Htoo and his two companions from the village council approached the Headquarters. They were confident that the commander would listen to their requests and accept what they had to say; they were, after all, the elders of the village and their words were listened to with the great respect that is always given to old people in Burma. They just had to be reasonable and all would be well.

On reaching the headquarters they were received by the soldier at the gate. Law La Htoo began in perfect Burmese, "We have come to see your officer. We want to talk with him about our village labour obligations."

"Wait here," answered the nervous young soldier, who went to speak to his superior, who then spoke to the officer in charge of the labour conscription. At length, the officer emerged impatiently from his quarters. He was expecting the new labourers today, then perhaps he would have some proper offices and barracks built so he wouldn't have to work in these cramped huts any more. He wondered what the problem was now.

Law La Htoo spoke first, "Sir, I would like to ask about the labour obligations for Daw Kler Leh Village. We would like to request that only men are sent to labour for you. We, as the village council, are unwilling to allow women on this occasion. Further, we want to ask for a reduction in the number of days required, since we have more than enough to do with raising our own crops."

"Just wait here," said the officer. This problem only added to his impatience with the situation. It was becoming very difficult to maintain the headquarters with few buildings and poor roads and they needed porters to supply the front line. They were desperate to bring proper control to the district and it could not be done without extra labourers. He marched quickly across to speak to the Major.

"Impossible," snapped the Major. "We must have all the conscripts. We cannot function without their work. We must make sure they comply. Take the old man as hostage until the labourers are delivered to us, then we can let him go. We must watch Daw Klaw Leh in future, it could prove to be a difficult village."

Law La Htoo's two companions hurried back to the village and reported to the rest of the council. "We have no choice, it seems. They want to build offices and barracks and a road. We will have to ask for volunteers from the village. If we don't have enough volunteers, then we must conscript."

The council members approached the families of the village and the numbers were made up with volunteers. The people of Daw Klaw Leh were strong and fit, they all knew how to work hard and they were not afraid to do so. Nga Reh went along as a master builder. He knew that he could leave his business in the hands of Thaw Reh for a month, and that if building was to be done he would be more capable and skilled than most.

Nga Reh was glad he went. He was older than the rest of the detachment but he felt that he could supervise the work, and keep an eye on the rest of the villagers to make sure that they were not ill treated. The work was hard and there was no pay, but Nga Reh was largely left to his own devices and was able to supervise the building work himself. The villagers were expected to cut trees and saw the logs as well as build the offices and barracks for the Tatmadaw. Nga Reh longed to get the work done, so that he could get home to his own business and so the group worked quickly and well under his leadership. As far as being able to supervise the rest of the villagers went he had been mistaken. For the whole of the month he saw nothing of the young women and half of the men. In spite of regularly questioning the officer in charge of the work detail, he was able to elicit no information as to their whereabouts or their well being. Sometimes he worried for their safety, at others he was so weary that it was all he could do to keep going himself.

The day came when they were given leave to go home so Nga Reh once again sought out the officer and asked about the other villagers. "We cannot leave without them," he said, the anxiety for them beginning to show in his voice.

Law La Htoo stared gloomily into space. He had returned safely to the village after being held at the LORC headquarters for a few days. They had intended to frighten him and had succeeded, but he had recovered from the ordeal, and was glad to get home. All had gone well after that. The villagers had helped and turned out to volunteer, more or less willingly. He thought back to the stories that his grandparents had told him many years ago. Stories of how the Karenni people and the Karens to the south used regularly to be taken as slaves, when battles would rage to and fro across the countryside. Even then, they had been known as hard and capable workers. Understanding the forests and the mountains, they could keep going far longer than those used to the softer life of the valleys and lowlands. No, the villagers had not let him down.

Then, the awful truth had come out. Those who had been working on the buildings had been fine, Nga Reh had seen to that. It was the porters and the women that had given everyone such a shock. One of the porters had not even come home. "He was sick," one of the young men had told him. "We asked the soldiers for quinine for him and we wanted them to let him rest. . . ." He stopped, unable to go on with the story. "They kicked him, sir," another of the boys continued, "they kicked him all over, then they left him there by the path. We tried to stay with him, sir, but they wouldn't let us." His mother and father had been distraught at the loss of their son and the priest had held a mass for him yesterday, but it was little comfort to them. They did not even have his body to grieve over.

All the porters had born the marks of ill treatment. One of them had been so delirious with a fever he had been unable to walk so Nga Reh had had to send his truck to bring the boy home. Swollen feet and bruises were so many that they could not be counted. The sight of them told the story more eloquently than any words could but their families listened with mounting horror, as they said how far they had had to walk with the heavy packs. They had been used to carry ammunition up to the front line for the Tatmadaw soldiers. By night they had had to sleep on the bare ground, with no shelter from the elements or the mosquitoes. Food had been meagre, but the worst thing had been the lack of water and the sheer exhaustion.

What had happened to the girls and women had been worse, much worse. They had all been very quiet when they returned. They had hardly spoken at all. There had been a strange atmosphere around them. Law La Htoo knew in his heart that something was very wrong. "It worries me," he said to his wife. "What do you think?" She was a nurse and understood these things better than him. "Perhaps you could talk to some of them. See what happened?"

"They made us cook for them," one of the girls said, and the others nodded in agreement.

"What else happened?" Law La Htoo's wife asked them quietly.

"Some of the girls had to go with soldiers at night."

"They wouldn't go at first," another girl had said. "Then they had to give in, they were so afraid."

"I was afraid I would never see my mother again," a weeping girl confessed.

But even so nobody was prepared for the horror of finding the body of one of them caught in the rocks under a high bluff jutting out across the river.

Now, Law La Htoo looked again at the new order that had been delivered to him. The headquarters were demanding more porters and more women workers. How could he send his people after what had happened last month? He knew that they would not volunteer this time, especially, as everyone knew someone who had been in the last detachment. The news of what they had had to endure had quickly spread round the whole village. And the Tatmadaw wanted this detachment of workers in two days time. Law La Htoo put his head in his hands as the troubles of the occupation surrounded him.

4

Law La Htoo had made his mind up. There was nothing else to be done. He would have to go to speak to the district officer in charge of labour once again to try to negotiate some better terms. His wife looked with concern at his tired face. It seemed to have drained of all hope. "What is it Law La Htoo?" She was worried for him He used to be so big in every way: big in body, big in voice, big in heart. Now he seemed to have shrunk, his shoulders slumped down, his ready smile turned into a mask of anxiety.

"What am I to do this time? They want more labourers, but how can I send people if they receive the same treatment as last month?"

"Perhaps you can persuade them to remember how well the villagers did last month, and this would make them see that they could be more lenient this time." She wanted to be helpful, but in her heart she knew it was no use.

Major Khin Maung was trying to gather his thoughts. He had received the delegation from Daw Kler Leh, and had decided to send them all away again. "This is typical of the sort of thing that happens in these far outposts," he said to his labour conscription officer. "The villagers are quite happy to help with the improvements to their country at first, but they soon

43

show their true colours, and prove unwilling to volunteer any more." He gave the officer a long hard look. They had reached this point together before now. "There's nothing else for it, we must send a company to Daw Kler Leh and take the villagers by force. I don't like doing it this way but they leave us with no alternative. There is no other way to properly establish control over the district. Who does this village headman think he is anyway, trying to tell us what to do?"

"Of course we can't work here without roads and offices and supplies," the officer responded. "The trouble is, these people have become too used to having their own way. Some of them are little better than savages of course."

"You're right," Major Khin Maung congratulated his officer on his clear judgement of the situation. "We must march on them first thing, the day after tomorrow. We'll take them by surprise and round some of them up."

The building work at the mine had been slow. Nga Reh had been out of the village for a whole month so Thaw Reh had had to carry on the business on his own. There had been other calls on his time, so he had not been able to visit the site as often as he would have liked, even though his youngest brother Ree Reh had been helping him.

"Now we are all back together again," Nga Reh said to his oldest son, "you can go to the mines and finish the work there. I can stay back here and catch up with the work. Ree Reh can help me." Thaw Reh was relieved that his father was home. He had enjoyed managing the business, he liked being his own boss, and Ree Reh, who was now sixteen, had been a great help. However, he had to confess that when it came to the real organisation of the work, his father had the edge on him. It was good to have him back. "You take the truck. We won't need it here."

As he drove along the rutted dirt road in the battered old truck, which had a whole door missing, and rattled with every movement, he felt a sense of peace and contentment, as if all was well with the world once again.

The tin mines had always been a source of employment for local people who were willing to travel away from their village to find work. The pay was good by the standards of Karenni State, and so some of the young people of Daw Kler Leh, like those of the villages around about, had moved in order to work there. Thaw Reh had delivered all the materials to the site, and the main building work on the new offices had been done. Now it was a case of finishing the work, fixing some doors and fittings, and making everything ready to hand over to the company. He thought that the work would probably take more than a day, so he had brought blankets, and his mother had provided him with some rice and vegetables in a metal can. He would sleep in his truck if there was nowhere else to go, although he guessed that he might well come across one of the village boys employed at the mines who would let him stay for the night.

As he approached the mines in his battered truck, he had to stop at a road-block. His heart pounded. The presence of soldiers was unmistakable. He knew that he had every right to be there, he had a job to do, he had a contract to fulfil with the mining company. On the other hand he also had a brother in the KNPP, and he knew that the chief object of the Tatmadaw was to crush the local armies by every means possible.

He had no alternative but to stop the truck at the barrier. He rummaged frantically in the front of the truck for the grimy sheets of paper that he knew were there somewhere. His father had established the original contract for the work, but they had forgotten all about the paper work in all the recent turmoil. Thaw Reh breathed a sigh of relief as he found them, and passed them out to the soldier at his side. He was allowed into the compound and he parked the truck beside the new offices.

As he sat for a few moments, he saw that the military had taken up residence in the main offices across the square. His heart sank as he thought of his father and the other villagers, and their treatment at the hands of men such as these. He suddenly wanted to go back to the safety of his own home, and his own family. This place seemed alien and threatening to him. At length he climbed out of the truck and walked quickly into the new offices. He felt better inside the building. He decided to get straight down to his work: no passing the time of day with the miners at the surface or the men in the offices. His work calmed him. As he concentrated on securing the doors, and smoothing down the steps and the hand-rails, he relaxed again and thought of happier times.

He had spoken to Suu Meh's mother and father about their marriage, and they were making plans for the wedding. Suu Meh would come to live at his parents' home, and he would build a new house for them, right next to theirs. He sometimes let his mind drift on and he imagined the beautiful children that Suu Meh would bear for him. He dreamt of their intimacy, he longed for the sight of her. Then he would hear a shout, which would wake him from his reverie, and he would remember that he must finish the work as quickly as he could, so that he could get out of this place, and back to the village.

At lunchtime, he went out to the truck to pick up his food.

"Hello there Thaw Reh." He turned to see Oo Reh, from his village, walking quickly across the square. "Have you eaten today?" Oo Reh asked as he reached the truck.

"Well, I was just going to."

"Join us, " said Oo Reh, "don't be afraid, they are all my friends" Thaw Reh realised his anxiety must be showing on his face. "What's happened?" He enquired of Oo Reh, as they settled down on the floor of the hut to eat their lunch.

"This is the Law and Order Restoration Council". Oo Reh's voice was heavy with irony as he told Thaw Reh about the soldiers' presence in the mines. "They are here to keep us Karennis in order, it seems. Making sure we work hard for our country. The Tatmadaw have taken over the mines. There is no mining company now, just soldiers. All our work goes to fill the fat bellies of the government in Rangoon."

"We've a contract with the company," Thaw Reh told him.

"Well, it's not worth the paper it's written on. You'll not see the money, I wouldn't even try if I were you. You should get straight back to Daw Kler Leh as fast as you can."

"What about you?"

"Me? I'm stuck here. Until these soldiers move on, none of us can do much. But you can, you aren't employed by the mine so you have no obligation to be here"

"Well, I'll finish the work. I probably need to stay until tomorrow, then I'm off home."

"Good man, Thaw Reh. Thank God for your father, he knew how to bring up his children. It's good to see you doing so well. I thought I would too, working in the mines. I wanted more money and a chance to get away from the village, but now look at me, a slave of this government. We are virtually prisoners here you know."

Thaw Reh could hardly believe what he was hearing. "Why? Can't you escape? Can't you run away? Why don't you leave with me in the morning?"

"Where could I go now? There are soldiers everywhere?"

That night, Thaw Reh went to the hut, which Oo Reh shared with several other miners. He hoped to put his sleeping mat down on the floor with them. All Karennis will share their home with anyone who needs to rest. He was confident that he would receive a welcome from them. The hut was almost dark inside. There was a fire in the centre of the floor, so the atmosphere was made worse by the smoke, which only partially found it's way out through the thatched roof. Then, as his eyes adjusted to the gloom, he saw the reason for Oo Reh's hopelessness and apparent reluctance to leave the mines. He lay on the floor of the hut, and he was not the only one. Together, the men were smoking themselves into a stupor with the opium that the soldiers had issued to them instead of their full wages. Thaw Reh entered the hut and sat for a while near the fire. One or two of the miners acknowledged his presence, but most just stared into the space in front of them, their faces masks of emptiness. He was not sure if Oo Reh knew he was there. After a long time of silence he reached out to touch his hand, and he felt some response in the movements the fingers, but Oo Reh had found another friend now, and he was beyond the reach of Thaw Reh.

The floor of the truck made a hard bed, but not much harder than the wooden floor that he slept on at home. Nevertheless, Thaw Reh woke, cold and stiff, before dawn but already aware of the fires that the miners had lit to warm themselves and cook their breakfast rice. He had wanted to get home, but although he had worked until after dark, he still had a couple of hours work to do. Now, as he remembered the disturbing scenes of yesterday, he was even more desperate to get away. Oo Reh's words about the payment for the work had circled his mind and he wondered whether he should present the bill to the commandant, or just drive away as fast as he could, and try to get thoughts of this place out of his head? He wondered if he could take Oo Reh seriously now, after what he had witnessed last evening. He decided he would visit Oo Reh once more before heading home, so picking up his rice tin he made for the miner's barracks.

"I can take you home; back to Daw Kler Leh " Thaw Reh offered, as they ate their breakfast. He wanted to help.

"No Thaw Reh. Don't worry about me." He said nothing more and they ate the rest of their meal in near silence.

It was with relief that Thaw Reh drove away from the mines in the middle of the morning. He had visited the commandant's office once he had finished the work and had spoken through an interpreter because he could speak very little Burmese. The commandant had seen the new offices and was pleased with them. "My father will present his bill for the work," Thaw Reh told the commandant. He had decided, on reflection, that this was the safest option, and now he was on the road again.

That morning the rattling, rusty old truck seemed to Thaw Reh to be the sleekest, most modern vehicle he could have dreamt of. It was carrying him home, back to his family, back to Suu Meh, and that was all that mattered. As he grew nearer to the village, he imagined he could hear his father berating his brother, about corners not properly mitred and wood poorly planed. Nga Reh had instilled the necessity for high standards into his sons and Thaw Reh had become grateful for that. He knew that his work was among the best in the district.

It took well over an hour to reach the village. The distance was not far, but the road was very rough, and he had to be careful to avoid some muddy patches. He didn't want to get stuck and risk not being able to get out. It was almost the hottest point of the day when he reached the outskirts of Daw Kler Leh. It was not far now; his home was on this side of the village.

He drove round the side of the yard, and was surprised by the silence. He would have expected to hear the sound of sawing, the clatter of tools, or some other sound that accompanied the work of a builder, but he heard nothing. He walked into the workshop. Still nothing. The place was empty and quiet. He walked round and through into the back of the house. Again, he could hear nothing. He stopped. There was a sound, perhaps a sob, perhaps a quiet cry. He went through to the middle of the house, where the family took their meals, and stopped as he took in the scene that was before him. His mother and grandmother were sitting on the floor, distraught, their faces twisted with grief, but what shocked him most was the sight of his father. He lay on the floor, with his head propped up on a pillow. He was covered with a blanket, but to the side, Thaw Reh could see a pool of congealing blood.

At first sight he thought his father was dead, but then saw a slight movement of his tongue in his mouth, and a small whimpering sound emerged. In one stride Thaw Reh crossed the room and knelt down beside him.

He was still alive, but only just. His forehead felt cold and moist, his eyes were closed, the lids lined with an appalling blue grey colour. His mother had a cup of water into which she occasionally dipped her fingers so as to moisten his lips; there was nothing more that she could do for him. There were no doctors in this part of Karenni State. There was a village clinic, but the staff there could deal only with the simplest of medical conditions, the miner's coughs, the pregnancies that were smooth running and without complications, the fevers of childhood. Nobody in this village could do more for Nga Reh than his wife was already doing so Thaw Reh joined the vigil that was quietly watching over the last minutes of his life.

"The soldiers came," his mother told him. "They were looking for all the young men to work as porters. They came to take Ree Reh." She stopped as she recalled what had happened.

His Grandmother continued, "Your father tried to stop them. They shot him. They shot him in the chest. He collapsed on the floor." Thaw Reh could picture the scene, as his mother and grandmother and young sister had struggled to drag Nga Reh into the house, and had tried to make him comfortable and keep him warm. He glanced around to look for his sister. His mother seemed to guess what he wanted, and she pointed in the direction of the bedroom.

They lost all track of time, so when Nga Reh finally slipped away, they had no idea when it was. The sun still shone hotly down on the house, but a cold chill ran through them all. A feeling of almost painful tightness in the chest came upon Thaw Reh. He ran out of the house, and across the yard. He went out into the paddy fields, dry now, but waiting for the rains so that the new rice could be planted. Gasping for breath he crossed several small fields before entering the forest that surrounded the village. The trees were thick, and he had to slow down. He stumbled on some roots, and collapsed onto the ground, screaming with pain and disbelief for his father, who had never done a bad thing in all his life, who had been everything to his children and kindness itself to everyone he ever met.

He sobbed loud and long, trying to rid himself of the nightmare. Perhaps it hadn't really happened. He would go back to the house now and all would be well. His father would be there, smiling and welcoming him home, telling him what a good job he had done at the mines and filling him with pride. No. He had seen it, his father was dead and he would never again hear him say how well he had worked. His father had been demanding. He complained about shoddy workmanship, he didn't like laziness. Oh to hear his father criticising, but then praising them over a job well done, how precious that would be.

Thaw Reh felt himself calming down a little. He sat up and took some deep breaths. He would go and see Suu Meh. She would help him; she would comfort him. He could talk to her and she would make him feel better.

He wondered whether he soldiers were still in the village. He decided it was best not to cross the square, so he skirted around the paddy fields. It was a longer walk, but he didn't mind that. He walked quickly, and eventually rejoined the road. As he emerged from the fields, he knew he had to be careful, but there were no soldiers about as far as he could see. Perhaps they were satisfied now they had killed his father and taken the young men of the village away. He felt another surge of anger, which he fought hard to bring under control. He was almost desperate to see Suu Meh, and was tempted to start running again, but he forced himself to move more cautiously.

The road was quiet. Where were the children that would normally be seen running about barefoot and grimy but always with broad grins on their faces? Where were the mothers with their babies sitting on the steps and chatting away the hours?

He opened the gate at the side of the road, and climbed up the steps. He started briefly, as he saw Suu Meh's mother and father sitting together. He felt a moment of embarrassment, and then he saw her mother's face. "They've taken her away, Thaw Reh."

"The soldiers took her," her father added sadly.

The pain returned, compounded with the shock of disbelief, and Thaw Reh froze where he stood on the verandah of Suu Meh's home.

5

That evening the men of the village helped Thaw Reh to dig the grave for Nga Reh. They worked in stunned and shocked silence as they carried him up to the graveyard on the cart, and the priest committed him to God's keeping. All was done tidily and properly; it was a sad and desperate attempt to hold onto something that spelt normality, sanity and the ordinary things of life.

The Mass for him was held the following night. Most of the village came: quiet and shocked and cowed, but seeking comfort from the familiarity of the wooden church, the words of the office and the closeness of their friends and neighbours. Nga Reh had lived in the village all his life and had been well liked. He had brought his children up to take part in the school and in the life of the village and as a family they had won the respect of all who knew them.

They all crowded into the dark interior of the church and took their places on the simple benches cut from the wood of the forest: children at the front, then the women, with the men standing at the back. The choirmaster sung the four notes of the harmony and the congregation joined in with the music, blending together in a harmony of deep and awesome sadness and filling the simple building with the sound of a bitter beauty. An observer might have thought these men were rough looking and poor, some of them ragged, even hungry. The ears of that same person would have heard something quite different. These were people of dignity and pride. Their faith and love displayed itself in their support and care for Nga Reh's family.

Thaw Reh felt numb. The words of the Mass may have helped others but they meant nothing to him. He was blind to the kindness and affection of the congregation. His mother needed him yet he hardly even noticed her. All he was aware of was the tight knot of pain that gripped his stomach hard and the terrible fear of not knowing where Suu Meh was. He tortured himself with questions. What was happening to her? Was she even still alive? He was standing immobile, surrounded by a blanket of cold hate and fear when he felt the light touch of a hand on his shoulder. He did not move, but the touch came again compelling him to turn around. It had come from his brother Sah Reh. Then they were lost in each other's arms, a tight embrace trying to discharge some of the pain of their loss.

"How did you get here?" Thaw Reh whispered.

"Never mind," his brother replied. "We heard what happened. The captain let me come home."

"Sah Reh. Take me back with you. Take me to your captain. I want to join up. I want to fight." Their eyes locked together and they each saw that same determination to somehow avenge their father's death and all the other cruel deaths that surrounded them in this hateful occupation.

"I can stay tonight but we must go in the morning before daylight. The Tatmadaw are everywhere but I know the way. We'll go together. I'll take you to the CO. You'll have to go through the training. It's hard, but you'll get on fine."

After the service their mother took Sah Reh and held him tightly; she hardly dared hope that he would stay at home now.

"I'm going to join the unit," Thaw Reh told her.

"What about you, Sah Reh?" She already knew what the answer would be.

"I must go now Mother. We must both go." She turned away so that they wouldn't see her crying. "We have to fight them. We can't let them take our country from us. And we must fight for the sake of Father. He would want us to go."

"So you are going to leave us. Am I to lose my husband and all three of my sons in one day?" They said nothing. There was nothing they could say. Their thoughts were only of revenge and hate for the soldiers who had torn their home apart.

Thaw Reh soon settled into the routine of a soldier's life. They drilled in the early mornings on the patch of grass outside the headquarters. Then they ran through rivers and jungle and over mountains so that the sweat ran into their eyes and soaked their clothes. He had been issued a uniform but the resources of the KNPP did not run to boots so his feet were punished further in the ragged canvas shoes, which were all he had. They were trained to carry heavy packs in the forest. They learnt to survive on what they could hunt and gather from the trees, plants and animals of the jungle. They learnt the importance of leaving no tracks, for fear of being detected by enemy patrols.

Thaw Reh discovered for the first time what true exhaustion was, but just to make sure that his fears for Suu Meh did not keep him awake and haunt him at night, he drank himself into oblivion every evening. Rice whisky and wine were easy enough to come by in the barracks and there were plenty of men to share with. The drink was not all that they shared; there was grief too. They had nearly all lost someone to the Tatmadaw.

After the two months of training the unit was moved to provide reinforcements to those defending the villages that had not been over run by the Burmese. These villages were largely KNPP strongholds and where they had recruited most heavily so support was unequivocal. "If these villages are ever taken by the Tatmadaw they are never shown any mercy." Sah Reh told him. "We've seen whole villages burnt down and the people forced to leave."

Captain Wah explained the strategy to the recruits. "We must defend our village strongholds for as long as possible. If evacuation becomes necessary then we must cover the village while the people retreat. We don't want any of them to get into the hands of the Burmese soldiers." It was well known that sometimes villagers hid in the jungle for many months at a time, finding what food and shelter they could, just to keep away from the enemy.

"Goodbye," Thaw Reh said to his brother.

"Goodbye," Sah Reh replied as they gazed at each other. For a moment Thaw Reh caught a glimpse of reality: he was no soldier. It had only been the presence of his younger brother that had sustained him over the weeks. Then he quickly brushed the thought away and set off on the march to the new location.

While they were still in territory that had not been taken by the Burmese, things went well. Their main difficulty was the extreme heat, for that year the rains that would cool the air were late in coming and in the daytime heat, the weight of their packs became almost unbearable.

There was another reason why they longed for the rains. The army of the Tatmadaw moved easily when weather was dry but the Karenni knew that once the rain began to fall they would immediately have the advantage over their enemies. They knew the forests and they knew how to survive when the invading army would only become hopelessly bogged down. The rains would halt the terrible advance of the Burmese for many months, allowing them to regroup and perhaps regain some of the ground that they had lost so disastrously during the dry season.

The column marched through the forest paths. Often they were cheerful and could almost forget that they were at war. Then the column would suddenly halt and the lookout would come back and warn of danger ahead. The message would pass back along the line and they would move back the way that they had come. On one such occasion they had begun to approach a village until the lookout saw the uniform of Tatmadaw soldiers among the trees. They had almost blundered into an enemy unit. The Captain ordered a retreat and the column rested in the forest until nightfall.

Captain Pula Wah was a wily old soldier. Thaw Reh and some of the younger recruits used to think he was too old but he knew his craft, he knew his men, and he knew his country inside out. He brought his NCOs together to appraise them of the situation. "We have to cross the Pon River and the Salween River." He showed them on the old crumpled map. "Upriver our way is barred now the enemy has moved further east than we were expecting. The long dry season has made it easy for them this year. The bridges are almost certainly taken, so we dare not cross by any of those. We will have to find a ford and cross at night. That is the only safe way. We may even have to resort to a deeper crossing."

The unit officer posted sentries around the group and detailed the rest of the men to sleep if they could. He could not allow them to even light a fire for fear that the enemy lookouts would see the smoke. Their supper was cold rice left over from yesterday's meal.

As night fell, the column continued its march down stream. They had a few torches but mostly they had to rely on the light of the moon. Sometimes the path was very close to the water but the sides of the valley were rocky and steep so there was no possibility of crossing. By midnight the countryside had levelled out again and the forward lookout saw the first few houses of another village. They walked round the outside of the place in silence for fear of the presence of another

Burmese unit. As they passed the last of the houses they turned back to regain sight of the river, which was much wider now, and began to look for a crossing point. Thaw Reh wondered how long this would go on; he was exhausted, cold and miserable.

Then the whole column halted again. They waited in the darkness but as no message came back down the line, they began to advance again, this time very slowly. As they moved forward they realised that a crossing place had been found and the advance guard had already gone out into the water. They had carefully stepped out into the gradually deepening river but they had not drawn any enemy fire. Once they had reached the other side they had signalled for others to follow.

The CO for their group allowed only a few men to cross each time. There was always the risk that this could be a trap. He didn't want to risk losing his men by sending them across in large numbers.

Then it was Thaw Reh's turn. He had bathed in rivers as a child but he had never learnt to swim properly; he had crossed many rivers on foot but never one this wide. Now he stepped cautiously onto the uneven bed and slippery rocks of the shallows. As the river became deeper the current was even and strong. He watched the back of the man in front of him knowing that if he kept him in view he would be all right. The water grew deeper so that it was soon up to his chest. He glanced back over his shoulder and saw that the bank he had left was further away than the one in front of him. He once again fixed his eyes on the man in front and grimly carried on, willing each leg to take a step and forcing each breath of air into his lungs. At last he could feel the riverbed coming up to meet him and it was with relief that he realised the water was getting shallower. Gasping, he dragged himself up the far bank, his heart thumping loudly. He would never have admitted to being afraid but he hoped that he would never have to ford a river that was any worse than that one.

At last the whole column had crossed. They moved away from the riverside, and set up camp in the forest for the rest of the night. The officer allowed the men to light fires to cook breakfast and they fell hungrily onto the rice as soon as it was ready. They packed some in tins in case they were unable to light fires again for a while; then they spread their clothes out on bushes and began to recover from the nights march.

By mid-day they were marching again. Now they had crossed the first of the main rivers they were able to turn northwards again. "We're back on our path again," the captain addressed the whole unit. "Our next problem is the Salween." He looked around at the grim faces of the men. "It's the old problem," he said ruefully "The rain helps us, and it doesn't help us." The men nodded in agreement. "The rain will send all those Tatmadaw running back to the city." Smiles and some laughter spread through the troops. "But then we get more than our feet wet." It was true that the Salween was a much bigger river than the Pon and the rains would make the crossing impossible on foot. "If all goes well, we should reach the river in two days. Then we must look for boats."

By the time the two days were through Thaw Reh's shoes were completely worn out. He abandoned them in the forest and like many others carried on with bare feet. It was only when they reached the villages that had not been occupied by the Burmese that they were able to come into contact with any human habitation. Up until then the unit had always skirted round places in the dark to avoid the enemy. Now they were able to enter villages, buy food and, almost as important, new shoes. They found only thongs but were grateful even for those.

They crossed the Salween at Namoon. As the captain suspected, the river was too high to ford even though the rains had still not started. Once the unit reached the bank he sent reconnaissance parties out to look for boats. Again they moved under cover of darkness and in small groups so that they could not be identified as a large column. They were all relieved when at last they marched into their new headquarters a full five days after they had set off.

Thaw Reh, ready to do whatever needed to be done, was still burning with the same desire for revenge that he had first felt after his father had died. He was always ready for work; so when the first detachment was sent out he was quick to volunteer.

Suu Meh's father had worked in the tin mines but that had eventually been his undoing. The dust of years had covered his lungs so he could no longer breathe easily. He could do small jobs around the house, but the breadwinning for the family was left to Maw Meh, his wife. But Maw Meh was a gifted woman. She grew vegetables and fruit on the land next to the family home and their quality was famed throughout the district. Suu Meh had always had to work hard. Her heaviest task was bringing the water up from the river in order to irrigate the fields. Maw Meh always insisted that the plants were well watered. "That is the only way to grow good vegetables" she would insist, when her children complained about the work.

"I wonder if we could buy a pump to water our vegetables. It would make things easier in dry weather?" Suu Meh would ask her mother. She was the youngest child in the family and like many other children occupying that particular place, her parents adored her. "We never have enough money," her mother always replied. And Suu Meh knew this was true. "My parents taught me not to borrow money. They always said that there was terrible suffering in Burma because people borrowed and could never pay the money back." Suu Meh decided that when she had her own business she wouldn't be so old fashioned.

After her day's work was over she would go to visit her sister and help her with her two little children. She loved to play with them, and made up songs and stories for them. She loved all small children but these two were very special.

Once a week Suu Meh would take the bullock cart to the markets in the villages around about and would sell the produce for her mother but it was in her own village that she had met Thaw Reh. This had seemed to her to be a stroke of good fortune, and she was to marry him very soon, so there was no need to leave her family. They would always be close neighbours.

Now, as the soldiers roped all the girls together to prevent them from escaping she held on to this thought. She was to be married to Thaw Reh: she would soon be home; only a few short weeks, and then they would be together. She often dreamed of him. She thought of how he sometimes kissed her, and how her whole body pressed against his. His hands were rough and calloused but his touch was gentle and she held onto the memory of it whenever she wasn't with him.

She was strong, far stronger than she looked. The years of carrying the buckets of water had made her lean, and capable of managing the baskets that she and the other young people of the village now had to carry for the soldiers. The evenings proved to be more difficult. As she lay resting one evening, the young guard put his hand on her leg. She pulled her legs up under her and moved away from him. "No, no," she whispered. She hoped nobody had seen what was happening. But he took no notice of her; now, he had moved closer again and was parting her sarong and his hand was reaching further up her leg. She felt her heart racing and pushed him away with another determined cry. He retreated, and looking at him she guessed that he was probably several years younger than she was. She thought how she would have felt pity for such a boy if she had seen him in the village.

He left her in peace and she breathed a sigh of relief and settled down to try to sleep. Then he returned, this time with another boy. Suu Meh's heart began to race again as they hauled her to her feet and marched her to their CO. He was a man much older than the other two and now she felt real fear.

"Undress," he barked at her.

"No! I want to go back to the barracks."

"Undress!"

"No." With her heart pounding in her ears, she tried to run back to the place where the other girls were resting. From the corner of her eye she saw the older man nod to the two others then before she knew it she was on the floor and they were tearing her clothes off her. She tried to scream and struggle, but the three of them overcame her.

"We wont hurt you if you let us."

"No!" It was useless.

After they finished she lay for a long time, her body wracked with pain. At last she dragged herself slowly to her feet; her arms and head hurt where they had been knocked against the wooden floor. Limping out to the latrine where there was a bucket of water, she tried to wash herself, but she felt so dirty and disgusting that she knew she would never feel clean again. She didn't want to go back to the other girls so she sat alone for a long while and then, when all was quiet, and she knew everybody would be asleep she crept back to the hut. She couldn't bear for anyone to know what had happened to her. Would they guess? Had they heard her screaming?

The shame was almost too much to bear.

6

The army of the Karenni National Progressive Party was always short of every resource. As far as guns, ammunition and fighting men were concerned they were heavily out-numbered by the Burmese. But by employing the element of surprise they were able to keep the Burmese on their toes on several fronts. What was more they knew that the Burmese were occupying a land whose population was largely hostile to them and that many of their soldiers were young conscripts who were very far from home and sometimes hungry. For the time being, the KNPP seemed to have stemmed the advance of the Tatmadaw by spreading themselves quite thickly on the ground.

The shortage of weapons meant that the KNPP regularly tried to capture the enemies' guns and Thaw Reh went on his first such expedition soon after his arrival at the headquarters. As the rains had begun at last they were confident of regaining some of the ground that had been lost during the dry weather. From their regular reconnaissance of the area the unit had a good idea of where the enemy gun emplacements were. "We approach at night," the CO told them, "and attack just before dawn when they are least expecting us. We need their heavy machine guns. Our reconnaissance party tells us they have Brownings. They're old but very powerful:

a few of those and we'll be well placed to defend ourselves."

As they waited in the darkness something disturbed one of the lookouts. He called out and Thaw Reh saw his face clearly. For an instant he was shocked at the boyish face before him, surely not even as old as that of his youngest brother. Then quickly banishing that thought from his mind he took aim and caught the boy full in the chest. The other lookouts were aroused but the KNPP were too quick for them. They released the gun and retreated as quickly as they had come. By the time neighbouring emplacements were ready to fire they had vanished into the forest.

So began an orgy of killing and destruction for Thaw Reh, followed by heavy drinking most nights. Sometimes he fell asleep where he sat with the other men and woke hung-over the next day, unable to remember what had happened. He began to get a reputation for drinking and, more than once, was hauled before the CO and given a warning. It made no difference. He continued to drink whatever he could find until one day he was so drunk that he missed the morning roll call. The patience of the CO had come to an end. "This unit is known to be one of the best in the KNPP." His face was a picture of restrained fury. "I will not tolerate such ill discipline. You will be shackled in the guard-room and if there is a repeat of this behaviour then there will be further punishment."

Thaw Reh had nothing to say. He knew he deserved everything that he got. The guard brought him some rice and water, and stood and watched him for a while.

"You think you're hard, don't you?" He leaned against the doorpost with his arms folded. "You are going to get yourself killed before much longer, then what good will you have done for our people?"

Thaw Reh didn't answer. He looked at the floor with a mixture of shame and defiance. The guard put his hand out to him. "Pee Reh". Thaw Reh looked at him and saw kindness in his eyes. He slowly extended his own hand and felt it gripped warmly by Pee Reh.

He spent four days in the guardroom. It gave him time to think. What had happened to his life and his ambitions, such as they were? He had only wanted to live in peace in his village. He had looked forward to seeing the business grow, marrying Suu Meh and bringing up a family with her. As he saw what had become of him he felt deeply ashamed.

He remembered his teacher, Khaw Htoo. Somehow that man had opened his eyes to something better than this. He had instilled in him and others the sense that whatever happened materially the mind could be free. It could never be destroyed. It could have a life of it's own that would go on whatever happened to the body. He couldn't alter the fact that his father had been killed in such an unjust way but what had happened to his mind? Hate and anger had twisted it so that it had become incapable of clear thought. Not only had the Tatmadaw robbed him of his father and his first love, he had allowed them to rob him of his mind, his conscience and his ability to do good. Pee Reh was right.

On his last day in the guardroom he woke shivering. The mornings were sometimes cool now the rainy season had started but he had never felt this cold before. The shivering was so severe that his teeth chattered and his head hurt so badly that he could hardly lift it up from the floor. When he tried to move he vomited, lurching helplessly, and then slumped back onto the floor again. There he waited until the guard came in. The medics unlocked the shackles and helped him across to the hospital block. He felt so bad that he was scarcely aware of what was happening to him. He knew immediately what was wrong with him. He had malaria.

He had had the disease before. It was common enough in Karenni State but years of exposure to the mosquitoes meant that he, like most people, had built up some sort of resistance, so that he had been able to almost ignore any attacks that he might have had. But here was different, they were closer to the river, deeper in the forest and several weeks of not caring where he slept had taken its dread toll

The medics lay him onto a mat and arranged the net round him working on the principle that it was important to isolate those who already had the disease. One of them took a blood sample from him and he began a course of quinine tablets.

"Once upon a time there were two brothers . . . ." His grandmother often told him this story. As he listened she rested her cool hand on his forehead, and immediately he felt better. "One brother . . .the older one

70

was a Karenni called Doh Say, and the younger was a white brother." Thaw Reh couldn't understand this. How could anyone have white skin? He knew what white was; he saw the white frangipani blooming in his mother's garden but how could a man have skin like that?

"One day, Creator God gave Doh Say, the Karenni brother, a book. It was a beautiful book, golden and shining. He told Doh Say to pick up the book, for it was very precious, but Doh Say was very busy. He had many trees to cut down for he had to prepare the ground for his paddi. After he had worked all day he walked past the book and saw that it was still there, but now it was all dusty and covered in leaves for he had cut down many trees that day."

His grandmother paused and offered Thaw Reh some cool water to drink. He took some for the fever had made him very hot and he was thirsty.

"The next day Doh Say had to burn the remains of the forest. All day he worked for he wanted nice clean ground for his paddi. At the end of the day he walked past the book, which was still there; but now it was covered in ash and black soot for he had burnt many trees that day. Now Doh Say had to break up the soil and plant his paddi but this day he decided he would look at the book. He went to the place for he had not forgotten it, but to his surprise the book was not there. His white brother had taken it. He had taken the golden book away far across the sea. Now it was lost and Doh Say would never see it again." Thaw Reh didn't like this part of the story. It made him sad. He wished someone would give him a book. If that had happened to him he knew he would never be too busy to pick it up, especially if it was a nice shiny gold one like the one in the story.

He reached out for his grandmother's hand but it wasn't there. He tried to find the folds of her *sarong* as she sat beside him but he couldn't. He was afraid. Where was she?

He opened his eyes. There was no grandmother. Through the net he could see other men like him, prostrate and delirious. Sometimes a medic was there to restrain the men who might otherwise have hurt themselves. One hurried across to him for his fevered dream had disturbed him.

Pee Reh came to see him and brought him fresh water to drink. Another time he brought a clean rag and a bowl of water and cooled his face and body with a wash then tried to warm him with a blanket when the rigors took hold of him. Thaw Reh tried to thank him but no sound came out of his mouth.

At last the fever abated and he was allowed to return to the barrack room to sleep. By the time he was well enough to return to active service he found that the front had moved westwards by some considerable distance. The Burmese had retreated from many of the villages and the KNPP had taken up several key positions in order to throw a defensive ring around them.

Thaw Reh was posted to one of these. He was glad to be back, especially when he saw that Pee Reh was also in the same unit. By day they patrolled the countryside and in the evenings they contented themselves with a quiet smoke outside their quarters instead of drinking. They talked about their families and their plans for the future and Thaw Reh began to put some order back into his life. He had grown in confidence as a soldier. His application for leave to visit home was turned down on the grounds that the journey was too dangerous but nonetheless he received word through his brother Sah Reh that his mother and sister and grandmother were all well, and his young brother had returned safely. But there was no word of Suu Meh and once again, his mind was tortured with fear for her.

The rainy season came to an end and the opposing armies began to flex their muscles once again: the Tatmadaw always trying to bring more of Karenni State under its control and the KNPP desperate to protect the villages and to survive as a people.

Thaw Reh's unit were defending one of the villages to the west of the Salween River. The advance of the Tatmadaw had been relentless for several days and the decision to evacuate the villagers to safety had to be made soon. It was their unit's responsibility to defend the village during the retreat. The villagers would then have to hide in the jungle the best they could or possibly try to reach the safety of Thailand and hope that they would be admitted to one of the refugee camps there. The ordinary villagers knew that they had a time of extreme poverty and anxiety ahead of them but this was better than losing their lives to the Tatmadaw. They also nursed the hope that they may be able to return to the village when the tide of war moved on and things went quiet again.

Perhaps they were off their guard, they who knew the terrain so well. Suddenly a small group of them were surrounded, with no hope of escape. They could try to shoot their way out but what would be the point? They would almost certainly all die in the attempt. There were six of them, Thaw Reh and Pee Reh among them. They hurriedly conferred and then seeing that there was nothing else to be done, they quietly surrendered.

Thaw Reh carefully looked around the group. He could see four guns trained on them by nervous-looking young soldiers. The Burmese disarmed their captives one by one and stripped them of their uniforms. There was no possibility of escaping alive. He felt sick, sick that he was out of action, sick that he had allowed such a thing to happen, sick when he wondered what was to happen to them. He glanced across at Pee Reh and saw that his face mirrored his own thoughts.

The commanding officer produced rope and tied the men's wrists behind their backs. They then began their march to the Burmese camp to await their fate. If they were to be porters then he knew they would have heavy work ahead of them. Thaw Reh knew what ammunition packs were like but they of all people should be able to carry them. Their own training in the KNPP had prepared them well. The one fear in the back of his mind, not just for himself but for the others too, was malaria; he had already had two more recurrences of the disease since that first dreadful bout that had laid him so low. He ruefully pondered the one thing that they could be grateful for. The dry season that had brought this ferocious advance of the Burmese had stemmed the activities of the mosquitoes.

7

Thaw Reh and his companions soon fell into the way of life of all prisoners wherever they might be in the world. Guards, whistles and orders regulated their days. Anxiety about the future took second place to the daily fight for mere survival. As they carried the heavy packs or hauled guns along jungle paths their minds concentrated only on the next section of the path. They thought only of the next drink of water, the next meal or the next opportunity to take a rest. Tomorrow was not important; they had only to get through today. They walked with guns trained on them knowing that to fall behind or stumble might result in a beating.

"Try to walk slowly whenever you can," Pee Reh said to the rest of the group on the first morning. "Not so slowly that they see what we are doing, but still, as slowly as possible." He was the one who kept their spirits up whenever he could. They had to march in silence but in the evenings as they rested around their meagre food it was he who talked and encouraged the others. He always seemed to be the one passing around cigarettes, he seemed to have ideas as to how they might improve their lot even just a little, and so they came to depend on him. The porter teams were always shifting and changing but when he was with Pee Reh, Thaw Reh always felt better about their situation. He also spoke Burmese so they turned to him when they needed to communicate with the guards.

"I was brought up by my uncle," he told them. "He was a mining engineer. He tried to get better conditions for the workers and for that they made him leave the mines and move right away to another part of Burma. We didn't see him for a long time. Then one day he came back and told my aunt that he'd become a refugee in Thailand. He took them all with him then, my uncle and aunt and my four cousins. I didn't want to go, so I went back to my mother . . . sometimes I wish I had gone with him. He was a good man."

Thaw Reh pulled back the shirt from his shoulder to inspect the skin. Pee Reh watched. "Ow," he grimaced. "How long has it been like that?"

"It's been bad for some time, but its worse today. I'll have to try to get some extra padding."

"I'll see what I can do, Pee Reh said. "You can't go on like that. The skin's badly broken. It must be painful."

Thaw Reh couldn't find a word to describe how painful it had become, but within the day, Pee Reh had produced a jar of balm and some extra clothing. True to form he had charmed the items out of one of the village women and Thaw Reh's spirits were lifted. But there were things that they could hardly bear to speak about.

The old woman's face was contorted with terror. The child who looked to be about ten years old, and was presumably her grandson, clung to her desperately. As they approached the pair they heard the shouts of the soldiers. "We need him . . . he must show us the way." The sounds of commotion grew louder as they reached the clearing in the forest.

"But he doesn't know the way," came the plaintiff cry of the old woman. Thaw Reh's heart thumped in his chest. The words meant only one thing. The soldiers suspected that the area around the village was mined and they wanted this child, small and insignificant as he was, to show them the way. The woman's cries grew frantic as the child was yanked away from her with a brutality that he would not have thought possible.

"Go home Phi Phi," they cried, mockingly, and Thaw Reh saw the rifle lifted and pointed towards her as she left the child with the soldiers.

When a fellow porter showed signs of fever or exhaustion others would try to help by carrying some of the load for him, adding to their already large packs but it was never enough. The man needed rest, medicine, good food and those things all depended on the whim of the soldiers in charge of the column. If he was lucky the man would get some respite, a chance to recover a little, and perhaps some quinine. Usually he would collapse by the path and would be left to survive alone, sometimes lucky enough to be helped by villagers living nearby.

Pee Reh stared into the fire that they had lit to warm themselves. The weather was about as cold as it ever becomes in Karenni State so they were grateful for the small comfort it gave them. "They will never let us go you know. They may let the villagers work for just a few weeks, but us? . . .No! We have to escape somehow, there's nothing else we can do. If we stay here, we will die."

"Where can we go?"

"We can get to Thailand. We could walk. We have to cross over the Salween, and then head due east. We could be there in a few days."

Then Pee Reh had fallen ill. He had begun to vomit as he walked back to the barracks and by the time he reached his mat he had collapsed with the pain in his head and his back. They brought the guard to him and asked if he could rest for a few days. Pee Reh's charm was legendary even among the guards and he was allowed what he needed.

The regular pattern of working meant that they marched from the military camp to one of the fronts, carrying weaponry and ammunition. This usually took a day. They then returned the next day to the base camp so Thaw Reh was away for two whole days at a time. As he entered the porter's barracks on his return he saw Pee Reh lying in his usual place. One of the guards was bending over him. Thaw Reh felt his breath quickening as he crossed the wooden hut to see what was happening. He had the impression that his friend had been talking with the guard but he was filled with relief as he realised that Pee Reh was well and in good spirits. As soon as he saw Thaw Reh the guard rose to his feet and left them. Pee Reh saw the question on his face. "That's Aung Gyi, he's been taking care of me." Thaw Reh didn't know what to say. "He wants to help us to escape. He wants to get away from the army himself. He wants to come with us."

Thaw Reh was incredulous. "You told him that we wanted to get away?"

"I didn't tell him. He came to me, and suggested it."

"You can't trust him. It must be some sort of trap."

"I don't think so," Pee Reh insisted. "Why would he want to do such a thing? Anyway, the Burmese soldiers are deserting all the time. There's nothing very unusual about that. They are sick of this fighting, sick of the army, sick of the non-existent rations."

Thaw Reh found this difficult to take in. He walked out to the back of the hut, took water and tried to wash the dust of the day out of his skin. Using a rag he bathed the sores on his shoulders; they never healed no matter what he did with extra padding and the balm that Pee Reh had found for him. The food was so poor that his body had little chance to recover. He could feel himself getting gradually thinner as the days and weeks went by. His skin was grey and he was beginning to see the outline of his ribs through his flesh. As he looked down at himself he wondered how much longer he could survive. Perhaps escape was the only option. If they died in the attempt it couldn't be worse than this.

But what could they do about this soldier? How did they know whether they could trust him? The answer was that they didn't know. But it was too late now anyway. He knew what they wanted. He was already in Pee Reh's confidence. Thaw Reh went back inside and collecting rice and water for himself and his friend he carried it to his side. As Pee Reh sat propped up against the side of the hut they talked quietly over their food.

"We have no option now, do we? We have to trust him."

"That's right. We've never been able to talk for long because of the other guards but we have begun to get some ideas together."

"What sort of ideas?"

"Well! First, we must make our move when there is very little moon. That could be next week sometime, it's still too full at the moment. Then we need to work round when Aung Gyi ends his watch. The one that ends at midnight would be the best. On the night that we go he will hand on to the next guard then he'll join us instead of going back to his barracks."

"How do we get out through the main fence?"

"We have been thinking about that. There is a small stream that runs through the camp. We can hide in the bed of the stream and make our way upriver until we reach the fence then it's under the fence and out. The problem is that the ground is very open. There are not many trees and bushes around the perimeter, so the stream gives us the best place to hide. They won't miss us until the morning roll call by which time we will be clean away. What do you think?"

"If it's such a good way to get out, won't there be guards there too?"

"That's why we have to go when there is no moon. What about it Thaw Reh? If we go, we go together."

The problem was finding the right time. They needed darkness and they needed a time when Aung Gyi was on the midnight watch. They also needed to know that the guard would be out of sight for the couple of minutes that they would need to get clear of the porters' barracks. It also needed to be a night when they were both there together.

Aung Gyi joined them by their fire one night during his duty. "Here's the stream, around the other side of the camp." He had drawn a map in the dust with his finger. "There's a patch of scrub here," he went on, "close to the porters' barracks. You can hide here, the prisoners' guards won't see you." He glanced up at Pee Reh to be sure that he had understood him. "Then you have to pass the main soldiers' barracks; that will be safe after midnight. The biggest problem will be the main thoroughfare that passes through the middle of the camp." They nodded, eager to hear his analysis of the problem. "The road bends at one end so the best answer may be to go and wait there. Then we can cross without being seen along the length of the road. After that its just a short distance to the stream."

Now they had to wait until the time was right. Each night they watched for the moon as it waned and the nights grew darker. There was still no word from Aung Gyi so that they wondered if he had been moved to another duty. Perhaps someone had noticed that he was spending more time than was usual with two of the prisoners. It was not impossible that one of the porters in their own barracks had been watching them closely. It would not be the first time that prisoners had traded information in exchange for favours from guards.

At last he came back to them. He hurriedly told them that he would be on the midnight watch for the next week and that they were to watch for the signal from him. As he walked past on his duty he would stop by the corner of their hut for a count of five, then he would move on. They were then to go to the latrines one by one and wait there for him to join them at the end of his watch. Pee Reh stopped him. "We only go together. If one of us is away we cannot go. You understand that. We go together or not at all." Aung Gyi nodded and disappeared into the night.

Two nights later conditions were as good as they were ever going to be. Clouds covered the sky obliterating stars and moon. They quietly rolled up their blankets, lay down as if to go to sleep and waited. Through a gap in the bamboo walls they had Aung Gyi in view as he paced to and fro during his watch. He disappeared back to his post for a while and then slowly returned to the corner of the barracks. He stopped. They counted to five slowly then watched as he walked away again. They had the signal.

Thaw Reh silently got to his feet, and slowly and deliberately walked out to the latrines. He waited for what seemed like an age until Pee Reh joined him.

Together they waited in the darkness, praying that none of the other prisoners would wake with the urge to answer the call of nature. Thaw Reh found it hard to breathe and he felt sure that the sound of his heart beating could be heard throughout the camp. Then the sacking across the doorway was swept aside and there was Aung Gyi. "I gave him some cigarettes," he said of the guard that had followed him. "He's lazy and he loves a smoke. That should give us a few minutes." He watched while the man's back disappeared round the corner.

"Now," he whispered. They slipped outside, across the patch of open ground and into the scrub. They crept along through the thin bushes until they reached the back of the main barracks. There was no sign of movement, only a radio playing. Clouds uncovered the moon again. It was only a small light but they dare not risk moving in the open. Thaw Reh began to think about how long it was going to take to get to the perimeter. They had until about 4.30am then the soldiers might begin to light their fires. They had to be clear before then.

They went deeper into the bushes again and moved further away from the barracks. Then the moon disappeared and they set off again, confident that they could not be seen in the deep darkness. They found the main thoroughfare and walked along the side knowing that they couldn't cross until they reached the bend, as Aung Gyi had told them. A dog barked. This set off a cockerel, which in turn set off others. The cacophony continued for some time while the fugitives waited until everything went quiet again. Suddenly Aung Gyi spoke. "Cross the road," he whispered.

Then they had reached the stream. Once in the small gully they flattened themselves on the ground and inched forward towards the fence. They could see a guard patrolling the perimeter so they watched him as he marched and Pee Reh quietly counted how long he took to cover his stretch of ground. "We have to go together," Pee Reh whispered. "If he sees a break in the fence he will know what's happening." Thaw Reh nodded in silent agreement. They had enough time but it meant that they had to stay very close together.

They crept closer to the fence. It was still comfortingly dark. Then they were right under the point where the stream entered the camp. The gap was not big enough for a man to get through so they had to find a way of deepening the channel in order to be able to climb under the fence.

The guard passed nearby. He stopped, turned, and then moved away.

Aung Gyi pulled a rock out of the bed of the stream. They all dug at the gravel with their bare hands. Then, another rock had to be moved. The space had enlarged and Aung Gyi was able to put his head through.

The guard came back. Again, he stopped. This time he lit a cigarette and stood for while looking up at the stars. Thaw Reh silently prayed that he wouldn't look down and give the stream the same sort of attention that he was giving to the sky. He could feel himself getting colder as the water of the stream washed over him. He began to shiver almost uncontrollably. At last the guard moved away. The hole under the fence was almost large enough to let them through. One last effort then they would be able to escape.

The guard passed again. They watched his back recede into the darkness. Then they were into the water and under the fence, tearing hands, faces and knees on the wooden posts and rocks. They stopped in a patch of reeds hardly daring to breathe. There was no sign of the guard so they continued their journey one at a time up the bed of the stream. At last they reached the shelter of the trees. In their relief they laughed. They could hardly believe that they had done it. They had escaped and they were safe outside the fence.

Their relief did not last too long. Aung Gyi brought them back to reality. "We have to be away from here as quickly as possible. Roll call is at 6am. We must put as much distance as we can between us and the camp. Pee Reh wanted to wait. "We don't know which direction to walk in. We can do nothing until daybreak."

Aung Gyi was determined. "At least lets get away from the camp. We can decide on our exact direction when it's light" Thaw Reh was inclined to agree with Aung Gyi on this point. The guards would almost certainly search for the three of them. They dare not be captured again; that would mean death for all of them.

Aung Gyi had a torch with him and a little rice that he had stolen from the barrack kitchen. They had no water but they were confident that they could find enough mountain streams from which to drink. Their only other possessions were the blankets that they had brought with them and these were soaking wet from the crawl through the stream on the way out of the camp. They would not last long with what they had. They knew they were dependent on being able to find sympathetic villagers to help them. They walked slowly and carefully away from the camp until the sky began to lighten. "We must walk towards the east, that's the way to Thailand." Pee Reh was thinking aloud as he surveyed the sky to try to ascertain where the light was coming from. They had been walking towards the north so they changed direction and began to turn towards the lightening sky.

As they walked they saw no homes and no sign of human life. Sometimes they were able to walk easily on what almost looked like paths but at other times the forest was thick and it was impossible to maintain their course. The sun began to climb up into the sky so they rested and ate some of the cooked rice. Aung Gyi took off his jacket, which he then buried deep inside a bush. He didn't want to mark himself out as a Burmese soldier, so he wore only a vest.

All that day they walked slowly and carefully, calculating the direction as best they could from the position of the sun in the sky. They drank from small streams as often as was possible and when they saw a building they skirted round it. In the same way, if they smelled a fire they stayed well away. They walked all day and part of the night, until they had to rest until the morning.

As the sun rose high into the sky they came upon a small house at the edge of the forest. There a woman was hanging out her washing on the bushes around her.

A sleeping baby was secured to her back and another small child played around her skirt. Such a picture of ordinary sweet domesticity pulled at Thaw Reh's heart. This was the first dwelling place they had seen since they had left the army camp. They didn't want to alarm this woman but they had to approach someone: they were desperately hungry. She came closer to their hiding place as she looked for fresh bushes for her clean clothes. At last Pee Reh stood up from his crouching position. "Aunty," he called softly "Aunty."

The woman looked up, unsure of the origin of the sound.

"Aunty!"

Now she saw him.

"Please can you help me? I am hungry. Please help me. I need some food." Since it is the custom among the Karenni to always give hospitality, even a stranger is welcomed, given food and a place to sleep for the night and so the three men were treated to refreshment and rest in the woman's home.

The little child hid behind his mother sometimes peeping out curiously to look at the three pale and dirty strangers. The baby smiled from the security of his pouch close to his mother but the woman was silent. She asked no questions and expected no explanations. Pee Reh ventured a question. "Is the Salween far from here?" The big river would give them the bearings that they needed. She told them that they would be there by the evening. Good news. Once across the Salween they would feel safer. The Burmese had never had such a strong foothold on the east side of the river as they did on this.

"What about soldiers?" they were almost afraid to ask.

"Yes," was her answer, "they have taken men from this village to work on the road. Now I think it is safe, but you must be careful."

8

Crossing the river was the most dangerous part of the journey. As the woman had predicted they reached the bank before evening, so while there was still light they began to reconnoitre. They needed a ford or a boat and could see neither. They dare not seek out any large habitation for the Burmese would almost certainly hold it. They needed a small independent boat operator.

Thaw Reh and Pee Reh saw them at the same time. Elephants! They were drinking and washing themselves in the cool of the early evening. "If the mahouts are friendly then we've done it."

"You two stay here and I will go and look for them," said Pee Reh.

It was quite dark when he returned. "The mahouts can take us across the river but we must wait until later so that there's less danger of a river patrol seeing us," he reported with a broad smile, "and look, one of them gave me some rice." So as they hid among the trees to wait they were able to satisfy at least some of their hunger pangs. "What will you do when we reach Thailand?" Pee Reh asked.

Neither Thaw Reh nor Aung Gyi had even thought about it. "My uncle is the headmaster. He will want me to go to school. I think he's right. I shall do what he wants and learn to be something clever, perhaps an engineer.

"I want to find Suu Meh if I can," Thaw Reh told them, "she was taken away by the soldiers to work as a porter. That was six months ago. That was the same day that my father died. I only thought about joining the army after that."

The other two exchanged glances.

"You've never talked about a woman before."

"True, I was so mad I only thought of revenge for my father's death. But now I wonder about her. I think about her every day."

Aung Gyi began to laugh. "There will be plenty of girls there in the refugee camp. Lots to chose from. Everyone says how pretty the Karenni girls are."

"Don't go getting any ideas," said Pee Reh. "My uncle is a very strict man. Very religious, you know? He keeps a very tight control on everything."

"He won't stop me. I can get through any fence. I've had lots of practice." Pee Reh and Aung Gyi laughed together Thaw Reh couldn't join in. Thoughts of Suu Meh were just too painful.

The other two fell silent. "Tell us about Suu Meh, then. What is she like?"

"It was serious. We were going to be married. Everything was good until that terrible day when the soldiers came into the village. Now I realise that I should have stayed at home. Maybe she would have come back safely, maybe I could have taken her place and then she would be free now. Maybe I could have done something to rescue her. But I lost my head, and then everything went wrong. Now I've lost everything . . . And yes, she is beautiful. She's beautiful in every way possible. She is all a man could want."

It was now thoroughly dark. Was it time to move again? "Ok," said Aung Gyi, "take us to the elephants, Pee Reh."

"Yes, perhaps it's late enough now. We have to at least try, and the mahouts won't go if it isn't safe, you can be sure of that."

As they got to their feet again Pee Reh began to feel slightly light-headed. He shook his head as if to clear it and began to lead the others down the path. "It's about a twenty minute walk upriver from here."

Thaw Reh noticed that something was wrong. His friend was weaving a little from side to side on the path. Then he held onto one of the trees for a few seconds. Thaw Reh put out his hand to help him and he felt Pee Reh's body lean heavily onto his. He dare not voice his fears but he thought them all the same. It could be another dose of malaria and they had no medicines at all.

"Is it far from here?"

"No, not far. If we can just reach there I shall be alright," Aung Gyi joined in supporting Pee Reh and they struggled into the elephant camp.

"Which one said he would help us?" Thaw Reh asked in desperation. He didn't want to ask the wrong man. Pee Reh couldn't be sure now. It was totally dark, the only light coming from the fires that the mahouts had lit. Someone saw them and came over to talk to them. He motioned for them to walk over to a wooden house, which was evidently where one of the families lived.

Perhaps this was the head of the mahouts. A wiry looking man with a deeply lined face came out and asked what they wanted.

"We need your help, we want to cross the river. Is it possible to have the use of one of your elephants?" Thaw Reh hoped that the man understood him. He seemed to know what they wanted.

"Yes. One hundred kyat." was his reply.

"We have no money and our friend is sick."

"No money, no elephant."

"We must get across" Thaw Reh tried not to sound desperate. "We know no other way." The man ignored him and went back inside the house. Their spirits sank. Then Thaw Reh turned to see a younger man at his elbow.

"I will take you." The young mahout motioned for them to follow him into the wooden house he shared with his family. He sat them down and gave them water. They laid Pee Reh down on the floor and tried to make him comfortable. "When do you want to go? "

"As soon as possible, but first tell us, are there any Burmese patrols along this stretch?"

"Yes there are. That's why you must go at night. Even then, we can't be sure. What about your friend?"

"He's just fallen ill again with a fever. We must take him with us."

"We can secure him on the top of the beast. The rest of us will be fine. I will find a seat for him." He disappeared into the darkness.

No one spoke. The rest of the family were obvioiusly beginning to settle down for the night. At last the man returned and they followed him outside to the back of the house where they found the elephant suitably saddled and ready to be mounted.

"We cannot thank you enough," said Thaw Reh, as they struggled to lift Pee Reh up into the seat. The mahout had rope with which they secured him so that he wouldn't fall. The rest of them would have to hold on. They set off back towards the river, the mahout on the head, Pee Reh behind and Thaw Reh and Aung Gyi behind him balancing on the wide back.

The elephant reached the water and stepped forward. Deeper and deeper he went, not seeming at all worried even though he must have been out of his depth. There was some gentle splashing then another sound cut through the darkness. Within seconds it was obvious that this was the sound of a motorboat coming ever closer. The mahout reigned in the beast and turned him back towards the bank where there were overhanging trees reaching into the water. If they could reach them they could wait in safety until the boat had passed.

Thaw Reh was surprised how fast an elephant could swim. Then the low branches were brushing his head, he ducked, and slipped off it's back into the water. The boat was coming nearer. It would soon pass, then they could get on their way again. But no! It seemed that the driver of the boat had seen something. Having been alerted by the fires of the mahout camp he came into the shore to investigate.

He knew where to go. Marching straight up to the head mahout's house he called him out. Once the officer in charge of the boat, had stepped ashore the mahout drove the elephant deeper into the trees with Thaw Reh holding onto his tail and Pee Reh still safely on the seat.

"Anything happening tonight?" asked the officer. "Smugglers, runaways, KNPP . . . you know what I'm looking for." The wiry old man eyed the officer inscrutably. He didn't care much for these runaways. Though perhaps he had been a little hard on the three that he had seen tonight. But why not? These people were always troubling him and wanting help. None of them ever had any money. But these were helping a sick man. And now one of the mahouts was out on the river with them. The mahouts and their beasts belonged to the oldest and most important occupation of the forest.

"No nothing, officer. All quiet tonight"

The officer knew better than to further disturb the peace of the mahouts. He was heavily outnumbered and this was a long way from his headquarters. "Goodnight then." The men exchanged a smile and a deep bow and the officer joined the boatmen. In two minutes they were out of sight. The Mahout helped Thaw Reh back onto the elephant and they resumed their journey. They came out of the trees and were soon in deep water again. The water lapped around their feet but Pee Reh stayed secure until at last they made the far bank. He then told them they would be safe for the night on this bank. They were to find a place a few yards from the river and they could rest there. Thaw Reh thanked him again.

"No problem. And God go with you." And he was gone, back across the river.

Thaw Reh turned to watch the mahout and his elephant as he swam out of sight again. He thought about his departing words. Perhaps the mahout was a Christian like him. If so, in his act of kindness he had shown the true love of God, love that was willing to lay down its life for others. He had saved their lives.

The forest floor offered them no shelter and Thaw Reh was soaked from his dip in the river so he took off his clothes, hung them over a low branch and covered himself as well as he could with leaves from the trees.

All any of them had to offer Pee Reh when he shivered with the fever were their blankets. The following days passed in a blur of hunger and exhaustion. Pee Reh had wanted to press on in spite of his fever so they did their best, mile after crawling mile. Then Thaw Reh felt the touch of the fever again so they had come to a halt once more. Another day, another night and Thailand seemed as far away as ever.

Thaw Reh woke again to the clatter of weapons and the sound of men's voices. He had been vaguely aware of footfalls and the rustling of the vegetation but now that awareness turned into alarm. Apart from the patrol they had encountered by the Salween they had seen no soldiers at all since they had escaped from the army camp. Now his spirits sank as he contemplated what their fate would be. He knew one thing. They were powerless to resist, as they were so weakened by hunger and malaria. Even Aung Gyi, who had not succumbed to the disease, had grown quiet and was unlike his usual cheerful self. Now he knew they were surrounded. He hardly dared open his eyes until he caught words that he understood.

He sat up as the realisation dawned upon him that this was his own language that he was hearing and Pee Reh was talking to them. "This is Aung Gyi. He's a deserter from the Tatmadaw. He escaped with us from the camp. How far is it to the border from here?" He was asking the C.O.

"If you can walk we can be there by this evening; we can do it if you are well enough."

"Yes, I'm better now," put in Thaw Reh, hardly daring to believe their good fortune.

The CO described the situation to them. "This dry season has been very hard for our people. There are many hiding in these forests. We send out our patrols now just to find people and help them to get to the border. Many are like you; they have no food, no medicines, nothing. We will send two of our men with you to show you the way. The rest of us will continue with our patrol."

They quickly picked up their few possessions and followed the two KNPP soldiers who had been assigned to escort them to the border. They had been walking for maybe a half an hour when the soldier in front abruptly left the path and turned off into the thick forest where they soon came upon some wooden buildings. "Breakfast," announced one of the escorts.

This was the local headquarters. Food, drink, a wash and they were soon ready to be on their way; true to predictions they were in Thailand by nightfall. Camp Duwa had a reception house, blankets, and food, and they spent their first night for many months, free and comfortable.

"I'm going to see my uncle tomorrow," announced Pee Reh. "I'm going to ask him to take me into the school. I think he will. He wants everyone to come to his school. What about you two, do you want to join me?"

Since that night by the Salween Thaw Reh had been thinking about his life. He had remembered back to the time when he had heard his teacher Khaw Htoo talking about how the children had to finish school at such a young age. He thought of how he had been happy in his work as a builder, yet inside he knew that there was so much more for him. He had reflected again on how he had started to learn to read English and how he had read books that had come from Khaw Htoo's library, such a distant memory, yet it had come to him then in the darkness. If only he could read more. As they had languished in the forest, wondering whether they would ever reach safety, he had decided to take whatever was available. If Pee Reh's uncle were offering him education he would take it.

9

The classrooms in the Camp Tewa School were of simple bamboo construction. They had earth floors and rough-hewn wooden desks and chairs. The upper classes of the school were built at the very edge of the camp where the ground began to rise to meet the foothills, so there was very little level ground to be seen anywhere.

The three young men had been quickly absorbed into the dormitory of the school. There were always new arrivals, many of them soldiers like themselves, so there was no problem with assimilation. Thaw Reh had met Uncle Kaw La Htoo and had found him just as Pee Reh had described, a good, kind and intelligent man. He lived in a small house near the school and he took the three newcomers there to talk with them. "Tell me about yourselves"

"We two were with the KNPP," began Thaw Reh," we were captured by the Burmese and have been working as porters for the last four months. We knew we would never be freed, so we had to escape. Aung Gyi here helped us. He was one of the Burmese guards." Aung Gyi was quiet. Kaw La Htoo seemed to read his thoughts.

"Don't worry, we have many soldiers here and we have some who have deserted from the Burmese Army. That is no problem to us. We are glad to welcome you. What do you all want to do? Do you want to join the school?"

"Yes, Uncle," said Aung Gyi, "but I have no English. I have never learnt it."

"We have classes for you, and we can help you as much as we can, but you must do your part. You must work hard, we have no place here for those who don't work."

"I left school a long time ago," Thaw Reh said. "I was fourteen. But our teacher helped me. I used to borrow English books from him and read them." Kaw La Htoo was intrigued. "How did your teacher have English books?"

"I believe his mother used to work for the British. When they left, they gave him some of their books because he used to want to read them so much. He kept them and used to lend them to us. I really would like to learn more English now. I thought I would never have the chance again, but now I have." He stopped as he caught the steady gaze of the teacher resting on him with a gentle smile. He felt his heart lift. Then the man's attention turned to his own nephew.

"What about you Pee Reh? Are you still breaking your mother's heart?" Pee Reh looked at him with a small frown, then he saw his uncle's eyes almost disappear into a wide smile.

"I don't know, I often wished I had come with you to Thailand. I joined the army but it did no good at all. We were lucky to get away with our lives in the end."

"Well this is a good week for us. We have some visitors from England. They arrived yesterday, so we are going to concentrate on English for the next few weeks. There's a whole group of them. We can spread them through all the top classes so they can help everyone."

Thaw Reh and Pee Reh took places to one side of the class. Kaw La Htoo introduced them to everybody and then he brought in the two English girls that had been assigned to their class. A buzz immediately passed around the room. Thaw Reh saw the boys' faces break into smiles as they welcomed the girls, but he was covered with embarrassment, not sure where to look. He had never seen a white woman before. He hoped they would not look in his direction. What would they see in him? He had never seen himself in a mirror but he could see Pee Reh's face, and from that he could guess what he must look like. He was pale with malnutrition and chronic hunger, his eyes were dark rimmed and sunken, the contours of his face sharply angled as a result of the weight loss. What had passed as normal when they were hiding in the jungle as lonely fugitives now looked appallingly pale and ghastly. He looked around at the rest of the class and saw clear eyes and good skin, and felt the shame of poverty and hunger. He wanted to get out of the classroom but he couldn't now. He just had to sit there.

An easy laughter was rippling around the room. The girls had introduced themselves. "Vicki and Katie from England." The members of the class were stumbling over their words but they all laughed together and nobody seemed to mind. They were enjoying themselves while he was filled with dread. Supposing one of them asked him a question? He wished he hadn't said he wanted to learn English.

He looked at the two girls. They looked so different to the Karenni people and yet they were laughing with the rest of the class as if there were no difference at all. Vicki had a round face with very light curly hair. He thought how kind she looked. She seemed to be the older of the two, and more confident, so at that moment she was doing most of the talking. The other girl, Katie, was quieter. She was watching Vicki carefully and seemed to be taking note of everything that she did. She had a smaller build than Vicki and short, dark hair and skin that was white, whiter than he had ever seen. She had a flush of pink across her nose and her eyes sparkled. When she laughed, it was as if a light came on in her eyes.

The girl they called Vicki was speaking; she wanted everyone to speak to the person sitting next to them in English. They were to tell their partner about themselves, then they were all to stand up in turn and say what they had found out about their partner. Did they understand? Vicki had spoken very slowly and carefully so even he, Thaw Reh, had understood. Then she wrote some questions on the board. "You can use these if you want to. You have five minutes to find out all you can about your partner."

Thaw Reh and Pee Reh began to try their English together. Their weeks together in the barracks and on the forest tracks working as porters had brought them close together, closer even than brothers. Now, they struggled to find English words that would describe something of their life. Then it was Thaw Reh's turn to speak.

"This is Pee Reh. He is 22 years old. He is a soldier. Now he wants to learn English. "

He sat down with relief.

"Thank you," said Vicki smiling. He smiled back. A first step and already he felt better. Nobody laughed at him, they were all glad to welcome him. Here, where everyone had lost home, or father, or mother, or freedom; all were equal, all were welcomed, all were brothers. This was his family now. Vicki led the class until near the end of the morning then she asked if any of them wanted to ask her or Katie questions. The members of the class who were braver or had a better command of the language excelled themselves and left the quieter element in peace for a while. Thaw Reh was glad just to listen and catch what he could of the banter that went round the class. He heard Katie speak for the first time. She told them how she was a nurse but had wanted to travel. They asked her about her home and family and she was trying to answer in terms that they understood.

By the end of the day Thaw Reh's head was spinning. He had been concentrating hard for many hours and could hardly take in the changes that had happened in his life in such a short time. In a few days he had gone from being prostrate with fever and almost starving in the forest to being in a place of safety with a floor to sleep on and food to eat. It felt a little strange being able to live his own life again after so many months in captivity, yet everything that he had once treasured so much seemed so far away. He thought about the rest of his family: his mother and sister and two brothers. Where were they? Were they safe too? Were they even alive?

Most of all he thought of Suu Meh. Now he was secure he had time to wonder about her again. He had heard nothing for months now and he tortured himself with fear for her life. And yet, it was just possible that she was right here in the camp. He resolved to begin looking for her. He would ask around the camp. He could start at the clinic and then maybe the other dormitories. Someone must know something. He would begin his search tomorrow.

Kaw La Htoo loved his work; he loved the school and everything about it. Each of the students had a special place in his heart and he would do anything to help them on their way in life. They were in a desperate situation. New refugees were coming over the border all the time now, each one with a story to tell. Large numbers of them had been forced away from their villages, into new townships that were controlled by the Burmese army. Sometimes when the army retreated, or released its grip, the people would run away and hide in the jungle. Eventually they would find their way to the camps on the border, where at least they were safe and had some basic food supplies and medicines, more than they had ever had in the jungle.

But in the end what good did that really do them? They could not travel or go into the towns to try to find work. The guards on the camp gate usually stopped them so they had to indulge in a sort of cat and mouse game, sneaking out through fences and across fields to get out and make some sort of living where they could.

Kaw La Htoo hoped that one day they would all go home: back to their villages, their farms and their businesses and live as free people again. He kept this hope in his mind because it nourished him when his spirits were low and when there was no money for books and no teachers for half of the classes. He needed such nourishment because he knew how much these children were desperate to learn. He had welcomed children from across the border that had never been to school. Even bright young people came to him with only two or three years of the simplest schooling behind them. He knew that if he could teach them and prepare them in some way for the future, he would have done something worthwhile with his life.

He thought back to the boys he had welcomed yesterday. They were bright boys, his nephew Pee Reh among them, who had willingly joined in an armed struggle that had been going on for almost fifty years. That was how long his people had had to endure the fight for their own survival. True, things had not always been this bad. It had only been in the last few years that the number of refugees had risen so sharply. The Tatmadaw had made some dreadful advances, which had sent the people running for the border in ever increasing numbers.

Pee Reh had always been headstrong, always wanting to go his own way in life. He had broken his mother's heart more than once, leaving her without a thought, but she doted on him and took him back whenever he came home again. Now perhaps his experience in the jungle would have taught him some sense and he would settle down and give his mother some much needed peace of mind.

The other young man they called Thaw Reh was interesting. He seemed very motivated and more serious than most about wanting to study. He had also seemed strangely driven in some way. He had asked for the names of the residents in the camp so Kaw La Htoo had taken him to the commandant; he had been looking for certain families. "Sah Meh, Ree Reh, Saw Reh?" The commandant sadly shook his head. All too often he had the job of trying to find lost relatives but telling someone that their families were not safely in any of the three camps never became any easier.

"Ku Shwe, Maw Meh, Suu Meh?" Thaw Reh hardly dared to ask; he almost knew he would be disappointed.

"No I'm sorry," the commandant had said, after a prolonged search through the lists. "But leave your name and if I hear anything we can tell you." Thaw Reh had turned away dejectedly. Nobody he really cared about had reached the safety of Thailand.

Suu Meh had been many months with the Battalion 501. When Thun Oo called for her now she went to him quietly. It was easier that way. The first few times she had fought and screamed but had ended up so bruised and battered that she could hardly bear the pain.

And anyway, once she let him have his way she did not have to endure the attentions of the other soldiers. He made sure of that. Sometimes he was good to her. He gave her some new clothes, some soap or *thanaka* that he had bought for her. Other times he acted as if he hated her and would not look her in the face. He was capricious and inhumane. Whatever he did she bit her lip and endured. She had no choice.

At first, she would think about her home, her sister, her beautiful niece and nephew, but that all seemed so long ago now. She was a different person to the one she had been when she had lived in Daw Kler Leh. She never thought of Thaw Reh; she couldn't bear to. What good man would ever want to be with her now she had lived like this? One night she dreamt that he came to her and she saw his face close to hers. "No!" she screamed, as she sat up. "Don't touch me." Then she looked across and remembered that she was in the hut with the other girls and she lay down again.

As she drifted back to sleep she was aware of a vague fluttering feeling deep in her belly. A few days passed and then she had no doubts at all about what she was feeling. It had been so many months since she had seen her periods that she had not thought about them. She had been exhausted and sometimes nauseated for weeks and had not dared to contemplate what it might mean.

Now she knew. There was no denying it to herself any longer.

10

It had taken several months for the group to prepare for their visit. Katie had put in extra hours at work in order to save towards the trip; she had never been so busy or so happy. As well as paying their own expenses the members of the group had tried to raise funds for the refugee camp school.

"There's a ten kilometre run coming up in a few weeks," Richard had announced one evening. "I'm going to enter and get some sponsors, does anyone want to join me?" Katie had looked around the group for a few moments wondering who else was going to respond, then suddenly knew that it had to be her. She could run, of course she could. She had proved that, months ago when she had been overwhelmed by the need to stretch herself against the crushing lack of a sense of self worth that Declan had left her with. "Yes," she said quietly. "I'll join you."

And she and Richard had spent the weeks of early autumn training in the park and relaxing together over a drink as the evenings slowly drew in. "It's Richard now is it?" Her friend Hannah laughed one day when she saw Katie going out in the rain wearing running gear. "He's good fun to be with, that's all," Katie had replied. "We're just training to enter for a run. There's no romance in it if that's what you mean?"

"Oh yes? I'm sure I can see your eyes light up every Wednesday; and isn't it Wednesdays when you go running?"

"Hmmm," she had answered. "Am I really that transparent?"

"Yes, Katie, you are," Hannah replied while her eyes twinkled. "But it's good to see you looking so happy again."

"I'm not going to get myself involved with anyone for a long time yet. This is going to be a time for me to find out what I want. Anyway, are you going to sponsor me for the run?"

Sarah had shown them videos of her previous trips.

"I didn't know what to expect," Katie had said to Vicki one evening. "I thought they'd all be starving or there'd be terrible suffering there."

"No, neither did I," Vicki agreed with her. "The school looked pretty good and they all looked quite healthy didn't they? Hey what is it?"

"I sometimes wonder what I'm going with you for," she had told her. "I feel as if I have nothing to offer."

"Katie," Vicki emphasised her name with such a reassuring tone that Katie found she almost always felt better. " We need you. The group needs you."

"How do you mean?" Katie asked.

Vicki had seemed to find it difficult to explain. "It's your personality. It's just you. You're quiet and you want to learn. I think that's the right approach for the refugees. They don't need people who know everything or can do things for them. They need people who are able to stand alongside them and learn with them, if you like." Katie had been nonplussed. "You're just the right sort of person. I know you are. Look at Richard; he's so tall and so noisy sometimes. Did you see on the video, most of the people were quite small and gentle? They probably find someone like him a bit overwhelming. But you, you're just right. You're small and quiet and you've got the right sort of attitude. I don't think you need to worry."

"Oh Richard's all right. He's fun. And I think he's the sort of person who'll get on anywhere."

She had enjoyed the experience of running with Richard too, but mindful of Hannah's comments, had decided that honesty was the best policy and one evening while relaxing over a drink, had told him about Declan. "Now I come to think about it, the worst thing wasn't that he went off with her, but that he made me depend on him so much. He was so good to me, or that's how it seemed at first. He did everything for me. And I didn't see it. Now I realise I was very immature and must have been flattered by him."

"Did you live together?"

"Oh yes, he thought it would be a good idea and I didn't argue. Perhaps I was frightened of losing him. But then I lost him anyway. He was deceitful too. He didn't tell his parents and I never told Dad. He didn't want me to and I accepted everything he said."

"He had you where he wanted you, didn't he?"

"Hmmm," Katie mused into her drink. "So . . . I'm being a bit careful at the moment."

"You don't want to get hurt again huh?"

"I can't take anything like that for a while anyway."

"And are you worried that I . . ?"

"Oh . . .uh . . I don't know," in her momentary embarrassment she wished she hadn't said so much.

"Don't worry. I just want to be friends, too. And when it comes to living together I have very strong views. I probably sound very old fashioned, but I don't agree with it. I've seen too many people get hurt and then nobody trusts anyone. That's not what relationships should be about."

"So you don't approve of me then?"

"I didn't say that. I've nothing against anybody. It's just the casual way that people drift into these things that I have a problem with." Katie met his eyes for a brief moment and saw no condemnation, just clear honesty.

"OK, sermon over. I've said enough. But consider yourself safe with me."

"And I'm just wanting to have a bit of independence for a while and this trip is going to be part of that."

"It's going to be good, Katie. Now how are we going to get Paul to relax and enjoy it too?"

She smiled with relief, glad to get the conversation away from herself again. Paul was the other medical student of the group: awkward, callow, and the one person who made Katie realise how far she had come in the last few months.

Now they were in the classrooms, two to each class. It had become school policy to teach English to all the students. This exercise was fraught with difficulties since there were so few teachers who had knew enough of the language to be able to teach it. However, the decision had been made because so many textbooks were written in English so the ability to read and understand it opened the students to a whole world of books and education.

This meant that the school was always very grateful for any who came to help them to improve their spoken English. Kaw La Htoo had, over recent years, found a few people from the English-speaking world who would help with this. Some even stayed in the camp for months or years. Some, like Sarah and her husband, would only stay for a few weeks but they were nonetheless welcomed for the invaluable help that they gave.

Katie and Vicki had decided to work together.

"I've never done anything like this," was Katie's plea.

"Well, watch what I do, and then you can join in later. Once we've introduced ourselves then we can divide the class into pairs and they can talk to each other. Then we get them to tell the rest of the class what they have found out about the other person. Sometimes people are less shy when doing things in pairs. After that we can encourage them to ask us questions."

"OK that's fine by me, I'll just follow you."

The whole group of English visitors met for lunch together

"How did it go Vicki, Katie?"

"OK! Good! I tried out a few ideas I learnt on the TEFL course. We'll try some more this afternoon."

"What about you, Katie?"

"Well, I didn't do much. I just listened really. I think I learnt a lot though."

"One of the main problems," Vicki added, "was their shyness. A lot of them seemed afraid to speak out so we had to help them."

"Some of the students have been in the school for only a very short time so they have a long way to go." Kaw la Htoo explained. "We are getting new refugees coming over all the time. It is very hard for them but everyone tries to help the newcomers."

"The biggest surprise to me was that some of the students were already in their twenties." observed Vicki.

"That's because most of them have had a badly interrupted education. Some left school at a young age, some have been soldiers and some have lived in the mountains where there is no school nearby. Now, they have a chance, so we do what we can for them." Kaw La Htoo told them.

Katie found La Meh surprisingly easy to talk to. "Tell me about your family?" La Meh asked her.

"Well, I have no brothers or sisters. I am an only child, and my mother is dead. It's just my father and me now."

"My mother is dead, too. She died when my youngest brother was born. He is ten now."

"Why did you come to the camp?"

"Our father died too, so we went to live with our aunty. One day soldiers came and said we had to move to another village. We didn't want to go so they made us go out of the house and then they burnt it down with everything in it. We lost all our things so we had to leave."

Katie gulped in disbelief. Sarah had told them that many people had very sad stories and now the first person she had really spoken to had had to endure almost unbelievable tragedy. The silence of understanding hung between the two girls and in that instant a friendship was sealed. Then La Meh spoke. "People were very kind to us and helped us, she paused. "Even though they had nothing themselves, they still tried to help . . . and God looked after us. Some Karenni soldiers found us and helped us to the border, so here we are."

Katie saw the certainty, kindness and what could only be described as serenity in La Meh's expression, and once again came face to face with her own inadequacy. "I'm afraid I didn't cope very well with my mother's death. Neither did my father. You see, at home nobody wants to talk about death so it can be very lonely. My father was ill last year and I'm sure it was . . ." Katie felt her throat closing painfully as tears rose into her eyes.

La Meh took her hand. "I shall pray for you Katie," was all she said and Katie was surprised at the comfort she found in those words.

Sarah Cassidy was pensive. The whole group were occupied somewhere. They were all teaching in one of the classes so she now had a chance to catch her breath and sit quietly for half an hour. She had never dreamt that she would become so involved in something that was so remote from her life in England. Sometimes she wondered if she and David should uproot and live out here permanently. They had talked about it often but they realised that they could probably do more by staying at home and trying to help people in England to learn about the problems of the Burmese ethnic minorities.

Their first visit had raised many questions in Sarah's mind. She was curious as to why there were so many refugees here when little was ever said about it in the world's media. Because of this she had resolved to read everything she could find about the situation in Burma. Then she had written letters to everyone she thought would know about it. So much so, that it became almost an obsession with her. She and David had given talks to all sorts of groups, and gradually they found that gifts of money came pouring in. Sarah hadn't intended for any of that to happen but, once it had, they had realised they now had the potential for doing something really worthwhile. They began to visit regularly and on each visit they took the money that they had raised with them and soon they had begun to see real improvements in the school. The teachers had started to write and print their own books and the school was able to pay them all a small salary. They built dormitories for the children who had no parents or home to go to and they planted vegetable gardens and reared chickens, so that the children could eat decent food.

After the first couple of visits, Sarah and David had decided to ask others to come with them. This was not always an unqualified success. Many westerners found it almost impossible to live without the comforts of home, electricity and running water. Sometimes the privations of life in the camp threw up other problems, and people began to call into question many of their long held assumptions about life. Sarah sometimes felt that what they did was rather shallow. What could they really achieve in a few short weeks? But Kaw La Htoo seemed very happy with things so they continued as they were.

Sometimes Sarah wondered if the situation would ever get better. She had been following it now for nearly five years and every year brought more refugees and ever more horrific stories. There were times when she could hardly bear to hear another story of killing and rape, of families torn apart, of children losing their parents and villages burnt to the ground: at others it seemed to her that it would be easier to just walk away but she would never do that now. It was as if these people were part of her own family and she would go to the ends of the earth for them.

And what about this group that she had brought with her? They all seemed to have settled in well and each one had found a niche somewhere, even Katie, who had caused her most concern at first. Sarah had been unsure about asking her to join the trip, but now she knew she had done the right thing. Watching Katie prepare for the ten-kilometre run had convinced her of that, it was as if she had come alive at that point. She had shown a determination that had surprised the whole group. It took some guts to train to run that distance and Katie had not once faltered in her resolve. She had asked colleagues to help with the fund raising, which many of them did very willingly, but they too were surprised when they saw how she had finished the course and raised several hundred pounds with just her entry to the run. She had turned out to be just right for this visit. Many westerners were so large and noisy by comparison with these small people with their quiet grace, but Katie's gentle nature didn't allow her to overpower anyone with the force of her own personality, she had instead slowly blossomed and had allowed others to do the same.

She found Katie one evening sitting looking at the stars that, away from the noisy light of cities, were visible in their thousands.

"Am I disturbing you?"

"No, not at all, I just love it here so much."

"Happy?"

"Ye-es. . .mostly."

"Oh? What's the problem?"

"I've decided that there's something I've got to do."

"Oh yes?"

"It's to do with my Dad. You know about my Mum dying when I was fifteen."

"Yes," Katie heard the gentleness in Sarah's voice.

"Dad took it so badly . . . well I did too of course. But Dad . . .well he's better now and he's met someone else. Theresa's her name. He wanted me to meet her. She sounded so nice, but I flatly refused. I was quite horrible about it, too. I wouldn't even go home at Christmas because of it. Well, being here has made me see how stupid and awful I've been to him. When I think what some of these people have been through my problems are nothing."

"Do you ever talk to your Mum Katie? I mean do you ever try to imagine what she would think about your Dad?" Sarah felt rather than saw the consternation in Katie. "Could you imagine your mother in a place where she was really happy, or . . .perhaps doing something she really liked?"

"That's easy. It would be her painting. . .in her shed. The studio, Dad used to call it. He used to laugh about it, but that was where she was happiest."

"Well, perhaps that's the place you should try and imagine her. What do you think?"

"Perhaps. I don't know. I'll have to think about that. But I know one thing. Coming here has made me want to sort out my priorities a bit."

"Yes, it does doesn't it? Look, there's something I really wanted to ask you about Katie.

"Yes?"

"When Kaw La Htoo heard that you were a nurse he asked me more about you. They really need someone to teach about health issues, and he is wondering if you would consider coming back and working for a few months. You can think about it, of course. You could come home with us, make your arrangements at home and then return in a few weeks or months or whenever you're ready. Our funds can provide you with the money that you need."

The sweet darkness of the tropical night enfolded the two women as Sarah waited quietly for Katie's response.

"Yes, Sarah, I would love to come back here again." The words were out before she had time to think, but to her own surprise, she heard the utter conviction in her own voice. And Sarah knew that she would. The two of them sat looking up at the sky once more, then Sarah got up quietly and left for her own room.

"Goodnight Katie."

And as Sarah left her alone in the warm darkness Katie closed her eyes. In her mind's eye she saw her mother wearing one of her father's old shirts on top of her faded jeans. Her straight dark hair was gathered untidily on the top of her head with a hair slide. She looked totally absorbed in her work, in love with her occupation. In her imagination, Katie moved around the studio so that she could see the painting.

The meadow was full of long grass. A riot of scarlet poppies lined the path to an old house and Katie could see herself on the path that led towards it. The door stood wide open, and she could see inside to the chequered pattern on the hall floor. An old man stood at the threshold smiling at her. He made her feel welcome . . happy, . . at peace. He didn't speak, but she knew by his face that everything was all right, and she had no need to be afraid.

Katie had taken to walking down to the riverside in the late afternoon as the brightness of the day was beginning to give way to lengthening shadows. This was the coolest time of the year, but even so, the heat could be intense in the middle of the day and she found it pleasant to bathe her feet in the water. She was also fascinated by sight of the women who would take their clothes into the water and, wrapped in a sarong, wash themselves, their children and the laundry in one exercise that struck Katie as highly efficient. Detecting a movement at her elbow, she turned to see Paul standing just behind her. He was the one member of the group that she had had almost nothing to do with. Intensely serious, she had at first found him intimidating. But now she detected in him a sort of deep unhappiness that she recognised had been in herself such a few short weeks ago.

"Hello," she uttered in her surprise, then became aware of the possible discomfiture of the women. "Perhaps we should walk along a bit, they might not like us looking at them.

"Yes. I'm sorry, I don't always think of these things. Shall I leave?"

"No, you don't have to do that." Katie suddenly saw how much he needed reassurance. "There's a path down here, I know it quite well now. I come down here every day."

"How's it going, Paul?" she asked by way of making conversation once they had put a reasonable distance between themselves and the women.

"It's good. I'm seeing a lot. Sometimes I don't feel as if I'm doing much good here. They've got their clinics and their mobile teams all sorted. I'm amazed at what they do. We've been going into Karenni State. They have a lot of land mine victims there. We did an amputation yesterday. That was pretty nasty and the chap was not much more than a child really."

"Anaesthetic?"

"We gave him a bit of Ketamine. It seemed to be enough, but the worst thing was that we had a lot of trouble stopping the bleeding. We had no fluids . . .nothing."

For a moment Katie thought of the patients that she had cared for back home in her hospital. Even in England, with every kind of medical equipment to hand, it was sometimes impossible to save the life of a patient who was bleeding heavily after a motor accident. She shuddered in spite of the heat.

"It's hard, Katie. How do these people keep going when they have that sort of thing to contend with? One of the medics was telling me that half of all the land mine victims die and lots of them are children. They step on them when they're playing outside in the fields and bushes." Katie watched helpless while he struggled with his emotions. "And in a few weeks we'll be going home . . . yet these people can never go home, or at least, if they do, they run the risk of stepping on a mine or being shot by the Tatmadaw."

"But they don't seem to let it get them down, do they?"

"No. In spite of it all, they seem to make the best of things. Amazing, isn't it?"

"Well it's certainly surprised me. Being here has done me a lot of good. It's helped me sort some of my ideas out. Did you know that Sarah's asked me to come back and teach here for six months, and I've said I will?"

"Yes, Vicki told me. Well done, Katie. You're another surprise. Out of all of us in the group, I thought that you would be the one to find this trip difficult, but you've come up trumps. If the truth be known, I think it's me that's found it hardest to fit in."

"Oh no, Paul," she wanted to reassure him, "don't say that. You've found out what the needs are, so now you can do something about them. Perhaps you could do some teaching, or raise some money to buy medical equipment or something."

"But that's such a small thing, and how does that deal with the situation? The real needs are so much bigger than anything that we can ever do anything about."

"Small things count though, don't they? That's all any of us can ever do. But it's always better that doing nothing." And Katie realised that she was talking to herself and knew more than ever that she had something to offer. "Look, we've gone half way across the fields already, and it's beginning to get dark. Shall we turn back?"

"Yes OK," he replied, seeming grateful for the change of subject, "and thanks. . . thanks for everything." And Katie just nodded. She didn't know she had done anything.

All too soon the weeks came to an end and they were exchanging addresses and promises to write. Katie couldn't take them all in. "I will be back soon," she tried to tell some of the students but they still pressed pieces of paper into her hands, as if that somehow signified that she was now their special friend. She was moved almost to tears, at the thought of what they were doing. It was hard indeed to walk away from these people that she had come to love in such a short time. She was already going over in her mind her plans for the next few weeks. She saw no need to delay something that she was so sure was right for her.

11

Thaw Reh soon developed a love for learning and lapped up every class that he attended. He began to make friends with David and went along to help him organize football classes for the younger boys. He found that it gave him enormous pleasure to see the children achieve some new skill on the dusty roadway that served as a football field and in return for his help David took him aside for English tuition every evening. "How long have you been here?" David asked as they drew to the close of one of their lessons.

"Just a few days. I was a soldier for a while . . . and before that I worked with my father. He was a builder."

"What sort of builder?" David was suddenly very interested.

"We built houses, offices, whatever was needed. A lot of people in the village built their own homes but he got jobs in the town, or at the mines, he was never short of work. He loved to do things with wood. It was his whole life."

"Did he make furniture?" asked David.

"Yes, but not for the business. Just for us. Most people had almost nothing in their houses, perhaps a cupboard or some shelves. But my father made chairs for my mother and my grandmother and cupboards and . . ."

"I work with wood too, that's my business. I restore old furniture." Thaw Reh's heart warmed as he realized that here was someone who understood how he felt about the life that he had shared with his father. "The interesting thing is," David continued, "I often come across furniture from this part of the world. People used to buy it when they worked in Burma years ago, then they brought it home to England with them. A lot of it's getting old now of course, so that's why it comes to me. But I love to see it. It's hard to work with but beautiful to look at and worth the effort. I didn't know I'd ever come to the part of the world where it all came from when I first started out years ago."

"Well there's not much teak left now," said Thaw Reh, "most of it's been cut down. It's almost the only way of making any money around here. My father did have one cupboard made of teak, but most of what we had was from the forest around the village. I remember he used to make me plane the timber until my arms hurt. Then I would have to rub it down, and still he would never be satisfied, so he would finish it himself. Then he would oil it and polish it. It had to be perfect."

As he spoke those words they brought to mind what he had loved the best about his father, and David watched as Thaw Reh suddenly turned away. He saw the angles of the young man's face become even sharper as he turned around to face him again. "He's dead, my father. The Tatmadaw soldiers shot him and I watched him die. I haven't seen any of my family since that day." And David stood quietly thinking how it would be if Thaw Reh were his own son and could work alongside him in his business.

Life as a porter for the Tatmadaw had been highly regimented and Thaw Reh had forgotten what it was like to be free. The freedom to choose had only been a distant dream for many months and he only slowly re-accustomed himself to the idea that he could do what he wanted. His talks with David opened up new possibilities and he began to see what old Khaw Htoo, his teacher long ago had been driving at; there was a world out there, far beyond his experience, a world of which he longed to learn something. But the visit from the English group was over all too soon. He asked for David's address and was given a piece of paper with all the addresses on it. "Katie is coming back in a few weeks." He had caught a snippet of a conversation in the classroom one day and his spirits lifted even more. He knew that she had not even noticed him. Why would a girl like that want to take an interest in him? Yet even so, he liked what he had seen of her and the memory of her quiet manner and ready smile gave him something to look forward to until she came back. Maybe he would even gather up the courage to write her a letter.

Then two events demanded his attention. He had not been in the school for many weeks when Kaw La Htoo had approached him; the older man was always concerned about the fact that he had so few teachers in the school. "I've been watching you in the classroom and I think you could help us by becoming a teacher."

"But sir, I need to learn more myself first. I haven't been here for long enough."

Kaw La Htoo had anticipated this reaction so had rehearsed his reply. "I have seen you with the younger children. You are very good with them. You are good at explaining to them in ways that they can understand and you are patient with them."

Thaw Reh's heart began to sink with disappointment. He had so much wanted to get some education for himself and now Kaw La Htoo was asking him to give it all up. "But, I wouldn't know where to start, I don't know the first thing about being a teacher."

"I would put you with another teacher for a while, until you are ready to work on your own." Kaw La Htoo tried to reassure him. "I would like to have a proper teacher training course. I have heard about what can be done to help teachers to be better at their job and in some of the camps further south they can do this, but we have no means of starting such a programme as yet. I hope we will before too long. Meanwhile, I have many classes and the teachers have to be shared out between them."

Thaw Reh said he would think about it. Sometimes it seemed unfair to him. Just as he was beginning to enjoy his classes and get to know the other students he had to leave them and begin working. At other times he felt honoured at being asked. It was true, he did enjoy being with the children: So much so that he had continued to help them with their football now that David had gone home and he was beginning to see real improvements in their abilities.

Kaw La Htoo had also mentioned a salary. It was very small, he had pointed out, but nonetheless it was something with which to try to improve his life a little. Eventually he had managed to negotiate some evening tuition in English with one of the teachers of the upper classes. Once he had done that he found it was easier to make the decision to go ahead and become a teacher with the primary children.

The second event occurred as he went into his classroom one morning and discovered that at last the camp commandant had a message for him. He could hardly bear to wait through the lessons until lunchtime and he forced himself to concentrate on what the class was doing, while all the time hoping that the news would be good. At length he was able to make his way along to the commandant's office. "Maw Meh has come into the camp. She is alone, but can I tell her you have been searching for her family?"

"Yes . . . yes," this wasn't what he had hoped for but it was something at least. "Yes, please tell her. She can find me in boarding house four. And thank you, sir."

Two days passed, and he received an invitation to Maw Meh's home, a small room at the side of her cousin's house. As the woman greeted him he had to stop himself recoiling in shock at her appearance. Her hair was streaked through with grey where once there had been rich, dark locks. Her face was etched with lines and she looked as if she had aged many years, although only ten months had passed since he had last seen her.

"How are you Aunty?" he asked her gently. She started to cry.

"Ku Shwe is dead. He couldn't bear it after they burnt the village. They burnt all our houses in Daw Kler Leh."

Thaw Reh's eyes widened in disbelief. "What happened?"

"They wanted us to move to another place. Law La Htoo asked if we could stay but they gave us a day to get out of the houses then they burnt them all. We had to walk to the new place but Ku Shwe could not walk far, his lungs were too bad. He died on the way."

"My mother and my sister?"

"They stayed in the new village. Your brother is with them. They are all right, I believe. I came to Thailand because my cousin is here. KNPP soldiers came and helped us to the border."

Thaw Reh was almost afraid to ask the question that had been on his lips from the beginning. "Suu Meh?"

"I haven't seen her. We went to the army camp to ask if she could be released but they would not let us near. Men with guns stopped us. We tried to give them money but they said it was not enough. When we went to the new village it was too far to go to find her. She never came back to us." Thaw Reh watched Suu Meh's mother's eyes fill with tears as she told him the story.

He had been nursing the hope that, either he would find Suu Meh safe and well in the refugee camp, or else she would be with her mother. But neither was true. He still had no idea at all where she was. He did not even know whether she was dead or alive. He could feel his stomach churning with nausea as he had to begin to face the fact that he might never see her again. Not knowing was the worst thing of all. He bade Maw Meh farewell with as much sympathy and compassion as he could muster and turned back towards the boarding house with a heavy heart.

As he walked he took a higher path that went up to the Chapel of the Queen of Peace. He passed the Chapel and reached the shrine that was little more than a deep cleft in the rocks. As he stood at the foot of the cliff he prayed quietly for all the people he loved, all the time wondering if the Virgin heard him. Did anyone hear any of the prayers of the Karenni people? It didn't seem like it, he felt nothing and heard nothing although he longed for some comfort or reassurance. He turned to walk back down the hill and saw Peter the catechist sitting outside the chapel. How long had he been there watching him?

"Can I help you?"

Thaw Reh sat beside him. "I've been thinking about my family and trying to pray for them," he said. "But I don't seem to be getting anywhere."

"I think we sometimes have to wait a long time for an answer. Who were you praying for?"

"Oh, my family, my mother and sisters and brothers . . .and my grandmother. The Burmese soldiers killed my father last year. And then there's Suu Meh, the girl I was going to marry, before she was taken away by soldiers."

"I'm sorry," Peter interrupted.

"And I've searched for her, and prayed for her, and nothing ever happens. Sometimes I wonder how much longer I can go on like this, not knowing where she is." he paused. "And what about all of us. We can't stay here forever. What sort of life is this? What's going to happen to us?"

"Well, some day there has to be a political solution. In some way or other we have to be reconciled, even with our enemies; that's the only way to the future. It will take a great deal of faith and patience . . . and we must never lose hope."

"But it's so hard to have hope when everything goes so badly for us."

"Perhaps that's what we need to pray for more than anything. Hope."

Hope? A fine word, but what hope did he really have of ever seeing Suu Meh again? Sadly he said goodbye to Peter and walked down the steep hill to his dormitory.

So the pattern of Thaw Reh's life in the camp began to take shape. For the remaining weeks of the school year he observed one of the teachers by day, sometimes taking over when the teacher left the room. By night he tried to help himself with the books that the High School classes were using. Sometimes he asked for help but mostly he relied on the weekly lessons that he had with one of the other teachers. He was always busy. Sarah had provided money for new dormitories that were desperately needed. So many refugees had crossed the border this year that the old accommodation was never enough for them. They used some of the money to buy building materials so Thaw Reh's skills as a carpenter and builder were much in demand as the dormitories took shape. It felt good to be working once again in the trade that he had come to love over the many years since his early childhood. As he cut and shaped the timber and neatly mitred the corners in the way that his father had taught him he began to recover a little from the experiences of the past months; it was as if his life regained some sense of order and purpose.

He visited the camp clinic to ask for ointment for the skin on his shoulders that had rubbed into deep ulcers under the pressure of the heavy packs that he had carried as a porter. The ointment helped and that, combined with the benefits of a better diet, brought about a gradual recovery of the skin. However the scars never disappeared; they remained as a constant reminder of his bitter experiences as a porter.

The other regular visit he made was to Maw Meh, Suu Meh's mother. Each week he hoped that she had somehow arrived in the camp and would be reunited with him but with each weekly visit that hope grew dimmer.

There was no denying it now; Suu Meh was pregnant. The child was growing in her body and announcing its presence daily as it moved and kicked inside her. But to her it was not a child; it was a growth of ugliness, a cancer conceived of hate and inhumanity. She didn't want her body to bear such a thing so in desperation she cast about for an answer to her predicament. "What can I do?" she asked Paw Htoo, one of the older women.

"Nothing! If you can feel it kick you then it's too late," was the woman's reply

"Please help me, I must get rid of it. You must be able to do something."

"I can't do anything. Ask him. You're his whore. Ask him to help you."

Suu Meh turned away in despair. Why had she left it for so long? The signs had all been there, why had she ignored them? But, she had seen the women and knew what they did to help one of the girls when she had required it. Some had gathered round so that prying eyes couldn't get too close but she had heard the screams and the cries of anguish.

She needed a sharp stick. Split bamboo would be the best, cut and sharpened with a knife. The knives were hanging by the fire in the kitchen; it would be easy to borrow one in the evening when all was quiet. She went out, selected a machete, pulled a piece of bamboo out of the pile of firewood and took everything into the latrine. Pondering the blade for a long time she held it against her wrist and thought how easy it would be to make a simple cut and end her life there and then.

No. In spite of everything she didn't want to die. She skilfully split the bamboo and sharpened the end as she had so many times as a young girl at her home in Daw Kler Leh. She carefully placed the machete down onto the ground, and with her fingers she sought the entrance to her vagina. Deep inside she tried to find the inner place, the entrance to her womb. She drove the bamboo hard into her vagina and up into her womb. A searing pain filled her whole body and blackness engulfed her as she slid unconscious onto the muddy floor.

12

And there he was.

She ran into her father's arms in the arrivals lounge. "How did you know which flight I'd be on?" she asked him.

"Oh, it's not too difficult, I knew which day you'd be coming and I made a few phone calls. You can't come all that way and have nobody meet you at the airport."

"And after I didn't even bother to come home at Christmas."

"Well, that's why I came to meet you. Look, how's this for an idea? I'll take you back to your flat, you can pick up a few things and then come back up to stay with me for a couple days. I guess you won't be going back to work until Monday. That gives us the weekend."

"Yes," he heard her hesitancy.

"Is that all right?"

"Yes . . .yes. It's just that while I was away I made up my mind that I was going to meet Theresa and stop being so stupid about her . . . and you." She saw him swallow as his hand reached across to tighten around hers. The picture of the painting on her mother's easel flashed before her eyes for a moment. She thought she saw the old man smiling at her. "Have you planned to meet her this weekend?"

"Only when you're ready. We can go and see her tomorrow if you want to."

"Yes. Perhaps not today, I'm pretty exhausted. Do you want to phone her and let her know?" He nodded. "I know you'll like her and she'll understand what you went through with Declan. Her husband treated her pretty badly before her marriage finally ended. Now! What about us? Once we're home and you're sorted out a bit, I thought we could go out for a meal early this evening in the pub just up the road from the house, just you and me to start with. What do you think?"

As the two of them sat bathed in the warm firelight of the country pub where they ate their meal Katie could, at first, ignore the vague ache that had begun to stiffen her shoulders and the slight soreness in her throat. But by the time they reached home the ache had turned to pain, her throat was raging and the prickling of oversensitive skin heralded a fever. She had no alternative but to submit to her father's ministrations.

He produced painkillers and bundled her off to bed, appearing from time to time with more tablets and hot drinks for her. She slept the clock round and for the first time for a very long time he knew the satisfaction of being able to care for her. If he possibly could, he wanted to make up for all those years when he had been silent and frozen. He remembered his own feeling of helplessness when he had been faced with Katie losing her mother at the age of fifteen. But he had hardly been able to deal with his own grief and had ignored her needs.

She sometimes slept lightly and found herself staring at the space above her head. She was unsure whether she could see the thatch of a bamboo hut or the ceiling of her childhood. Although it was winter she felt claustrophobic sleeping in a room with walls and windows and would fling her clothes away from her, then wrap them around herself again as the intense chill of fever gripped her.

Once she woke to find a strange woman sitting on the bed about to take a blood sample from her arm and surmised that her father had called the doctor. "He's worried that you might have picked something up on your travels," said the woman.

"I don't think so," murmured Katie. "It feels like an attack of 'flu. Maybe I caught something on the plane."

"Well I'm going to get a test done for malaria, since you were in a part of the world that's notorious for mosquitoes."

"But I was always careful. We slept under nets the whole time, and I wasn't bitten."

"I'm still going to be careful and test you. Just to make sure."

As she drifted on through the zone between sleep and wakefulness she slowly became aware of daylight coming through the curtains, but she had no idea what the time was. She heard a soft tap on the door and it quietly opened to admit her father bringing another cup of tea and some juice. He sat down on the edge of the bed. "I don't think you'll be back to work on Monday. We'd better phone in and tell them you're going to be off for a few days at least."

Katie had no trouble agreeing with this suggestion. She caught a slight movement in the corner of her eye, and painfully pulling her head round to look at the doorway saw a strange woman walking into the room. She was of medium height and slim build. Her hair was short and neatly cut, a very pale blonde. Her face was made up and she gave the impression of someone who always took great care with her appearance but never overdid it. Perhaps 'sophisticated' was the word that could be best used to describe her, especially when one saw her from a distance, however, her smile was gentle and welcoming. Her eyes lit up her whole face with warmth whenever she was speaking.

"Katie! This is Theresa."

"Hello, how are you feeling now?"

Katie tried to smile a response, a weak, exhausted smile. She could see immediately that there was something very attractive about this woman. "It's good to meet you," she tried, "but I just feel like death at the moment. You'll have to excuse me." Her father plumped up some pillows behind her and she gratefully took the tea and began to drink while Theresa left the room again. "I'm sorry Dad, I know I said I'd meet her but I just can't face anyone at the moment."

It took most of the week; the 'flu lingered on and on. Her father took care of her although he had to work for most of the day. She had a lot of time to think, and she even confided in Theresa, discovering that if she thought of her as an ally rather than as someone competing for her father's affections, they got on very well. She told her all about her problems with Declan.

"You could say I've learnt a lot about bad relationships," the older woman said with more than a touch of bitterness in her voice. "After my ex-husband had his first affair he begged me to take him back. That didn't work out either. It nearly destroyed me. I found it hard to accept that my marriage was over. In the end, I had to be quite hard. I had to grit my teeth and walk away. It was very difficult, and very lonely at first, but I've come through it a stronger person."

"Yes," Katie mirrored the laughter that she could see on Theresa's face.

"I can see what you're thinking. What a strange way to meet someone? But life's full of surprises and things happen when you least expect them it seems. Someone gave me a piece of advice; they suggested that I accept every invitation that came my way. 'If anyone wants to help then let them,' she said to me. That's how I got through in the end. I took all the help I could get and found I had more friends than I ever knew."

"I've found the same," Katie found herself agreeing with Theresa. "Just when Declan dumped me, I was invited to go on this trip. It's the best thing that ever happened to me. And there were plenty of surprises there too."

"Tell me about it. I would love to hear what happened."

"Hmmm, where do I start? There's so much. I had no idea what to expect at first, I was dreading seeing the place. I was travelling with such an incredible group of people and that was the thing that kept me going."

"What happens in a refugee camp; is it run by a charity or aid agency?"

"Oh no, they seem to manage everything themselves. They have a kind of council with someone running the different departments such as schools and health. They even have a justice system and a lock-up for offenders. We worked in the education department. They do all the work themselves but they have to have funding from charities. Sarah provides some of the money for the school but there are others from different places in the world. It's very interesting."

"And you father tells me you're going back again."

"Yes, for six or seven months this time. And I can't wait. I've fallen in love with the place . . . and the people."

The first letter arrived remarkably quickly.

Jan 25th 1998

Dear Katie

I am so glad you are my friend. I cry when you leave me. Please write to me. I want you to help me with my English. . . . . . .
La Meh

Jan 31st 1998

Dear La Meh

Thank you for your letter. Your English is very good. Kaw La Htoo has asked me to teach about health to the students and to the women in the camps. I will need someone to interpret for me. Will you do that? It would mean that you could not go to school on the days that you are helping me. Please ask Kaw La Htoo if you can do that. I would love for us to work together. You've been such a good friend to me.
Katie

And there were others. Students asked for medical books, dictionaries, songbooks. . . the variety was endless. She had some work to do before the next trip. One letter in particular interested her for the precise request it contained.

Jan 30th 1998

Dear Katie

I want to talk to you, but I am afraid that my English is not good enough. I want to make it better. When I was at school I read a book by Thomas Hardy. It is called 'Tess of the D'Urbevilles' I read only a few pages. It was very difficult for me but I want to read this book again. Please bring it for me. I know you are coming to our camp again soon . . . . .
Thaw Reh

13

In less than three months Katie was back in that narrow strip of land where over a hundred thousand refugees eked out their meagre living.

She often wondered why she was doing this. True, in that short visit to the camp she had fallen in love with the people and she had met others in the camp who had all encouraged her to come back. Was she running away from something? It looked as if she was on the rebound from Declan and she had looked carefully into that question. But deep inside her she knew that particular door was well and truly closed now and she was relishing her newfound freedom.

This time her bags were heavy; full of the things that the students had asked her to bring with her once they discovered she was coming back. Books were the bulkiest items, including several that were needed to help her with the teaching that she was to be involved in. There were so many that she had asked her father to send some on by post but still she carried a large number with her. It had intrigued her that almost the first letter that she had received had included a request for a book by Thomas Hardy so she had bought the one that had been wanted although, to her shame, she had not even read it herself. She decided that she must do so before she passed it on to the person who had asked her for it although it also occurred to her that she didn't even know who they were. She just hoped that they would make themselves known when the time came.

La Meh came to the little airport to meet her with Kaw La Htoo. "Welcome Katie. It's so good to see you again." Katie was overcome as La Meh took her hand and held it. "I'm so glad to be here at last. It takes so long from England but I'm so excited about everything."

From the back of the truck she saw the familiar territory that she had come to love during her first visit. It seemed incredible that this place already felt like home to her. "You have your own room in one of the houses, Katie," La Meh was saying. "You will be sharing with Caroline, but she is at home in Australia for the holidays. Now you are a teacher you live in a nice place."

Katie was unsure about this apparent elevation of her status. "I will miss you all then. I liked being in the boarding house with the rest of you."

"Don't worry, we are all close by. Now I am your interpreter I have my own room too. I am in the house next door."

Her first visit to Thailand had been in January, the coolest time of the year when sometimes they had had to wear jumpers and wrap themselves in blankets at night. This time there was an obvious change in the temperature; it was now April and from the moment she had first stepped off the plane she had felt the oppression of the midday heat. Now on the windswept truck she was glad of the cool breeze, which blew through her hair and provided some sort of relief. The leaves on the trees hung brown and dry in testimony to the heat, where they had been bright green only a few weeks before, and the truck disturbed clouds of dust, which blew up into their faces once they left the metalled road for the track to the border camps. She could feel the heat of the sun burning down on her head and wished she had brought her hat.

As they entered the camp and alighted from the truck the noise of the cicadas was almost deafening. She had been aware of them during her last visit but this time their sound served to heighten the burning intensity of the sun. The heat and the long journey pressed down on her, so that by the time she had reached the house that she was to share with Caroline, keeping cool was the only thing on her mind. The students had helped her with her bag but even the effort of walking had exhausted her. She was sticky with sweat and the dust from the truck ride and longed for cool fresh water.

She stood in the centre of the room that was to be her bedroom for the next few months. The walls of the room had been made by weaving different coloured bamboo strips into a pattern that was reminiscent of the weaving that she had seen the women do on their traditional looms. The floor was of the same split bamboo construction, which meant that it had some bounce to it. This made for a reasonably comfortable bed when covered by a mat and a folded blanket, as Katie had done during her first visit. There was a window to the outside with a simple wooden shutter providing privacy, but at the same time, allowing fresh air to pass through in times of extreme heat. Above was a roof thatched with leaves the same as all the houses of the camp. Outside the door was a small veranda that was surrounded with another wall to waist height, which would enable her and Caroline to sit outside but still have some privacy. The whole house was set on strong posts and was about four feet above the ground, while wooden steps at the side led down to ground level.

The kitchen was in an adjoining wooden construction, which was shared by some of the other teachers who all cooked together. The washing facilities were simple in the extreme, consisting of a large tub of water in a small hut, so that there was some privacy. She remembered how, during the last visit, she and Vicki had gone down to the river to wash with some of the other girls. This had involved wearing a *sarong* into the river while carrying soap, flannel and plastic dipper, all the while hoping that the inexpertly tied garment would not fall down. The local girls had also brought their own clothes to wash in the river and the whole occasion had turned into a watery ritual. They had then washed themselves while trying to stop the soap and dipper floating away in the current that suddenly seemed a lot stronger than they had thought. Then, after the washing they had climbed out of the water and had had to carefully change into a clean, dry *sarong,* which was no mean feat to the uninitiated. The whole occasion had been accompanied by fits of giggles and watched by youthful voyeurs who were greatly amused at the sight of two white women struggling to do something that to them seemed so ordinary. She laughed to herself as she again pictured her clumsiness compared to the grace and comeliness of the Karenni girls, but this time there was no Vicki to laugh with.

She suddenly felt acutely lonely as she remembered that Caroline was away. It was the school holidays. 'Of course, how silly of me to assume she would be here.' It was perfectly natural for her to be away, but Katie still felt a twinge of disappointment, which was almost turning into anger. 'She could have at least been here to welcome me.'

As she turned around slowly and took in her surroundings she saw nothing that was familiar. That excitement she had felt on leaving the plane had been replaced with an acute homesickness. What have I done?' she thought, as something like panic welled up inside her. Now she was alone. She had no group of westerners surrounding her. She was here with these people that she had so much wanted to get to know but now she saw that in fact their encounters so far had all been quite superficial. She wondered how it would feel to really have to depend on them in a crisis. What about all that superiority that was sometimes assumed almost unconsciously by westerners? It was as if all that was being stripped away, leaving her feeling naked and alone. Now she needed these people more than they needed her, she would have to accept what they said and fit in with their plans. Then there was the heat. There was no doubt that the temperature was a lot higher than it had been a few weeks ago and she wondered how she would cope with working when it was like this.

La Meh had noiselessly entered the room. "Sit down and rest Katie." She was very attentive as she handed her a cup of water and Katie tried to make herself comfortable on the floor. A few weeks ago living without furniture and other home comforts had seemed like fun. It had been, in part, born of rebelliousness, a determination to manage without all those material things. Now she wondered how she would survive for six months with no chair to sit on or bed to lie on. "You can have a sleep now. We'll cook supper for you so you don't have to do anything, just unpack your bags."

She willingly obeyed La Meh's suggestion. "Thanks. You won't believe how tired I feel and this heat is almost too much for me."

"It is hot today. Even for us it feels very warm." Katie felt somewhat comforted by these words. 'If even the locals feel hot, then it's no wonder I do,' she thought.

"You'll soon get used to it, and you'll be fine in a few days. It's because it's still dry. Once the monsoon starts the rain cools everything down."

Once left on her own, Katie tried to unpack a few of her things. A bamboo pole served as a rail for clothes but as soon as she saw it she remembered that she had brought no coat hangers. She started to cry and slumped down onto the floor again. She couldn't believe her own stupidity; why was she getting upset over such a trifling issue? Here she was surrounded by people of her own age who had lost their homes, their parents, or both, and she was crying over nothing. Giving herself a good figurative shake, she tried half-heartedly to find a place for a few items and then, overcome by the heat and exhaustion, she at last lay down to sleep.

A light tap on the wooden door woke her and La Meh came quietly into the room. "It's supper time soon. Please join us. It's nearly ready." Katie turned over to look around her and at La Meh. She saw the strip lighting was already lit. She must have been asleep for several hours. "You want tea?" La Meh laughed.

"You remembered. Yes please."

"And then after supper some of the teachers are coming to my house. You are invited. Then you can meet everybody again."

Katie smiled. She was feeling better for her sleep, and as darkness began to envelop the camp the air cooled down a little and it became more comfortable. The evenings were what she had most enjoyed about her last visit. There was always a welcoming atmosphere among the students and teachers. They would sit for hours talking or playing guitars and singing together, and they always included visitors, especially those who were in their age group. Without bars, nightclubs or television they had to make their own entertainment but they did so quite successfully in her estimation.

The evening passed gently. For a brief moment she was reminded of the times she had spent with Declan in Mac's listening to the musicians playing and relaxing together. The memory felt easier now and she smiled inwardly wondering what Declan would think of her, here in this place. The guitar was being passed around and anyone who wanted to could sing. Some sang solos but Katie enjoyed the group songs best. The students seemed to be able to break into harmony at a moments notice. They sang both in English and in languages that were quite unknown to her and she felt somewhat ashamed that she did not possess anything like the same level of creativity that nearly everyone here seemed to have. She sat quietly at the side with La Meh just drinking in the warmth of the company.

"This is Meh Ong," Kaw La Htoo introduced her to a pleasant, middle-aged woman, at the beginning of her first full day in the camp. "She is the senior nurse at our clinic. She wants to invite you to come and see the clinic as you will be working there sometimes."

"Hello." Katie extended her hand, and the woman took it in greeting.

"You can come and see what we do. You can spend the day with us if you like. I will look after you." The woman spoke excellent English. Katie had noticed that many of the older people spoke English well.

"Yes, I would love to come along." In truth, she was glad to be kept occupied. It helped her to resist the pangs of homesickness that threatened to overwhelm her at almost every turn. La Meh, who had offered to come with her, was good company and an enormous help as an interpreter. They spent the morning watching and listening. Sometimes the nurses asked her what she thought about a case but she tried to keep quiet; she didn't want to interfere with their work if she could possibly avoid it.

It was during the morning clinic that she saw one of the young men that she recognised from last evening's party. He stood out from the women with their babies and the old men with chronic coughs and as soon as he saw her he smiled at her in recognition. She returned his smile, glad to see a face that she knew. It was a kind face, open, with even features and good teeth. He was taller than many of the Karenni people that she had met so far and lean, perhaps a little on the thin side while his black hair was thick and slightly wavy   He wore a dark green striped *longyi* with a grey tee shirt. She guessed that they were about the same age. When his turn came, the nurse took him into a separate room and Katie wondered why he was here in the clinic, when he patently looked so well to the casual observer. She busied herself with some small children while their mother was occupied with a baby although they fought shy of her at first.

"The children are frightened of people with blue eyes," La Meh told her.

She moved her fingers in the shafts of sunlight that streamed in at the side of the building, throwing shadow patterns onto the floor and the children came and watched her. This was how she was occupied when she became aware of someone standing beside them and turning round she saw the same young man. He had been seen by the medics, and had come over to join them.

"Hello Katie . . . La Meh," he extended his hand. She took the hand offered to her. "Hello. I'm afraid I don't know your name."

"Thaw Reh," he told her. I'm a teacher in school." He spoke slowly and carefully.

Thaw Reh? She wondered where she had heard that name before or perhaps she had seen it written?

"I write you a letter."

"Yes." She suddenly felt foolish. She had hardly taken note of the name of the person who had written to her. In truth, she had not even known if they were male or female. Now she was lost for words.

"I wrote to you to ask for a book."

"Yes . . . Yes. I have two books for you." She laughed. She had never dreamt that the shy letter writer would be someone like this. He bent down to one of the children, the little boy, who then climbed up into his lap and began to playfully wrestle with him there on the bench beside them. "Can I call this afternoon for the books?" He went on, as he restrained the wriggling child.

"Yes. I'm here for the day, but I'll be home later, after I've finished."

He played with the child some more and then freeing himself he rose to his feet, and made to leave. "I see you later, Katie. And thank you for the books."

"Bye. See you later." She brought her mind back to the work going on in the clinic. She remembered that she had to talk to Meh Ong about teaching in the clinic itself and wondered how this was going to work. She felt better now about teaching people younger than herself but wasn't so sure about older women. She would have to think more about how she would approach them.

It was soon lunchtime, after which Meh Ong explained more about what was needed in the way of teaching for mothers. Katie tried to concentrate but she found her mind wandering. To her surprise she found herself thinking about Thaw Reh and looking forward to seeing him again later.

They had seen enough for one day, so as soon as was decently possible Katie asked if she might go home again. The afternoon was already well on and she was hot and sticky although she had done very little physical work. She wanted to have a wash and freshen herself up before Thaw Reh called to pick up his books.

She doused her face and hands with cool water and put on some clean clothes. She had brought a mirror with her, so fixing it onto one of the wooden frames of her room, she carefully combed her hair, feeling relieved that it was short and easy to keep tidy. She looked through her toiletries to find her make up and dabbed on a smear of eye shadow and mascara; she didn't want it to be too obvious. Studying her face, she decided she still looked very pale from her long journey so taking a brush she dusted the lightest powdering of blusher onto her cheeks. Then she wondered if she had overdone it so she stopped herself.

'What am I doing getting excited about a boy coming to collect his books?' Breathing deeply, she forced herself to calm down. She decided that a bit more unpacking and sorting out would have the desired calming effect and was part way through this process when a knock disturbed her. It was La Meh bringing her a cup of tea.

"Oh Katie. You look very pretty. Very nice"

"Well thanks. But is it too much?"

"No . . .no. It's fine. Can you show me how to wear make up? I have never tried it."

"OK, lets sit down out here and we'll have a go," said Katie, grabbing her bag. "I'm waiting for Thaw Reh" she put in, while painting La Meh's toenails.

"He's nice," was the reply "We all like him."

"What's he like?" she asked, trying to sound as natural as possible.

"Well, . . he's quite serious. He's very kind and he's quite good fun, especially when he's with his friend Pee Reh. They came to the camp just a few months ago. He's very clever too, that's why Kaw La Htoo asked him to be a teacher."

They were so deep into their analysis of Thaw Reh's character that they hadn't noticed the approach of the object of their discussion. He knocked on the wooden post and climbed up the steps. Kicking off his shoes he joined them on the wooden floor and Katie welcomed her first guest into her new home.

14

Thaw Reh's mood had lifted a little. The medic had been pleased with the appearance of the sores on his shoulders and had said the dressings could be left off and that he did not need to attend the clinic anymore. Then he had had the good fortune to meet Katie there. She had then returned his greeting with a smile that had given him such pleasure that he could hardly contain his happiness as he left the clinic.

So it was with a light step that he walked back to the teachers' houses. He had some work to do this afternoon on one of the new dormitories; the high school students were far too crowded in their old boarding houses, so the building was something of a priority before the new school year started. Some of the students were helping him but they needed his supervision. They were inclined to be in too much of a hurry and they usually tried to cut corners, so he couldn't afford to be away from the site for too long. Sarah's generous gifts of money meant that they had been able to buy some decent lacquer to paint onto the walls and floor and he was beginning to look forward to seeing the finished building.

Then another question had arisen which Kaw La Htoo had approached him about. "The orphanage needs to be extended. They need much more space for the girls now," he explained. Thaw Reh had been up to see the site and was worried. The whole camp was built into a narrow valley and the orphanage was situated at the bottom of one of the steep sides. "The ground is so steep here, uncle. We'll have to dig right into the hillside. I don't think it will be safe. Perhaps we could build in a different direction."

Kaw La Htoo had been a mining engineer and he was well aware of the problem. "One way is the school. We can't build there, we have no space."

"Well what about going towards the fish farm?"

"No, that's impossible. We are short enough of food as it is, we daren't take anything from there. I'm sorry, it has to be this way."

Kaw La Htoo could be stubborn. Well so could he. "Well, if you insist then the only answer is to dig right into the side of the hill, and then we shall need double the number of posts just to make sure the whole structure is secure. I shall need extra help for the digging and we'll have to get more posts."

"All right, you shall have all you need, Thaw Reh, and I'll make sure you have plenty of students to help you."

However he promised himself he would go to see Katie and collect his books. He had only asked her for one book so he wondered what else she had brought him. He had washed carefully after his afternoon's work and had selected a clean shirt out of his rather meagre collection of clothes that half-filled a cardboard box in the corner of his room. As he approached the house that Katie now occupied he saw her head bent closely together with La Meh's; 'intent on some mystical feminine confidence,' he surmised. They were so deep in conversation that he was almost reluctant to disturb them so he hovered for some moments and then, stepping forward, he rapped his knuckles on the woodwork.

"Tess of the D'Urbevilles and The Return of the Native. That's also by Thomas Hardy," Katie explained as she handed him the books. She had found them in a bookshop in the Charing Cross Road as part of a series of books adapted for students of English as a foreign language.

"Thank you." He had wanted to say much more to express his gratitude but he didn't know how. Words didn't quite seem enough. His eyes met hers in what was supposed to be a short glance but turned into something just a second or two longer. In those seconds passed a great deal of gratitude.

"Would you like some tea? coffee? water?" she broke the silence first.

"Yes, yes. Thank you. Coffee."

Katie busied herself with hot water, spoons and mugs for a few minutes. "I was very surprised that you should ask for a book like this."

"Why . . . why are you surprised?"

"The language is quite difficult in the full book. It was written over a hundred years ago. Some of the English is a bit old-fashioned now. That's why I bought this one specially written for students." She hoped that he would not feel insulted by the fact that this was not the whole book.

La Meh picked up the book and began thumbing through the pages. "There's a lot of reading for you here Thaw Reh," she put in.

Thaw Reh was not going to be put off. "I borrowed this story from my teacher once. It is the only English book I have ever tried to read. I want to read it properly now."

"Have you read all of it?"

"No. Just small parts"

When Katie had received Thaw Reh's letter she had decided to read the book "Tess of the D'Urbevilles" for the first time. Indeed, she had never read anything by Thomas Hardy before, and had been shocked at the depth of the tragedy and the injustices that were contained in the story, as well as being impressed by the sheer beauty of the descriptions of the countryside and the people. La Meh was right. Thaw Reh was very serious . . . and he must be quite bright, she decided.

"Will you help me read it please?" he was asking.

"I can try but I don't know much about literature or books." She suddenly felt that she had very little to offer him.

"Then we can learn together. Are you feeling better today?" he continued after a pause during which they sipped their coffee.

"Well, yes. I was just exhausted yesterday. The journey was so long, and then the heat. I found it difficult. But today is better."

"I think it's hard for white people to come here. You come from a place where everything is nice. Here we have a difficult life."

Katie smiled at his perception of life in Britain or indeed other parts of the western world. "Well, it's not that simple. Life isn't that nice. There's a lot of crime. A lot of people are very greedy. And people aren't always happier because they have more things than you have." She found it hard to explain to his satisfaction.

He looked unconvinced. "Tell me about yourself, Katie,"

"All right, I will tell you about myself, and then it will be your turn. You must tell me about yourself." She could see that he wanted to hear all she had say. There was something about his eyes that told her that even the minutiae of her life were of interest to him. He was hungry to hear from the outside world and he took in everything she told him. La Meh shared with most females the ability to read the clues of human behaviour and once she had drunk her coffee she soon decided her presence was superfluous, so quietly made her exit.

In that short hour of the late afternoon Thaw Reh found that he and Katie shared more than he had ever thought possible. "My mother died when I was fifteen," she said, "but the worst thing was that my father was so sad. He hardly spoke to anyone. He wouldn't let me speak about her. For many years I was just very, very unhappy and I never told anybody about how I felt."

Thaw felt sorry then. Sorry that he had made the assumption that westerners have everything easy. "I have never spoken about the death of my father since the day it happened," he said. It had seemed so difficult when there was tragedy all around. What was his loss when measured against the sum of all the losses that had been sustained just in his village, let alone the rest of Karenni State? "We had no time for anything. We had to get on and fight for our people." Katie heard the edge to his voice. As he spoke he remembered with shame, the terrible anger and the hate that had driven him to such excesses when he had been a soldier.

There was a long silence. "I was very angry, so angry that I wanted revenge. That is why I went to be a soldier. There were many like me. Some of them were very young . . . still children . . . small boys." Katie tried to form a picture of what he was telling her. She had heard about child soldiers, but she hadn't ever thought about the reality and hadn't known that such a thing happened here. It hadn't occurred to her that Thaw Reh might have been a soldier himself. "I'm sorry." He was apologising to her. "I'm sorry. This is too hard for you to hear."

"No! You must talk about it. If it's a part of your life, I want to hear it."

But he remained silent. He had said enough and the door that had opened just a little snapped shut. "What about you? What happened to you? What happened to your father?"

"Well, after many years I found someone who helped me. That was Sarah. That's why I am here. She was such a help to me when I needed her, so when she invited me to come here with her I decided I would. She always seemed so happy, such a good person. Perhaps I wanted to be like her."

They sat for a long time, hardly aware of time passing and dusk was already beginning to enfold the camp when a slight flash surprised Katie.

"That's the generator coming on," Thaw Reh said. "It will be supper time soon." He got to his feet and crossed to the communal kitchen. He came back shortly and announced that they would be eating with a group in one of the other houses in a few minutes.

Katie was amazed at how food was shared and organised in a way that she hadn't yet come to understand. She saw people bent over smoky fires and then meals appeared in numerous places and she wondered whether she ought to volunteer to help, but the whole thing was such a mystery to her. For the time being she willingly submitted to the arrangements as they were presented to her.

"Later tonight I want to begin to read my book." He picked up the two small volumes.

"How about you read Chapter One, then we can talk about it together? What about tomorrow?"

He smiled his agreement. "I'll see you then."

15

Food! That was to be the first topic for her health classes. She knew well enough how hard it was to eat a good diet here in the camp but at least she could give the students some basic principles to work towards and it seemed a good starting point. She had checked with Kaw La Htoo and he had agreed. Still bothered by the extreme heat in the middle of the day she had found that concentration levels were at their best in the cool of the early morning. Now she was used to going to bed early she was finding no difficulty in rising, like everyone else, at five am when the fires were lit.

At first she had been disturbed by the sounds of the construction site: hammering and masculine voices calling. Thaw Reh was working with the other boys in the early morning trying to finish the last of the new dormitories and the orphanage building. The new school year was soon to begin so they needed to complete them as soon as possible. They were also about to celebrate *ka thow bow* so they wanted all the building work finished.

Katie had brought paints and paper to the camp with her and had now taken them to the end of the veranda. She had discovered that if she sat there she could see past the teachers' houses to the site where Thaw Reh was working and as she prepared visual aids for her classes she sometimes looked up and caught a glimpse of him, shirtless with his muscular brown body glistening with sweat in the bright sunlight. She smiled inwardly as she caught herself watching him; she hadn't thought of herself as a voyeur, but she liked what she saw.

"What are you looking at?" Caroline's question broke into her reverie

"Oh, nothing, just dreaming."

Caroline came round and looked at where she could see Katie's eyes had been directed. "Ah."

During the first couple of days in Camp Tewa Katie had been desperately homesick. That had had the effect of forcing her to find friendships and solace among the Karenni students and teachers. There had been no fellow westerners to help her, so she had relied on the refugees themselves and had been overwhelmed by their welcome. They had drawn her into everything they did, and La Meh and Thaw Reh had become real friends to her very quickly. They had seen her vulnerability and had answered her need generously.

Now Caroline had joined her, with her assumed superior knowledge and with advice that she wasn't sure that she wanted to hear. "You're watching him."

"Yes, " Katie replied somewhat sheepishly, but with a smile on her face that she could hardly disguise.

"You must be careful," Caroline said in a lecturing tone, " You know they have very strict rules about love and sex here." Katie tried to listen patiently for what was to come. "You know sex outside marriage is a complete no-no. It's not like with your English boys . . . And they never show affection in public. They would think that was in very bad taste." Katie did know that.

Sarah had explained enough to her. "Look, he's just a good friend. He's been very kind to me."

"Well I think you're getting too involved."

Katie could feel agitation rising. How dare she interfere like this? "All the teachers have been very good to me. I was on my own when I got here. I didn't have anyone else to talk to. They all just helped me to settle in."

"Look, Katie, I'm just telling you to be careful. A lot of the men here want to find a foreign woman to marry them. Some of them just want to get out of here."

Katie felt hurt that Caroline should think she was that stupid. She would see through anyone who tried to do that wouldn't she? She didn't see that attitude in Thaw Reh or was she just being naive? She was irritated that Caroline should be forcing her to question her motives, and his. "What about Rachel?" she replied. "She's married to Yeh Htoo and they live here in the camp. He didn't marry her to just get out. They have both stayed here."

"OK, but that's just one example." Caroline drifted away. She seemed to have tired of the argument but Katie was left inwardly seething.

It wasn't so much the subject of the argument that bothered her, but rather that Caroline had been so parental towards her. It sounded as if she didn't think that Katie could look after herself. That was how Declan had been. At first she hadn't minded but now it infuriated her to think that she had once been so naive that he had just taken advantage of her. Now Caroline was treating her in the same way. What was it about her that made people think that she was incapable? Yet that hadn't been true of the people she had met in the camp. They were treating her with respect and as an equal. Perhaps that was why she was so happy here: they were all so kind without feeling the need to be overbearing in any way.

She had been so looking forward to Caroline's return to the camp after her holiday. She had been expecting a kindred spirit; someone with whom to share her life for her time here. Now, to put it bluntly, she was disappointed. If anything she had brought a sense of heaviness with her. Katie hoped that everything would be better when the school year began and they were both busy.

Meanwhile the thoughts of everyone were on the *ka thow bow* festival tomorrow. La Meh had promised to take her to the poles and explain it all to her. Eventually she returned to the posters she was making. She had to get on and finish the first few lessons at least. It sounded as if she was not going to get much work done during this festival that they were all talking about. Once that was over she was straight into the school term. She found it hard to settle to her painting again. Caroline's words had unsettled her, so when La Meh appeared later in the morning, Katie could hardly disguise her relief. She packed her work away carefully while La Meh explained what was going to happen.

"It starts tomorrow morning so we must all be up early."

"But what's it all about?" Katie was curious, and more than a little excited at the thought that she had been invited.

"Well it's a sort of New Year celebration for the Karenni people. But some people say that it's for us to pray for rain too. Some of the old people say that if we don't celebrate *ka thow bow* then people get all sorts of diseases and the children die. I don't know if that's really true but some people believe it."

"Is it kind of a religious festival?" Katie asked.

"Well, it is, sort of." was La Meh's reply. "Some people give offerings to the spirits, like food or drink, and they tie chicken bones onto the pole. I'm not sure why they do that. It's a tradition, I suppose. But lots of people go along and celebrate, and they're Christians, so it doesn't seem to matter. I'm a Catholic. Lots of us are, but we still go along."

"What else happens?"

"Well the whole day is taken up. There's a big group of dancers who dance through all the camp. That's what I like best. They stop at lots of the houses and have a drink at all of them."

A vision of an extremely tipsy dance troupe rose before Katie's eyes. She laughed. "I'm surprised they can still stand after all that drink."

"I think if one of them gets too drunk then someone else takes over." La Meh's shrugged her shoulders. It didn't seem to be a problem. "We have a volleyball competition at the school too, so there's lots to do. You'll love it Katie," she enthused. Katie thought so too, as long as she could take the pace, in the ever more oppressive heat.

"You're not going to that?" Caroline's response was hostile. "It's nothing but a load of mumbo jumbo."

"Well, La Meh invited me, so I thought I'd go along." Katie said defensively.

"But it's pagan, all spirit worship and things like that. I don't like it."

Katie tried to suppress the growing sense of unhappiness she felt about Caroline's attitude, not only to her, but to the students as well. It seemed that she assumed a superiority to everyone else. At first, she, Katie had felt belittled by it. Now she just couldn't understand it. "I'm going anyway. La Meh is calling for me first thing in the morning." She decided that to stand up to Caroline was the best policy.

It was soon after five that La Meh arrived. To Katie's surprise she was wearing a black outfit, the top half of which was covered with several bead chains threaded with cowrie shells and coins. The bottom half seemed to be a kind of *longyi* made of more black material, with an ornately decorated white apron. She wore a black hood and her face was framed with more shells.

"This is beautiful!" Katie exclaimed.

"It's is our national costume. My family is from the Yinbaw group. This used to be my mother's, but now I keep it and wear it on special days."

The two girls walked together through the camp up to the site of the poles. There were parts of the camp that Katie had not seen yet. She had so far spent most of her time near the school and the dormitories, which were themselves quite extensive. Now they passed through a large area where families lived and she was fascinated to see women in different costumes.

"Karenni State has many small tribes," La Meh explained as they walked along, "and many times they don't all agree. You see these women? They are Kayan." Katie could see the women wearing a form of dress, which included black bands around their knees and ankles. "Then, there are the Padaung. They are the most famous because they wear brass rings round their necks. Tourists come to take photos of them. They call them the long necked women and they live near the edge of the camp."

Two gongs and a drum played incessantly with an almost hypnotic quality. For hours the dancers swayed and dipped to the rhythm without ever taking a break. Katie, now intoxicated by the strong rice beer followed the crowd through the camp, La Meh at her side the whole time. She hardly noticed the heat of the sun on her head or the strange sensation in her stomach until the dancers stopped for a brief respite for refreshment.

"You must rest, Katie," the ever-solicitous La Meh suggested.

"No, I'm all right, really."

"You look tired. I'll get you a cup of tea." Before she could stop her, La Meh went in search of the host. "Aunty! Aunty! Can we have a cup of tea for my friend?" Katie was mystified. She already recognised some commonly used words. "Is this really your aunty?"

"No. We call all women Aunty in our country. It's kind to call them that, I think."

"Yes," Katie had to agree.

She sat on the floor of the house and took her drink gratefully, although with its large floating black leaves, it bore no resemblance to tea as Katie knew it. Her head was spinning with the strangeness of the day and she suddenly knew she could take no more.

"I'll take you home. It's no trouble. Then we can see what they're doing at the school later if you want to."

She willingly submitted to La Meh's ministrations and allowed herself to be led home. Once they reached the main street that doubled as football pitch, volleyball pitch, and anything else that was required of it, Katie felt she was on familiar territory. She knew her way from here on. They paused for a few minutes and watched some of the students playing volleyball. Katie was pleased to see Caroline among them. 'Well at least she's joining in some of the fun,' she thought. She also spotted Thaw Reh among the players.

La Meh suddenly stiffened. "Listen," she hissed. Katie could hear a distant whining noise, barely audible above the noise of the festivities.

"Motorbikes! It's the police," she exclaimed while hauling at Katie's arm and dragging her into one of the pathways that led off the main road. The two girls ran to hide behind one of the huts as the motorbikes came closer and the sound of guns firing into the air rang out. Katie was dumbfounded. "You are not supposed to be here. If they find you there'll be trouble."

Katie was suddenly afraid for Caroline. La Meh seemed to know what she was thinking. "Caroline knows to hide. Don't worry," she cried, as they sped through the twisting alleys of the camp.

16

It was a sound to strike terror into the hearts of illegal immigrants, refugees, ghetto dwellers and marginal peoples wherever they might be in the world, the noise of the approach of police, and gunfire in the streets. The children scattered, their game soon forgotten. The gongs were silenced and the dancers paused. Drink that had begun its journey to lips was put down again, food never reached mouths.

Thaw Reh knew what they were looking for. They wanted to find people who weren't registered, to find evidence of drug trafficking and if they could find the drugs themselves then that was a bonus. They wanted to see if any more people had slipped across the border and indeed what better time to enter a country than during the apparent chaos of a festival. Most of all they wanted to remind the refugees that they were a subordinate people and that they need not have any notions of getting too comfortable in their new homes. Katie! He was suddenly anxious for her. She wasn't registered; she wasn't supposed to even be in the camp. She had entered by the back door so the authorities did not know she was there. He had not seen her all day so he just hoped that she was well out of sight.

Although the sight of the police was supposed to be intimidating for the refugees, the truth was that they rarely ventured away from the main road so they never looked into the homes of the ordinary people. They approached the home of the commandant. "Grandfather. We see that you have a lot of beer today and food. How do you buy this? Where do you get the money?"

He knew what they were looking for. The presence of the extra food and drink was evidence of prosperity. "Officer," he began respectfully, "we have saved for many weeks for the food and we make the beer ourselves. You can see in our homes. There is nothing here that shouldn't be. We have nothing to hide."

"You will be sure to let us know if you have any unregistered people here won't you?" The officer tried another line of questioning. "We are also looking for any narcotics that may be coming across the border. This is an increasing problem for our country and we need your cooperation in the matter."

"Of course, officer." The commandant was the epitome of politeness. He had been dealing with the local border police for a long time. "Immediately we notice anything, we will let you know."

"Good. Now Grandfather, we would like to watch your volleyball tournament. Please bring your children back onto the pitch so they can continue their games. Then perhaps we can see your dancers. It will be good entertainment for my men."

The commandant called out to a small boy. "Go and get *thra*. Tell him to start the game again. The officer wants to watch you play." At length, the game restarted and the gongs began to play. *Ka thow bow* was underway once again. Maybe a little more restrained, now the refugees had been successfully reminded who they were and what their place was in the scheme of things.

The day of the *ka thow bow* festival had been Katie's first experience of illness in the camp. The heat combined with the unfamiliar drink had given her an intense nauseating headache.

"Dehydration," diagnosed Caroline, who had followed close behind them. For once Katie didn't mind what she said or did. Caroline might have irritated her with her rather parental, know it all, tone most of the time, but now she did not care one bit. Caroline bustled about finding boiled water for her. She added some salt to it. "That's because you've probably lost it in sweating and you've got heat exhaustion. The cure is to add salt to everything for a while." After half an hour or so, Katie began to feel that the situation was under control. She had plenty of water and yes, she would add salt to it.

"Why don't you and La Meh go back down to the games? They might have started again and I don't want to spoil your fun."

"I don't know," said La Meh. "We don't know if the police are still here. Sometimes they stay for a few hours. They want to keep an eye on what's going on here. They like to watch us." She spat the words out, her voice displaying the disgust she felt. "And they don't want us to have white people here. That's why you have to stay out of sight."

Katie felt foolish about the way she had been at the *ka thow bow* and more than a little shamefaced. She had wanted so much to join in and be part of the fun and she had tried so hard, but had simply made herself ill in the process. It took a couple of days before she fully recovered. "It doesn't matter too much,." La Meh had laughed, "lots of people have to rest for a day after *ka thow bow*. Many of them feel ill."

"At home we call that a hangover," Katie said.

"Hangover? Well, we have lots of hangover here." And the two of them laughed together.

Now she had to concentrate on getting well enough to begin the new school term. She was to teach the older classes in the school and then one day each week she was to work in the clinic. The nurse had arranged for her to teach a class of students in the morning and then a mothers group in the afternoon. This last was the one that worried her most. She wondered what she could really say to women who were older than her, and much more experienced. Would they really want to listen to her for an afternoon?

"But they don't have enough to do here," La Meh assured her "they haven't any land and they can't all get work so they want to do something with their time. I think they will enjoy the classes and what they learn will help them." La Meh was her ever-cheerful self. Katie was realising more and more what a good friend she had. She never seemed to show any sign of being depressed or troubled about anything.

Katie began her classes. At first, all the students sat quietly; they wanted her to teach them, and they took in all that she had to tell them, but as soon as she tried to ask them questions she met her first disappointment. They all sat mutely at their wooden desks.

"They aren't used to being asked what they think," Caroline had told her after the first day. "You have keep on trying. Don't give up." And she had been right. At first only certain of the students would take part and then others became braver. She learnt to reword things and simplify them so that everyone was able to get involved. "What foods should we give children to make them grow strong?" The mothers in the clinic knew the answer to this. She wrote on the board for them, as they told her long lists of fruit and vegetables, rice, roots, fish, eggs, meat. She asked them if they knew why each of these foods was good. "Now let's paint them all onto big charts." She showed them what she meant. "Foods for health, foods for growth, foods for energy, a chart for each one. Then we can hang them up in the classrooms for the school children."

The women set to. Katie realised that she was older than many of the mothers who were already burdened with two or three young children. Some had already suffered the pain of widowhood and she wondered how she could have been afraid to meet them. Now they began to look upon her and La Meh as friends. The women laughed together over their efforts at painting but, in truth, they produced some work that surprised her. Katie now began to think that she would soon need to go to town to buy more supplies. Painting and drawing had become so popular with all her classes that she was fast running out.

Both she and Thaw Reh finished their day of teaching around three o'clock and met around an hour later. That was to become their time until supper at around six o'clock. "How was school today?" She would ask him. The question became a sort of ritual. "I've so much to learn," he would reply. "I stand at the front of the class, and tell them what they should know. That's what lots of the teachers do. But I'd like to try something else. I'd like to tell the children a story, and then ask them questions about it, or perhaps I could get the children to write their own stories. You see, they learn things but do they really understand what they're learning".

"Having the children write their own stories sounds a great idea. Don't they do that now?"

"No, they only learn what the teacher tells them and I'm sure there must be a better way."

"Perhaps they could remember some of the old stories that their parents used to tell them," Katie suggested. "Or they could even write about some of the things that have happened to them. Then, if you could get them to do drawing or even painting they could do some pictures to illustrate their stories." She glanced across at him as she spoke.

"Yes . . yes, I could," he smiled at her.

She swallowed hard, uncomfortable in the awkward silence. "Now what about our book?"

"I read chapter one this morning," Thaw Reh told her on their first day

"Don't you find some of the words difficult?" Katie wondered how he had coped with the colloquialisms of nineteenth century English, even though they had been simplified somewhat in the edition that he was reading from. "Do you realise that the language is from a certain part of the English countryside that Hardy wrote about?"

"Well, I can see that it's not modern English but it's not too bad. I want to ask you something though. "Why does the parson use the name Sir John? What does it mean?"

Katie racked her brain for a way to explain the English aristocracy in plain language. For a moment she wished she hadn't taken this on. "Some people in England are called Sir or Lord. It's a title . . . err . . . some people are thought of as better than others. If you're called Sir, then it means others will look up to you. Or they used to. Lots of things are different now, though."

"We call our teachers *thra* and our leaders *phu,* meaning grandfather. Perhaps it's a bit like that?"

"Maybe. But your teacher or leader has probably done something to deserve the title. That isn't always true in the English system. In this story the title Sir is nothing to do with what the man has done in his life. In fact, they are a very poor family but it seems that perhaps the family were important in the past. This is the theme of the book. Hardy seemed to be interested in the way that society worked at that time. John Durbeyfield seemed to think that being a Sir would help him in some way, but it doesn't. In fact Hardy shows us that the divisions in society are quite strong, so it's very difficult for people to better themselves."

"I can see that. I remember thinking that when I tried to read this book before."

And so they fell into a pattern. They would both read a chapter each day. Thaw Reh would read his as soon as there was enough light. He would take his copy of the book and warm himself by the fire outside, brewing his coffee as soon as the water boiled. Katie would read hers at night. She bought some candles and would set them up inside the mosquito net so that she could light them as soon as the generator was switched off plunging the whole camp into darkness. There, cocooned in her very own world, she would read until sleep overtook her.

"Listen while I read this bit to you," she said. 'The cradle rockers had done hard duty for so many years under the weight of so many children, on that flagstone floor, that they were nearly worn flat, in consequence of which a huge jerk accompanied each swing of the cot, flinging the baby from side to side like a weavers shuttle, as Mrs Durbeyfield, excited by her song, trod the rocker with all the spring that was left in her after a long day's seething in the suds." As he tried to understand, she was struck by the comedy of the picture that was being drawn, and she began to laugh. As he looked across at her she caught the expression of sadness in his eyes. Did he think she was laughing at him? "The story is funny. As I read I can picture what's happening. I'm laughing at it. I'm not laughing at you. I wouldn't laugh at you. Everything you do is far too good for that."

By the time they reached Chapter Ten, Thaw Reh had the measure of the story. As he thought about the dangers facing the fictitious Tess, his mind strayed to the very real dangers that Suu Meh might be in among strange and hostile people. He had never talked about her to Katie but reading the story had brought the painful possibility to the forefront of his mind once again. He wondered how he could pass over it without too much comment.

"We know what is going to happen to Tess, don't we?" Katie said ingenuously.

He nodded his head slightly. Did Katie notice his uneasiness? If so, she didn't say anything.

Katie wanted to talk about Chapter Fourteen, "He makes the countryside sound so beautiful, don't you think?" After a pause, she added. "You know, it really is like that. Although there's darkness and unhappiness in the story it really is as beautiful as he says."

Thaw Reh saw the far-away look in her eyes that reminded him of how different their two worlds were. "This is your home he's talking about, Katie. I can see how much you miss it."

"Yes, I do miss the countryside. And it'll be beautiful now. It's early summer and I'm not there to see it. But I'm happy here too." With a slight movement of her head she shook off the longing for home and moved on to the next part of the story. "This is my favourite part of the whole book. It's where she baptises the baby. It's so sad and yet so real at the same time."

"I can see what you mean. It's very clear isn't it? It's as if we are right there in the house with the children. He draws a picture for us with the words he writes."

"That's what makes him such a good writer." He watched her face as she described what she liked about the scene in the book. He wanted to reach out and touch her, to run his finger across her cheekbones and over the top of her nose where tiny beads of sweat glistened in the hot afternoon. She looked up then and smiled at him and his heart missed a beat.

"You're spending a lot of time with the *Kolah wah,*" Pee Reh observed, as they sat smoking on the veranda. The rain had cooled the air down and it was a pleasant evening. "How did you get so lucky?"

Thaw Reh said nothing. He watched the clouds of smoke rise into the air.

"You know she could help you get out of here. It's been done before."

Thaw Reh felt a stab of irritation. "I'm not thinking about that at all." he didn't want to discuss Katie with anyone at the moment.

Pee Reh persisted "Does she know about Suu Meh?"

They sat for a long time in silence. "What would you do Pee Reh? What would you do if you were me?" At length, Thaw Reh broke the silence. "I know what I think. Katie won't want me once she leaves here, and goes back to her own country. I shall never be more to her than a refugee. That's what we are Pee Reh, we have no country, we can't go anywhere. In four months she'll be gone. What will a girl like her want with someone like me then? Tell me that?"

17

The summer rains had begun, an event eagerly awaited by people who had been increasingly short of water for many weeks. By early June, the steamy heat of the monsoon had replaced the dry heat of April. The rivers and streams had been yielding an increasingly meagre flow with every week that passed. Women had become used to washing in the tiniest trickle at he bottom of the river bed and insects had buzzed languidly; even they couldn't move at their usual pace.

Now the opposite was true. The rain turned dust into mud. Clothes could be washed but took days to dry. Rivers swelled, insects multiplied once more and the hot dry air turned to steam. Katie was more than glad to sit down at the end of each afternoon. Often the air seemed so thick that she felt as if she could hardly breathe; sometimes she found herself gasping as if there wasn't enough oxygen. Then there would be a roaring sound and the rain would fall in torrents onto the thatched roof, quickly filling the little drainage channels beside the path outside each house and pouring down in rivers past the boarding houses that were built up the side of the valley. The rain always brought some relief from the intense heat and washed the air clean for a few hours.

But to Thaw Reh who had lived with the rhythm of dry and wet seasons all his life none of this presented any problem. Now he had finished all the building work that was planned for the year he was content, and what really pleased him was the fact that at last he had time for his own study. When once his day had consisted of building before the school day even started he could now give that time to reading. He was well on with Tess now, and each day he looked forward to meeting with Katie and either discussing the book or some other aspect of the English language that he needed to improve on.

And Katie was thrilled with what her classes were beginning to do. "They're making posters to hang up in the schools and clinics. The first ones are about food, but then I thought we could go on and do some about disease prevention, perhaps about AIDS or malaria. They've got some great ideas. Perhaps your children could do something like that."

"I think they need someone to get them started. They don't seem to have much confidence on their own. Perhaps you can come along to some of my classes too," he laughed, and she joined in as she felt the gentle persuasion to spend ever more time with him. "And I need some paints and paper. . . and pencils."

"Perhaps the money from Sarah would help. You must ask Kaw La Htoo. Now," she hastened to change the subject, "we're onto Chapter Sixteen."

"Yes, teacher," he laughed again and try as she might, Katie could not keep her face straight. "OK. Shall we have a cup of coffee?"

"Or what about a bottle of beer? I've got one hidden back in my room. Shall I get it?" Katie gulped.

She had been to the shop and also had some idea of how much Thaw Reh earned as a teacher. The beer would have taken a substantial part of his monthly salary. She nodded knowing well that to refuse any sort of hospitality would be deeply insulting. He disappeared for a few minutes, then on returning with the bottle he poured the precious liquor into two china mugs and handed one carefully to Katie before returning to his book.

"Things seem to get better again from Chapter Sixteen. It's as if Tess makes a fresh start. She goes to work on a farm and makes some new friends."

"When I read this I want to go and see your country," Thaw Reh was serious now.

"I hope you will one day. I really hope you will. You'd love it . . .except for the cold in winter of course. You'd have to come in spring . . or summer. Can you imagine it, just from the way he writes? Of course it's easy for me. But what do you see?"

"I see a man who loves his country . . .and loves the people. . . and it seems as if the whole chapter is full of hope for the future."

"And there's humour too. I can see how he finds humour in the way of life," Katie added, "look at this bit. 'Mrs Crick, the dairyman's wife - who was too respectable to go out milking herself, and wore a hot stuff gown in warm weather, because the dairymaids wore prints - was giving an eye to things'. It's so subtle, but Hardy says so much about society, in just a few words."

"How do you mean?"

"Well, it's where you are placed in society again. Mrs Crick thinks she is above the dairymaids so she won't wear the same sort of dresses, even though the weather's very hot and she would be much more comfortable in their clothes."

"I see . . . and subtle?"

"Subtle? Oh sorry. That means he describes something without saying it too strongly. Perhaps it means he is being gentle, slightly humorous . . . not too obvious. But the meaning is still there."

"I've been reading the chapters that describe the farm, I'm finding that I am understanding more now. It's clear how Angel and Tess get to know each other . . . . and slowly, they come to like each other more and more each day." He swallowed hard. Her eyes met his for a long moment.

As the weeks went by she looked forward to her afternoons more and more. She caught herself watching him as he tried so hard with the story. Sometimes he looked up and she realised that she had been staring at his face for a long time. Then he would smile at her and she would be hypnotised for a moment by his eyes, so close to hers and of the richest chestnut that she had ever seen. She longed to touch him. She wanted to rake her fingers through his rich black hair. She longed to kiss his neck, from his jaw, all the way down, and along his shoulders, inch by inch, lingering at each point, for sheer pleasure. The air was laden with repressed sexuality. Or was it? Was she imagining it? Was she going mad? Perhaps it was the heat.

Sometimes their differences seemed as nothing. Sometimes she wished she could just step across the yawning cultural divide that seemed to separate them. 'He just wanted to read,' she told herself, 'that was all,' while she sat watching and trying to control the ever present tingling that had settled itself deep inside her stomach, her intestines, at the end of her fingers, all over her body. She didn't know where, she couldn't pin it down.

The chapters leading up to the wedding had taken a few weeks to cover. Thaw Reh's initial enthusiasm for the book never flagged. The tension of Angel's hopes for a happy future as against the growing anxiety that Tess felt over whether or not she should confess her past, weren't lost on him. Katie never ceased to be surprised at Thaw Reh's grasp of the concepts within the story. "You seem to understand what's going on in the book so well, probably better than some English people."

"Perhaps that's because I come from a place that's a village. We're surrounded by forests and sometimes no outsiders come to visit us for many weeks. It's as if I can understand this way of life because back in my home it was like this too."

"So you can understand life in nineteenth century England, perhaps better than I can."

She turned back to the story. "They marry and Angel confesses his past. Tess then thinks it's safe to tell him what's happened in her life. It's the turning point of the whole book. It's a tragedy from then on."

Their hands brushed as they both reached for the book together. A surge of longing pulsated through

Thaw Reh's body. "A tragedy?" His hand found hers again and rested lightly on her fingers while the tingling rose to a crescendo inside her.

"Yes. It means the story is very sad." She looked up at him, her lips parted just a little. He reached over to her and their lips met in a soft caress. She leaned in to him and rested her head on his shoulder while he put his hand under her chin and lifted her face up to his and kissed her again. Her body melted into his, yielding softly to his embrace. She had willed him to kiss her and then she knew she hadn't been alone. Those stolen glances and the meeting of eyes had been full of meaning for him too. Suddenly there was nothing to be afraid of any more.

"I wonder where Thaw Reh is?" Katie asked of La Meh "He's usually here by now for his English lesson." Over the past few weeks the pattern had become a familiar one. Katie came home from the school or the clinic feeling hot, and dirty. She always had a wash in cold water to cool herself down. Then she would sit and read quietly and recover some energy before Thaw Reh arrived.

"Sometimes he goes to visit Maw Meh . . . perhaps he's gone there and he'll be along later."

"Maw Meh?"

"Yes. Thaw Reh and her daughter . . . well . . but she was taken away by soldiers. He hasn't seen her for a very long time, over a year, I think."

In spite of the steamy heat of the afternoon Katie felt a sudden chill. Of course Thaw Reh would have a girl back home in his own country. He was the sort of man that any girl would find good company: kind, intelligent and good to look at. What a fool she had been to imagine otherwise. Of course she wouldn't be the first one in his life. She remembered Caroline's words "He wants you so that he can get out of here." The words had haunted her ever since she had heard them all those weeks ago. Maybe he was using her. But no, that didn't make sense. If he really had someone else back in Karenni State then he wouldn't want to leave here, would he? "What do think La Meh? Do you think this girl will come back?"

La Meh gave a deep sigh. "I don't know . . . many people get lost . . . lots of people never see their families again. It's a big problem for lots of the students. I don't know what to say . . . " There was a long pause. "You like him a lot, don't you?"

"Mmm, " Katie's face glowed at the thought. "I didn't expect something like this to happen. I thought I would come here for the six months, then go home and that would be the end of it. But. . . now. . ." her voice tailed off. "Perhaps I should ask him about this girl. Do you think he'll tell me? What do you think, La Meh?"

"Mmmm . . . I'm not sure."

"Yes, I will ask him, what ever you say. At least I shall know then how he feels."

She decided to wait until he settled down on the veranda before she confronted him with the question. She had watched him walk up the steps and thought how tired he looked. He greeted her happily enough with his usual warm smile but there was something about his whole being that spoke of disappointment and deep sadness. She'd made him some coffee with the usual generous spoonful of condensed milk; the only way she had of sweetening anything. "Who is Maw Meh?" she asked

"How do you know about her?"

"La Meh told me. She told me that you go to visit her sometimes."

He stared into his coffee cup for what seemed like an age while the humid air pressed down heavily on them both. She had been watching him but now she turned away confused. She wanted to shrink away and leave him to his thoughts: more than anything she regretted asking the question. She turned back to look at him. Could she see tears in his eyes?

After a long time, he spoke. "Yes. . .I was to be married to Maw Meh's daughter." he swallowed hard, regaining his composure, "but she was taken away by soldiers. It was the same day that my father was killed. . . And I haven't seen her now for over a year. Each week I go to see her mother and each week I'm disappointed. Nobody has ever seen her. She hasn't arrived in the camp. I just don't know what has happened to her."

Katie looked across at him. She wanted to put her arms around him and comfort him. She wanted to make it better for him. This man who had lost everything, his family, his love, his home. It was then that she knew she loved him.

18

The whole school drilled together in the yard between the classrooms. They sang the anthem as the precious flag of the KNPP was raised and then Thaw Reh led his class of nine and ten year olds inside to begin their lessons. They began with the usual chanting of arithmetic. This was the way they had always done it. He wished he was confident enough to try some different methods of teaching, but he had no idea where to begin as far as arithmetic was concerned. However today he was going to try something new.

"Now, I want you to write something for me to read," he told them. "You can call it 'My Story'. You can write about anything you like. Perhaps your mother told you a story when you were younger, or perhaps something has happened in your family that is interesting. I want to see what you can do, but first I will give you some ideas." He turned to write some sentences on the blackboard.

'A long time ago . . .'
'One day I was with my. . . '
'On Saturday I like to . . . .'

He stood back and let them see what he had written. "These will help you," he told them. "You can start your story like that. Now take out your books and your pencils and you can begin. Remember you can ask me if you want me to help you."

The usual clamour and clatter ensued as the boys settled themselves down. Some were obviously full of ideas; some restlessly looked around them giggling with their neighbours and unsure what to do. "What's the matter Law Reh?" he addressed a fidgeting boy.

"I can't think *Thra.*"

"Well can you write something about your family? What about your mother or father, or brother or sister? Or what do you like to do; can you write about that? Or animals, do you have a dog . . . or a pig, or chickens?"

"My father has an elephant *Thra.*"

"Well perhaps you could write a story about your father's elephant. I would like to read that sort of story. I think even the whole class would like to hear it. You see what you can do." Thaw Reh walked to the back of the classroom to see how they were all getting on. He had to take care as the earth floor was rough. "What are you doing Eh Nye?"

Ey Nye was on the verge of tears. "I can't write *Thra.*"

Thaw Reh's heart sank, then he perched himself on the edge of Eh Nye's bench. "Well, you tell me something about yourself and I will write it down, then you can copy my writing. Now go slowly and I will write big letters and you can write yours underneath."

Eh Nye began his story and Thaw Reh wrote for him. As the boy began to copy he stared across the yard, his mind beginning to wander. "Honesty. That was an important theme of the story," Katie had said as they had read Hardy's book together. "It's interesting how much of the story is taken up with the question of whether Tess should tell the truth, or not."

"Would it have been better if she had kept the secret?"

"Well, I suppose the story would have been less tragic, but they would never really have known each other, would they?" She had said.

And then he hadn't known what to say, because he knew he hadn't told her everything; before he could even begin to, events had overtaken them both. Both the depth of his relationship with Katie, and the speed at which it had developed had taken him by surprise. Now it seemed as if there was no way back. He had been wondering how much to say to Katie about Suu Meh. At least she now she knew about her existence. It was also clear that some people had observed his growing friendship with Katie, Pee Reh for one. There was bound to be talk now. There were few enough topics of conversation in the close confines of the camp and the gossips would soon be at work.

And what about the issue of forgiveness? Yesterday they had talked over the terrible consequences of Angel's attitude to Tess after she made her confession in the story. "If only he had forgiven her then they would have been happy," Katie had said. "After all, she forgave him."

"Forgiving. It's a very hard thing to do," he had replied, "I can never forgive what they did to my father. When I think about it I feel such hate. It eats away at me." And sure enough last night he had tossed and turned until the early hours of the morning as the picture of Nga Reh's dying moments had flashed before his eyes every time he closed them. 'How can anyone be expected to forgive that?' He thought again as his stomach tied itself into a knot, just as it did every time.

Honesty and forgiveness; words that Peter, the catechist was always using. Sometimes Thaw Reh went to the chapel hoping to find some help or comfort or an answer to his prayers but instead he had to listen to Peter talking as if it was easy to forgive . . .and be honest and do all the other things that religion required. Katie would be happy with what Peter said, she seemed to have no trouble with such things. But he'd seen too much, and suffered too much, and religion asked too much of him and gave too little, and he wasn't sure if he believed anything any more.

A scuffle broke out on the far side of the classroom.

"He hit me *Thra*."

"He broke my pencil."

Thaw Reh hauled the two culprits out of their places to the front of the class and placed them where they couldn't interfere with each other. "Let me have your pencil Oo Reh," he said wearily as he fumbled in his bag to find the penknife which he had bought from the camp shop with some of his first month's salary. He carefully sharpened both of the broken ends of the pencil and handed them back to the boy. "There, now you have two pencils instead of just one, so get on with your writing. I will want to hear your stories soon and if there's any more noise there will be no football class this afternoon."

The heavy rain had turned the steep hillside into a quagmire. Suu Meh struggled uphill with her pack, which was lighter now the other girls were helping her out because she was so near to the end of her pregnancy. One patch was especially slippery and they all reached out to grasp onto the small trees at the side of the path. The lump in her belly, combined with sheer exhaustion, slowed Suu Meh down even more than the others. She felt a hand take her upper arm in a strong grip and urge her onwards. "Nearly there, Suu Meh. Just a few more steps and we're at the top. It's easier then. Keep going."

She turned to see Paw Htoo at her side. Ever since that day when she had tried to end the life of the child inside her Paw Htoo had been kinder to her. True she had refused to help her then, but it had been too late anyway and there was nothing she could have done. But when one of the women had found Suu Meh collapsed on the latrine floor Paw Htoo had immediately taken charge, brought her back into the barracks, found water to wash her with and had generally supervised their care of her. Suu Meh's feeble attempt to procure an abortion had been unsuccessful, for the child was deep inside her body and had remained safely clear of any damage that she had tried to inflict on it. She had bled for a few days but the most enduring effect was the guilt and misery she felt at her own actions. 'How could I have done such a thing?' she thought, for she had always been taught that a child was a gift from God and each one was precious in his sight.

Another of the girls, Maw Nee, had wanted her to pray. "God forgives," she would say, "God forgives everything if only we ask him."

Suu Meh had tried to pray, but she couldn't believe that God would forgive her so she had asked Maw Nee to pray for her. Perhaps the prayers of a good person like Maw Nee would help.

Each day they crossed the Salween on a raft and then carried the supplies towards the front line. This year the *Tatmadaw* had remained resolutely on the east side of the river, refusing to be beaten back by the KNPP, which had always happened in previous years, once the rains had began.

Suu Meh couldn't take another day. The child pressed down hard inside her and she found walking difficult. As they climbed she stumbled and fell. Paw Htoo rushed to help and Maw Nee joined her.

"Let her rest, sir, she can't walk anymore," they pleaded with the guard.

"Walk on Aunty," he made as if to swing at the women with his rifle.

"No sir, please let us help her."

The young soldier was afraid of his superiors and wouldn't let them stop. "No, Aunty, you must go on." His voice rose to a shout. When the party had all passed he took the basket away from Suu Meh's back and with a violent kick, pushed her to the side of the path. The girl screamed and braced herself for another blow, fearing what was going to happen next. She was so scared that she dare not open her eyes, instead she waited while the pain subsided. All had gone quiet so she carefully looked over her shoulder. Nothing. The porters and the soldiers had all moved on and left her alone. As she sat and tried to gather up enough strength to get up and walk she felt a strange sensation pass through her body. It was as if all the muscles of her belly tightened for a minute, then the feeling passed off and she felt better again.

She was alone in the forest. It took some moments for the truth to dawn upon her. The column had moved on and there was nobody near her. After a year as a slave of the *Tatmadaw*, she was free. As she sat trying to take stock of her situation she felt another pain take hold of her. She reached down with her hand to try to massage it away and drew it back again with a start. It was smeared with blood. A sudden urgency seized her; she had to get away from the river. There were too many soldiers around the landing stage. And she had to get help if she could.

She turned her back to the river and away from where the soldiers were making for the front and began to walk. The tight feeling gripped her belly again, this time harder and more painfully. She held onto a tree until it passed and she was able to set off again. All day, she kept going. She found a stream and lay down beside it so she could drink some water, then followed it upstream. Her pace was desperately slow because she had to keep stopping; and all the time the waves of pain grew in intensity until at last she had to rest. She sank down on the forest floor unable to walk any more. Exhaustion washed over her and she heard an animal of the forest making a strange noise. Again, the sound came, louder and fiercer. Fear gripped her as the noise grew harsher then she realised that it was coming from her own mouth. Again it came, but this time more piercing, a scream of indescribable agony.

"Woman. Sit up woman. Sit against this tree." Hands were half carrying her, half dragging her to the side of the path. "We can help you. We've had many babies." Two women were with her there in the forest clearing. She gripped the hand of one of them while they tried to make her comfortable and then she opened her eyes. Through a blur of pain and exhaustion she saw the two of them and a few curious children around her. "We stay here in the forest. We had to leave our village so we made our home here." one of them told her. The strength of the contractions increased until she was immersed in a sea of pain, regularly punctuated by an intense stabbing that was now lower and sharper and moving downwards. "Your baby will be born soon," one of the women told her. "Now you must give a push. Each time you have a pain, you must push."

Suu Meh had no strength left. "Water," she gasped, "water." The women sent a child back to their shelter for something with which to carry water from the stream. She tried to push when the women told her but collapsed back against the tree; she could do no more.

"You must, you must," she heard their voices, insistent and encouraging, "keep going." Then a searing pain cut through her. With one final effort she pushed just to get it away from her; she could bear its presence no longer.

It was over. One of the women gave her something to put in her mouth. "Go on, you must bite the cord. Bite through it." Suu Meh did as she was told; she had no strength to do otherwise. But there was no other sound. The other woman took hold of the grey, lifeless infant and a wave of panic washed through her. She blew on its face and gave it a small slap but to no avail, for the tiny girl did not breathe even once. She never knew anything of the sad and desperate world that her mother lived in.

They worried for the girl, for she only whispered one thing to them "Bap . . ."They heard. They crouched closer, and strained to hear. "Baptise . . . please."

"She wants us to baptise the baby." Suu Meh wanted to do what she could for the infant and the women understood that, for they were of the Christian faith, as were so many of the displaced people in this forest. They fetched water from the stream and sprinkled some onto the child's head. Then they sent one of the children back to their shelter for a hoe so that they could dig a small grave for her and do things decently.

As they placed the infant in the tiny grave a howl of anguish arose from the forest while the life of Suu Meh began quietly to trickle away, for the kick that she had received from the soldier had not only killed the child, it had also torn the afterbirth so some of it had remained inside her body, with disastrous consequences.

19

"Your classes are all going well." Meh Ong's impeccable English rang out across the makeshift classroom. "They love your lessons, they talk about you all the time."

Katie was trying to clear up at the end of the afternoon. She could feel that her body was running with perspiration and her head was beginning to ache. It hadn't rained for almost three days and the heat was oppressive. "Thanks. I never learnt to be a teacher, I just enjoy it that's all."

"Still, it shows in what you do. And the posters. We're so pleased with them all. But I wanted to talk with you about something."

"Yes?" Katie was unsure what to expect.

"We have another clinic in Camp Duwa."

Katie had heard about it; how the people there were so much poorer than in Tewa. This was because many of them had been hiding in the forest, sometimes for months at a time. "We need some extra help there and we are asking if you could go there to work for some time."

Katie gulped. Suddenly she didn't relish the thought of being away from Thaw Reh even for as long as a day. How long did Meh Ong want her to spend there? La Meh joined them. "It's hard there. They need a lot of help. It would be good if you could go. And I'll come with you."

"How long would you want us to go for?" Katie voiced her worry.

"Well we are thinking that if you could come for two weeks that would be a great help. Then perhaps we can get some of the other Tewa nurses to help out too. Will you think about it Katie, please?" Meh Ong was very persuasive.

At last Katie managed to get away and she and La Meh walked back to the house, both of them longing for the rain to cool the air. Once home she went out to the tiny washroom, took off her clothes and threw some cool water over herself. She quickly lathered up the soap, washed and rinsed with some more water. She wrapped herself in a clean sarong and went back to her room where she dressed in her lightest clothes and lay down on her mat with the sarong resting on top of her. She knew Thaw Reh would be visiting later but she just needed to rest for a while.

She began thinking about Camp Duwa. What were the people like? She had heard that many of them were in a very poor state of health. What would she see there? Surely it would be unkind to refuse to go when they obviously needed all the help they could get. Gradually she drifted off to sleep in the hot, still air. "Katie," she heard a whisper and was aware of someone entering the room. Thaw Reh! She knew it was him by the way he moved and the scent of his body was unmistakable in the thick unmoving air. She shifted languidly under the sarong and vaguely took note of the slight click as he pushed across the tiny bolt on the door. Then his mouth was on hers, warm, rich, moist, his tongue moving slowly and deliberately between her parted lips. She clung to him, savouring the sweet longing, the arousal and the heat of his body pressing hard against hers.

"Meh Ong has asked me to go to work in Camp Duwa for two weeks," she told him, as he lay down beside her. "I'm not sure whether or not to go."

"Why aren't you sure?"

"Because I shall miss you, that's why."

"Well, I think you should go."

"Why? Won't you miss me?"

"Yes, I shall miss you, but I still think you should go." He leaned back on his elbows and laughed. She sat up and reached into his hair. She kissed his face, his high, angular, cheekbones and found his mouth with her lips.

"Why do you want me to go? Have you got another woman that you want to see?"

His face hardened and she felt the tension run through his body. "Oh, I'm sorry. What have I said? I'm sorry, Thaw Reh."

"It's all right, Katie."

But she knew it wasn't all right. How could she have joked about such a thing?

"I'm really sorry. Truly I am."

"It's all right, really. I want you to go because it will be good for you. They do more in that clinic and you'll meet some good people there. And I'll visit you. I can come on Sunday to see you."

"You're sure?"

"Yes, I'm sure."

She wanted the afternoon to last forever, there in no man's land, safe from the prying eyes of the rest of the world. She felt that she loved him more than she had ever loved anyone else before. There was no world outside the camp, there was no world outside the room where they rested together. She wanted to break all the rules for him, to stay with him for always, whatever happened.

The morning for departure soon arrived. It was a short journey to Camp Duwa but they had a lot of things to pack onto the truck. Large bundles of clean clothes had been collected for the new arrivals and Katie and La Meh gathered stocks of medicines with which they could refill the cupboards of the clinic. There were no doctors available. The medical team would be visiting in a few days so they would just have to do what they could for the time being.

Camp Duwa was very close to the main camp but it was considered to be something of a sensitive area so westerners were not often able to get in there. Security was very tight, mainly because the far edge of the camp was only just over a kilometre from the border with Burma, so of all the places this was the most unsafe, both for the residents and for anyone who tried to help them.

They drew up at the clinic and began to unload the boxes. Already a queue had begun to form consisting mostly of weary looking women and desperately pale, ragged children. Her heart sank at the thought of the long day ahead. Precious little could be done for these people. The clinic had only the most basic medicines and the food was very little more than rice, salt and eggs. At a glance she could see that most of the women were showing obvious signs of severe anaemia and many were coughing repeatedly.

They set out the simple equipment and it was as the nurses began to call the patients in that Katie saw her. Hollow eyes stared out from a face that was mask of fear and hopelessness while her skin seemed to be almost impossibly pale. She wore a filthy *sarong* that was caked with blood and a ragged vest hung round her thin frame. A nurse led her to one of the simple wooden beds and motioned her to lie down and rest. The head nurse spoke to her and took down some notes.

Katie had her own work to do. She helped to manage the medicine supplies with one of the junior nurses but eyes kept on returning to the other side of the clinic. This was a young woman of about her own age. Her face bore the imprint of almost unfathomable sadness, yet her dark eyes seemed full of intelligence and dignity.

The head nurse, together with two of the other nurses, would take histories and try to diagnose as much as they could with their limited knowledge. They would sometimes consult with Katie and ask her opinion, and together they would decide what could be done for each of the patients. Katie and her helpers would then count out the medicines and see what other ways they could help them. Sometimes a mother needed clothes for a new baby, and they would peel the old rags off the child and watch the mothers face light up as her infant was dressed in something clean and new. A recent visitor to the camp had thoughtfully donated a large box of soap and all the women laughed as they received such a simple but beautiful gift. They had a box of vitamin pills, but not enough to give a large quantity away so they counted them out carefully, and each family was given a few precious tablets.

By early afternoon the crowd gradually began to thin out, and the staff relaxed a little. As they drank their tea together Katie asked Baw Gyi, the chief nurse, about the girl that she had seen earlier in the day. "She was a porter for the Tatmadaw," he said, "and it seems she has been raped by soldiers." His voice fell to a whisper. Katie had heard this story many times before. It was almost commonplace. "She was pregnant," he continued, "when she couldn't work any more, she was kicked in the belly by one of the soldiers. Then they let her go. She was found by some of our KNPP medics so they brought her here. The baby was born dead and she is still bleeding very heavily."

Katie felt suddenly afraid for this woman. At her hospital in England such a case would have immediate attention. There would be expert help available, doctors, surgery, the right medicines. A woman with such a problem would have no need to fear for her own life. But what could they do here? She needed surgery, and quickly before she bled to death. Yet they had no doctor. The doctors would be visiting in two days time but that could be too late for this girl. And they did not even have a phone to get any outside help. Katie looked anxiously at Baw Gyi.

He saw her face. "We need to evacuate her uterus. I can do it, I have done it before," he said, trying to sound more confident than he really felt. "If her uterus is still intact, then she should be all right. If it's already ruptured, then there is nothing we can do. But I think that is not the case. She would be dead by now if that had happened." He paused while his mind turned towards the practicalities. "We have some Ketamine, we can use that."

Katie had worked with anaesthetics in England but there had always been a doctor present. She raked through her mind to try to remember all she knew. What were the basic principles? What could she do to try ensure that this girl survived her ordeal. She needed to have had no food and drink for a few hours for a start.

Baw Gyi had been thinking ahead. "I will leave the rest of the clinic to the others now so we can get ready. We had better do this as soon as possible, she has had nothing to drink since the early morning." He asked one of the juniors to wash the worst of the blood off the girl's skin and get her ready while he assembled the instruments and dressings that he would need, so that they could go into the pressure cooker that they used as a steriliser. Then he went to the locked cupboard for the Ketamine. He counted the vials and took one out, noting it carefully in the book. Katie looked in the cupboard herself to see what else might be useful. "Have we anything to contract the uterus?" she asked peering inside to look for Syntocinon, or something similar.

"Nothing!" was Baw Gyi's reply

She took out some Adrenaline, in case of cardiac problems. There wasn't much else to be found. She vaguely remembered that people who have had Ketamine sometimes have bad dreams when they wake up so she looked for a sedative and picked out a small ampoule of Valium. There was an oxygen cylinder in the clinic with a single mask attached to it so she checked that it still contained oxygen. She didn't know what she would have done if it had been empty. It was the only one.

Katie measured the girl's blood pressure. Low; perhaps dangerously low! Her pulse was rapid and weak. That and the low blood pressure were sure signs of serious blood loss. She noted her findings into a note book that she had found then she asked Baw Gyi if they could use one of their precious intravenous infusion bags.

Having satisfied herself that everything was ready she turned her attention to finding a vein in the girl's arm. This was made difficult by the fact that the blood loss had resulted in her extremities becoming very cold and clammy. In the end she was able to place a cannula into the crook of her arm. She had always been taught that this was not a good place, but there was nothing else she could do. She then connected the intravenous fluid to the cannula and opened the clamp, allowing the fluid to trickle into the girl's arm.

She filled a syringe with the Ketamine and looked across to Baw Gyi. He had taken the pressure cooker off the fire and opened it to allow the contents to cool down. Meanwhile he was washing his hands and preparing to put on the rubber gloves that the nurses had washed and re sterilised many times.

She placed the syringe on the cannula and squeezed a small amount of the drug into the girl's vein. There needed to be just enough to make her go to sleep and feel no pain, but not enough to stop her breathing. If that happened there was nothing that Katie could do. She held the girl's wrist and noted her pulse as she drifted into a light sleep. After a couple of minutes she touched her eyelids and saw no response; the girl was deeply asleep. Katie watched the rise and fall of her chest; she was still breathing. She put the mask onto her face and adjusted the flow of oxygen, then she nodded to Baw Gyi.

Baw Gyi parted the girl's legs and passed one of the dilators. There was no resistance so he carefully introduced a curette. The girl began to stir. Katie pushed more of the Ketamine into her vein. She quietened again and Baw Gyi was able to complete his work. She pushed the syringe again and soon afterwards Baw Gyi pressed hard on her lower abdomen and squeezed all the contents of the uterus out. Katie began to breathe more easily. Baw Gyi was thorough and careful. She had seen many surgeons at work and this barefoot paramedic with his second hand instruments worked with the same sort of devotion and care that she had seen at home, among highly trained, professional people.

He took some gauze and wiped the blood away, and Katie took the syringe out of the cannula. She drew some of the Valium into another syringe and gave that to the girl to try and help her to wake up peacefully then together they turned her onto her side. The intravenous fluid continued to trickle into her vein and the girl's breathing deepened until at last she began to stir. Katie stayed by her while Baw Gyi cleared up around her and the girl gradually woke up from her deep sleep. She glanced out of the window. Already the sky was beginning to darken.

She found her own bag and started to rummage through it until she pulled out one of her own tee shirts and a cotton sarong. She picked up one of the bars of soap and collected hot water from the fire at the back of the clinic, then carried everything into the room. Closing the simple bamboo door she carefully took the rest of the clothes from the dozing girl, checked to make sure there was no fresh bleeding and then washed her again with the warm water and dried her with some clean rags. She sat her up, pulled the clean tee shirt over her head and carefully negotiated the sleeve round the drip and the cannula. She took hold of the sarong and held it to herself, remembering for a moment that this was the one that she had worn when she had been with Thaw Reh only a few days before, then she put it round the girl. She went to the store and found her a blanket, then to the kitchen to look for the boiled water that they always kept ready for drinking. Supporting the girl with one arm she held the cup to her lips and allowed her to sip some of the water. Then she left her to rest for a while in the care of the juniors who were still tidying up after their long day.

Katie had been given a place to stay in the building behind the clinic, so she went there now to join the others for their meal. The students had cooked their simple supper of rice with fried eggs, boiled green beans from the garden and a dish of fearfully hot chillies. They shared this meal with all the helpers. After their coffee Katie found a small dish into which she put a little of the rice and some of the egg. This she took through to the girl and tried to feed her a little of the mixture. The girl was very weak and hardly able to take in even the smallest morsels. In the event, she could only manage sips of water.

Baw Gyi passed through and stopped by the bed. Katie stopped what she was doing and looked up at him. "Do you know her name?" she asked, realising that all day she had never thought to find out.

"Her name is Suu Meh."

"Suu Meh," Katie whispered, as she held the girl's hand and felt the glimmer of response. "Suu Meh," The girl opened her dark searching eyes and looked straight at her.

Katie silently said a prayer for her.

20

Katie could see why she had been asked to help in the camp Duwa clinic for a few weeks. The work was relentless. There was a constant stream of mothers and children and a smaller number of men waiting every morning as they opened the doors and the queue was always there until the afternoon. Many of the complaints were relatively trivial. It seemed to Katie that most of the mothers were in need of reassurance as much as anything else. Sometimes the greatest problem was anxiety, and it was no wonder, given the stories that some of them had to tell.

She was also worried about Suu Meh. The girl had stopped bleeding and, clinically, she was making a good recovery from her ordeal. However, she would hardly speak to anyone, and barely ate a thing. Katie had visited her at least twice a day as she lay on her hospital bed in the small building adjoining the clinic, and had tried to encourage her to eat, but to no avail. And there was another concern: Suu Meh did not seem to have any relatives. What were they going to do with her now she was better? She couldn't stay in the hospital all the time and yet she hardly seemed well enough to go anywhere else.

When Sunday came round Katie was glad of the rest. She ate lunch with the nurses and then excused herself and went into her room to lie down. The heat was heavy at this time of day so if it was possible to rest she made the most of the opportunity. She was missing Thaw Reh. She reflected on how much she had come to depend on him and how lonely she felt without him. During the week she had been so busy that her mind had been fully occupied. She had been too tired at the end of each day to think about anything other than sleep, but now she was alone and the day was quiet he occupied her every thought.

As she began to doze she became aware of the sound of male voices and laughter outside the veranda. She peered out through the doorway and saw Thaw Reh. He had walked from Camp Tewa to visit her. Immediately her heart was leaping with happiness. He was talking to Baw Gyi and some of the other men outside. As she waited for him to come into the house to see her, her happiness became tinged with anxiety. The world that he belonged to was so different from hers. These were his people, his friends, and she would always be an outsider. Meeting with Thaw Reh in the intimacy of her own veranda was one thing - but what about wider social encounters? Would she ever understand all the cultural nuances that were always waiting to trip up the unwary? And what about the language? Even if she learnt it, surely a long time would pass before she could catch all the shades of speech and those small gestures that often were full of meaning.

What was happening to her? Already, he had some power over her. He could make her happy or miserable, by the way he spoke to her, looked at her or kept her waiting . . .Then he was beside her. He gently pushed her back into the room and she was in his arms, resting her head on his neck. She smelt his warm masculinity, slightly tinged with sweat. His smell. And she was secure, content, what could she possibly be afraid of?

She went to find water for him as he walked back outside again and sat down on the floor of the veranda. "You came to see me . . . I was missing you so much."

"I miss you too. What's been happening here?"

"We've been very busy; there's been so much to do. I haven't really stopped all week."

"Well, it's very near the border here, so the people always have many problems."

"Then we had a very bad one last Tuesday. A girl was very sick. Her baby had been born dead and she nearly bled to death."

"What happened?"

"Well, Baw Gyi operated and I had to do an anaesthetic. At home I wouldn't be able to do that, it's always done by a doctor, but we just had to. There was nothing else for it. She might have died if we had left her. It was very frightening at the time but it all worked out well. Now she won't eat, but we keep trying to encourage her." He reached out and took hold of her hand, entwining her fingers in his. "I love you Katie"

Their eyes met, and rested awhile, unembarrassed, unafraid while her heart danced. "I love you too, Thaw Reh"

"You've been here three months already, Katie. Three more months and then you'll be going home."

"I don't want to think about it. Please don't make me. I'm so happy here."

"Katie," he paused, trying to work out what to say. "You can leave; you can walk out of here any time you like. And I can't. If I leave here, it has to be back to Karenni State. I can't go anywhere else. I can't get a passport. I can't get citizenship. If I even go into the town, I might get arrested."

Caroline's words came back to her. "Do you want me to help you get out, is that it?"

"No, Katie. You don't understand. I don't want to get out. I'm content to stay here. And I know you have to go back home. But I shall miss you more than I can say. I love you, Katie, but I can't hold on to you. And I think about that all the time."

"Well, I have things on my mind too. I feel such an outsider here. Everyone's been very kind, and welcoming, and I love the work. But there are things I feel I shall never understand. Things are so different here. I feel as if I shall never belong."

"But it's the same for anyone who goes to a new place. If I came to your country, I would be an outsider at first. It would be very hard for me. That's not unusual." She had to concede that he was right.

"Katie," his voice had softened almost to a whisper, "will you stay here with us? Please?" He wanted to say "Will you stay here with me," but the words would not form themselves in his mouth. Her steady gaze met his as they both tried to read the future.

Thaw Reh left Katie before darkness fell. Although he knew the way, the trees grew thickly, so the light of the stars or the moon didn't always penetrate to the forest floor, and he didn't want to run the risk of falling in the thick undergrowth. As he walked his mind turned over the events of the day and he realised that he was somewhat unsettled by his time with Katie. The week that they had spent apart had made it clear that their friendship had moved from a light hearted enjoyment of each others company to the point where he found he craved intimacy with Katie more than with anyone else in the camp. In spite of their differences she satisfied his need for human closeness in a way that he had dared not admit even to himself. He saw now that he had come to rely on her for love and affection, but he had no way of holding on to her. How could he? He couldn't easily leave the camp. And what could he ever offer her? He had no money, nothing with which to keep her by his side. And yet it had all occurred so quickly that he hardly knew what was happening to him. His thoughts jammed together in his mind like logs in a crowded river, and he was so distracted that before he had given any thought to where he was, he was walking through the main street of the camp towards his house. He climbed the steps and was just kicking off his sandals when his attention was suddenly caught by the presence of someone sitting in the semi-darkness of the veranda.

"Thaw Reh," the voice was unmistakable. Then they were in each other's arms.

"How are you little brother?"

"Not so little now. They made me a lieutenant. I have my own platoon. And you?"

Thaw Reh told his brother the story of his less than glorious military career. "I never wanted to be a soldier. I went into it for all the wrong reasons. But we make the best of things here in the camp. I teach in the school and I supervise the building projects when they need me."

"You always were clever," Sah Reh had thought well of his older brother even when they had been young children.

"Have you seen any of the family? What about Ree Reh?"

"Ree Reh is well. He went back home. And I've seen them all. They had to move to another place, one of the townships. Daw Kler Leh was burnt down." He spoke matter of factly: the story was all too familiar." But they are well. Grandmother too."

"And you? How did you get here?"

"We're working close to the border at present. We've been finding a lot of people in the forest and bringing them across to the camps. There's something I have to tell you." His face was suddenly serious and Thaw Reh instinctively felt his flesh creep with dread as he wondered what his brother's news might be.

"We ambushed a Tatmadaw column. There were some women porters among them and they were in pretty bad shape. The soldiers must have been very slack because there weren't many guards, so we were able to rescue them. They told us that someone called Suu Meh had been with them until just a few days ago. They were worried about her because she had fallen over and didn't seem able to get up again. They wanted to help her, but the guards wouldn't let them. They fear she may be . . ," Sah Reh swallowed and watched his brothers face turned helplessly into a mask of disbelief.

"And they said she was . . . "

Thaw Reh took hold of his brother's arms as if to shake him. "They said she was what?" Sah Reh only stared in horror at his brother as the grip on his arms tightened. "What did they say?"

"They said she was pregnant. She couldn't work any more . . and she fell . ." Sah Reh's voice tailed off and he watched as disbelief turned to grief and then to cold rage. He felt the hands fling him aside with such force that he stumbled and fell against the bamboo wall. Then his brother was gone, jumping down off the veranda and away from the house, pausing only to put his shoes on again.

Thaw Reh walked blindly down the little paths that he knew so well until he reached the main street. There he turned away from the river and Camp Duwa, from whence he had so recently come, towards the other end of the camp. This ground was not so familiar to him, but here in the open there was sufficient light to enable him to see his way. At the end of the dirt road he turned onto a path that he knew would take him through the trees and into some low hills. Here he had to slow his pace as the path became steep and the trees meant that less light reached down onto the path. At last he had to stop out of sheer exhaustion. He paused to look through a gap in the trees where he could see the roofs of the camp houses bathed in the silver moonlight. It was as if every ounce of energy had suddenly drained away. He had no idea what was happening to him. He didn't seem to be able to see properly. He felt so nauseated he imagined he would vomit at any moment; a sharp pain was piercing him around the middle of his chest so he tried to rub it away with his hand. He seemed to be losing control over his mind.

The snap of a breaking twig pierced his consciousness and he turned around to see a small light coming towards him. As the light came closer he recognised his brother. He felt the weight of a reassuring hand on his shoulder and took the cigarette that Sah Reh had lit for him. They found a place beside the path and the two of them sat looking down across the camp while Thaw Reh began to feel some sanity returning to his tortured mind. "No," was all he could say, "she can't be. No. She can't." Time seemed to have no meaning for them. Sah Reh had no idea how to comfort his brother so he just sat beside him trying to imagine his pain and confusion. After what seemed like hours he spoke.

"Perhaps we should go back down now," he suggested helplessly. "We could try to find something to eat." Thaw Reh said nothing, but allowed his brother to lead him down the path towards home. Once there they found food in one of the student's kitchens, but Thaw Reh turned away and would not eat. "I'll stay with you," Sah Reh offered.

"Don't you have to . .?"

"No, the C.O. knows I'm here. He knows what I had to do." And for the first time, as their eyes met in the long gaze of anguish Thaw Reh realised the affection that his brother had for him. Then he turned away again and stared into the darkness until it was time to lie down for the night.

Sleep eluded him for much of the night. Every time he turned over he thought of Suu Meh and tried to conjure up a picture of her in his mind. Sometimes he couldn't and in the middle of the night when terror and exaggeration took hold, he was afraid that he might never even remember what she looked like. As morning approached he settled a little but was woken again by the first of the morning fires being lit. He went out into the damp early morning, it was pointless trying to sleep on.

"Coffee?" his brother came out and sat beside him."

"Yes please," and they sat and smoked while they waited for the first water of the day to boil, staring into the fire and finding some small comfort in the warmth it offered.

Kaw La Htoo came to see him, summoned by Sah Reh, and told him to stay at home and rest, which he did for one day only. Having nothing to do only compounded the agony, so he went back to the school and, finding that the company of the children helped him a great deal he slowly began to recover some of his equilibrium.

Katie's second week passed with no more serious incidents. There were cases that the nurses could not deal with but they were able to wait until the visiting doctor attended. As the week wore on Katie's greatest concern was still for Suu Meh. The girl was slowly getting stronger and the dreadful grey pallor began to disappear, her skin regaining some of its colour, but sadly the same could not be said for her state of mind. The girl remained with her face turned towards the wall for most of the time. She was reluctant to look anyone in the eye and it was becoming clear that she needed expert help of the sort that was simply not available in the camps. Gradually, the important question began to form itself in Katie's mind: what was to be done with her?

Nearly everyone who came into these camps had a relative somewhere. They were almost all part of some sort of extended family. Baw Gyi had questioned her, but Suu Meh did not seem to be part of any such network, or if she was, she was not saying. There was nowhere she could easily go. She obviously needed some sort of care, but where was it to be found?

As Katie awoke one morning she had a sudden flash of inspiration. Rosa! Yes, Rosa would help. She ran a small orphanage; a much-needed institution in places such as Camps Duwa and Tewa. She had spaces for about twenty children, most of them too young to go into the school boarding houses. They needed the care of a mother figure and Rosa was certainly that. What better place for someone like Suu Meh? The more Katie thought about it the better the idea seemed. She just had to hope that Rosa would agree. She determined that she would ask Rosa on her return to Camp Tewa at the end of the week, then would try to arrange for the girl to be brought across in the truck that the doctors used.

"Can I talk to you about something?" she asked Baw Gyi that evening. "It's about Suu Meh. I think there is someone who can look after her in Camp Tewa. Do you know Rosa?"

"Yes, I know Rosa. But Rosa only takes young children. She won't want this woman." He seemed disinterested. Katie felt a surge of irritation at his apparent lack of concern. It seemed as if he no longer cared about Suu Meh.

Katie persisted. "But Rosa would be a good person to take her in. She could do with the help to look after the younger children. Suu Meh could go there and give Rosa a break when she needs it."

"I don't know about that. We have to ask Rosa first. We can't just take the woman to her."

For the first time she could hear her voice increasing in pitch. "I know that. But have you got any ideas? What else can we do with her? She has to go somewhere."

"No I haven't any ideas, Katie. Ask Monique when she comes tomorrow. "With that he ended the conversation. It was obvious that he had no idea what to do with Suu Meh and he did not want to be bothered with her either.

Well, she would ask Monique. She would approach her first thing in the morning the minute she arrived from the town to start her clinic. Monique was a volunteer doctor working with Medicins sans Frontiers. Katie liked her very much. She had a direct, no-nonsense approach to all the patients, but she also always seemed to have time for them all, time to reassure an anxious mother, time to listen and time to deal patiently with the chronic complaints that were clearly never going to get better. She taught the students to thoroughly examine each patient and diagnose most of the conditions that they were likely to come across on a regular basis so that when she was not there they could carry on without her. Katie had found her presence comforting on occasions. However happy she was with her life in the camp it was good to meet another European and share together some small cameos of home.

"I'm worried, Monique," she helped the doctor unpack her things from the truck. "It's Suu Meh. What are we going to do about her? What can we do?" Monique was quiet. She always measured her words carefully, so Katie waited.

"I find I can never get to the bottom of this problem. It's possible that she tried to get rid of the baby, or she may have fallen or been kicked. There are so many terrible things happening to the women back there over the border. The problem is that they will never speak about them. There's so much shame attached to the whole subject of rape that they are afraid to talk. They won't talk to their own people because they are afraid that someone may tell their family. They won't easily talk to us because they don't have the language or they don't trust us."

"But if she could only talk to someone, I think she would begin to recover."

"Yes, but part of the problem is helping the women to learn to listen to peoples stories when they tell them. It's not just rape, it's forced labour, children seeing their parents being killed, losing their homes, and so on. All those things need to be talked about if people are to begin to get over them."

"I was wondering about Rosa. Do you know her? She runs an orphanage. I think she might take Suu Meh, and she might be the best sort of person to help her too. I don't know what you think?"

"I'm afraid I don't know her, but if you think it might work, then she's worth a try. You could ask her when you go back to Tewa tomorrow. As long as Suu Meh herself is happy with the idea, and Baw Gyi, of course, then she can go there. I can't do anymore for her here."

So Suu Meh travelled back to Camp Tewa. Katie had first been to see Rosa and, as she had predicted, the woman was more than happy to help so willing was she to take in anyone who needed her.

Suu Meh often thought about the women in the forest and how they had helped her. "The children had gone to collect water from the stream," one told her, "they left the buckets and ran to find us." They did everything for her and took her back to their shelter in the forest where she rested for a few days. Then paramedics had come from Thailand and had taken her, still bleeding, back with them. She remembered very little after that. She knew she had slept for a very long time.

Sometimes faces appeared before her and then they drifted away. A *kolah wah*, a white woman, had been there many times as she had floated for so long between sleep and wakefulness. And now she had come to a place of safety where a kind woman allowed her to live. There were no whistles, no shouted orders, no heavy baskets to carry and no soldiers to threaten her at night.

To Suu Meh it seemed as if all these people were like angels. She didn't know any of them but they were all there when she needed them. Her prayers had been unspoken; they had not even formed themselves into coherent thoughts. Perhaps that meant that someone else had been praying for her. Whoever it was, she knew that they couldn't possibly know what she was really like or what she had done. These good people would never want her if they found out.

21

"That's the fifth time I've seen you look at your watch in the last ten minutes. What's the matter with you kiddo?" Caroline's voice broke into Katie's thoughts. It was true. Clockwatching was never an important part of life here in the camp. The almost unvarying length of the tropical day, and the fact that there were many parts of the camp with no electricity at all dictated the way that time was understood.

"Can't you guess? Thaw Reh hasn't called yet. I thought he'd be here some time this afternoon. He came to visit me in Camp Duwa, so you'd think he'd come here. La Meh came in yesterday didn't she?"

A slight look of consternation glanced across Caroline's face. It looked to Katie as if Caroline was as surprised as she was.

"You can never be sure can you? Things are so different here in some ways."

"Yes, that's exactly what I was thinking. I daren't go and visit him, I might make a great fool of myself. Sometimes I feel as if I've done enough of that already. And I've broken rule number one haven't I? I let myself get too involved."

"You're thinking about what I said to you when you first came here aren't you?"

"Maybe . . . I er . . ."

"Well, I'm sorry. I spoke out of turn then. I think you're very suited to each other, and I can see how happy you are together. I shouldn't have said some of those things."

"Apology accepted. But I'm still left with the question: What do I do now?"

"Well, concentrate on your classes, I suppose, and keep yourself busy. That way you won't have so much time to worry about him. And how about asking our resident spy to see what she can find out? She always seems to have her nose to the ground."

Katie laughed. "You mean La Meh. That's a good idea. And tomorrow afternoon I think I'll go and visit the girl we brought back from Camp Duwa with us. I'll see how she's settling in with Rosa. Then if he calls he'll see that I don't sit around all the time moping about him anyway."

"Great going Katie. Now what about our supper?"

Rosa had the sort of personality that seemed to fill the room whenever she was present. In her middle years she had a strength of purpose quite undreamt of in her youth. Once she had had a happy family with a husband and two healthy boys. Then soldiers had come and made them leave their home so that overnight, they became destitute. Her husband took one of the sons and went to try to find a new place to live but he never returned. It was weeks later that she was told that his body, and that of the son had been found in the mountains. She had never found out how they had died.

She had made her way to the refugee camp in Thailand with her younger son and there she poured herself into caring for the children who had lost parents during those terrible years. Her home was soon full of all sorts of children from tiny infants to teenage boys, including Aaron, the son she still had. Her reputation had quickly grown throughout the camp, and whenever the nurses in the Camp Duwa clinic encountered a homeless child her family would grow once more. She never tired of opening her home to all who needed it. But hers was not an easy love. It was a love born out of grief. It was a love that knew it needed to be strong in order to fight against evil.

Rosa had two dormitories, one for boys and one for girls that had recently been extended. Each was a simple room, lined with split bamboo where the children laid out their mats for sleeping each night, and then everything was tidied away by day. They had few possessions so this was easy to do. Adjoining the boys' dormitory was a room with tables and chairs: this was where they ate, and did their homework each day at the end of school. At one end of this was a raised area - perhaps it could be described as a tiny stage - where she taught the children to sing. One of the older boys could play the guitar and that was the evening entertainment.

At the back of this building was a lean-to structure. To one side of this was a long open fire on which the children's food was cooked, while ranged alongside were the large pots and cooking utensils. The lean-to stretched across the width of the building and was often inhabited by the extended family of chickens that added valuable supplements in the form of eggs and occasional meat, to the refugees' simple diet. Beyond the lean-to was a small yard, behind which stood the recently extended girls' house.

She found room in her heart for all her charges but none vexed her as much as Suu Meh. Katie and Baw Gyi had brought the girl to her in desperation, they did not know what else to do. "She was alone," Baw Gyi had said. "She gave birth to a baby in the forest but she has said nothing about a husband. We don't know what has happened to the rest of her family." She had nowhere else to go and Rosa simply couldn't say no. She had her suspicions about Suu Meh's story but she hardly wanted to think about them let alone try to decide what she was to do about them.

She had heard women talking in hushed tones about how girls had been treated by some of the soldiers when they had worked as porters for the Burmese. No woman ever said that it had happened to her. The shame was too much to bear. But it seemed to Rosa that this was the most likely reason for her extreme distress. And yet she felt that if only Suu Meh could speak about it her burden might be easier. As it was, it almost broke her heart to see such a beautiful young girl looking so withdrawn and unhappy and even now Suu Meh seemed to be making very little progress towards a recovery.

Still, she had found her niche in the orphanage. With the growing numbers of children the daily chores were becoming increasingly heavy for Rosa, so once she had regained some of her strength Suu Meh quickly turned her hand to fetching water, seeing to the chickens, cooking the supper and the myriad other tasks that needed attention when there were so many children to look after. Best of all, Suu Meh had a gift for tending the tiny garden that was beside the new dormitory. She knew what to do with the plants, whether it was thinning, cutting, or watering, and the vegetables flourished in her hands. And as she worked Rosa would sometimes see a look of contentment on her face.

"Your brother told me what happened," said Pee Reh as he and Thaw Reh sat together late one evening. Thaw Reh stared silently into the middle distance. "I'm so sorry to hear the news." He watched while his friend squeezed his eyes tightly shut and then shook his head as if to rid himself of all that had happened. "Have you told Katie?" he ventured after what seemed to be a reasonable interval.

"I don't know how to. What can I say to her now? I don't know what to do. Sometimes I just want to run away."

"You've run away in the past, remember. And it didn't help you then either."

Thaw Reh sighed deeply. Pee Ree was right, he had a tendency to want to get right away when he didn't know what to do about something.

"You have to face up to seeing her soon, after all she's been back from Camp Duwa for a few days now."

Thaw Reh made no response. "And you can see her now with a clear conscience after all that's happened."

"Hmm, I don't think I can yet . . . sometimes I think women are just too much trouble." he added as a bitter afterthought.

"You didn't say that a few weeks ago . . . and don't be unfair to Katie. You must tell her. She's been very good to you, and it's not as if she ever did anything wrong."

"You're right, Pee Reh. . .but then you always are." And Thaw Reh managed a rueful smile in the direction of his friend before his face turned grim once again. "Did Sah Reh tell you the whole story?"

"What? About the women saying that Suu Meh was dead?"

"Yes, but did he tell you why they had to leave her there?"

Pee Reh shook his head as he heard the anger rising in his friend's voice.

"Sah Reh told me that they had to leave her because the guards wouldn't let them help her and . . . she was pregnant Pee Reh. She couldn't go on because she was pregnant. And she was with those soldiers for a year. She died carrying the child of one of those men."

Pee Reh gulped hard as Thaw Reh's voice became a whisper. "And if I ever meet that man I'll kill him. I'll kill him with my bare hands."

22

In spite of the intense afternoon heat, which meant that her thinnest tee shirt was sticking to her with sweat, Katie had climbed the hill at the far end of the camp so that she could be alone with her thoughts. She had come up here because it seemed as if aloneness was almost impossible to achieve in the camp. When she had first arrived over three months ago she had wanted company and had always found it. If she ever wanted to be alone she had had to shut herself in her room which she never actually did, much preferring to be outside on the veranda whenever possible. She was alone at night of course, shut inside the cocoon of her mosquito net with her candles and her book but that was never for long; busy days in the steamy heat of the monsoon and early morning rising made sure that she usually fell into an exhausted sleep after just a few pages. But she wanted to be alone now after what La Meh had told her.

"I went to see Pee Reh," she had said. "I thought that would be best. I asked him what had happened to Thaw Reh and he told me. His brother came to see him. It seems that some women brought him a message about the girl he once knew. They told him she'd fallen and the soldiers wouldn't let them help her so she was left for dead. That's why Thaw Reh hasn't been to see you. I think he's too upset."

"Of course, he must be," she had replied. But she hadn't known what to think. It was only just over a week ago that she had been with him and they had been so happy together. Somehow she had always managed to keep the knowledge that Thaw Reh had had a previous relationship shut up in the back of her mind where she could avoid facing it. And it was true that at the beginning she had no idea that there was anyone else. But Thaw Reh had happily allowed their friendship to grow into love hadn't he? Even though at that time he had believed the girl was still alive. Was he so desperate for closeness and intimacy that he was prepared to ignore his conscience, and allow himself the luxury of a friendship that just happened to turn into love before either of them had realised what was happening? How had it happened anyway? It was as if everything between them had come from nowhere.

Her head began to ache with the confusion of her thoughts, made worse by the oppressive heat. If only Sarah were here. She would know what to do . . . and to say. As she thought about Sarah, Katie pictured in her mind what she had done before. She had sat down with her and made her talk, and gradually, as if from nowhere, an answer had come. That was something Sarah always said. There's an answer to every problem, you just have to look for it until you find it.

She brought the picture of the painting on her mother's easel into her minds eye. She saw herself on the path that was lined on both sides with a riot of red poppies growing among the grass and smaller meadow flowers. It was the height of summer and the way to the house was almost dazzling in it's brightness. She wanted to get to the house because she knew there would be a welcome there; the look on the old man's face had made that clear to her. The door was partly open so that she could see the chequered tiled floor. The man stood at the doorway. She could see by the look on his face that he loved her and wanted the best for her but he wouldn't open the door fully, so she couldn't see right inside. She wanted to put her hand out to open the door but something stopped her; it was as if the time wasn't yet right, and she didn't want to do anything that the old man wouldn't like. She looked at his face as if to question him about the inside of the house, but he seemed to be telling her not to worry about that. It seemed at that point that all she could do was look at him. And as long as she did that, then everything was all right and she had no need to be afraid.

She stared down over the roofs of the camp for a few moments, not sure whether she was in a bright field of poppies on an English summer's day, or in a refugee camp in a remote forest in the tropics, when spots of rain on her arm brought her back to the present. Such had become her familiarity with tropical storms that she knew she had no hope of reaching her house before the rain had soaked her through. Still, she started along the path, which she knew would quickly become slippery once the rain began to fall heavily. Walking carefully and holding onto branches of trees she made her way down until she reached the main thoroughfare, where she turned left and began to hurry along the road, which was well trodden and much safer for walking. The path to the house that she shared with Caroline was some distance along the road and she knew that there would be a short cut somewhere, possibly several. The house was up to the right where all the student's dormitories and teacher's houses were and there was a whole maze of paths that was used by them all. The rain was now heavy, and pouring through her hair and her clothes. Several people looked out from their verandas and some even motioned for her to find some shelter with them but she pressed on. She was anxious to get home now and change out of her wet things.

She knew the direction and that there would be a path round both sides of the school so as soon as she reached the playground she turned left and hurried along the edge. She had reached more familiar territory at last.

"Katie, Katie." There was no mistaking the voice. She looked up to see Thaw Reh watching her from the shelter of the back of his house. "Come in here. You'll get so wet out there."

Then she realised what she had done. She had been to the house that Thaw Reh shared with another teacher before, but had always approached from the front so hadn't recognised it from the back. She left the path, reached the bottom of the steps and hesitated there with water streaming though her hair.

"Come up quickly, you're soaked,"

Meekly accepting his invitation, she climbed the steps and kicked off her sandals, which by now were squelching with water, while he went inside for a moment, reappearing with a clean *longyi* in his hand. Wordlessly he wrapped the large piece of fabric round her so as to absorb some of the water. "I heard what happened," she said. He started to pat her wet hair with a corner of the *longyi*. As he touched her it was as if a series of electric shocks were pulsating through her. Still he said nothing. "You haven't been to see me . . . I've missed you."

"I'm sorry Katie . . . I just don't know what to do. I can't read . . . it's too difficult . . and . .''

"It's like that when someone you love dies," her voice became a whisper, "it's hard to concentrate, but you don't have to read. You can come and see me anyway."

His hands that had been busy with their ministrations became still and then slowly encircled her in an embrace that needed no accompanying words. She carefully freed her arms from the *longyi* and held him. At last the rain stopped and the sound of rushing water died down. "Katie," he said, "I'll come and see you tomorrow . . . and I'll bring my book."

"You don't have to, not if it's too much."

"Yes, I will. I want to. I think it'll make me feel better . . . You'll make me feel better." And their eyes locked together. Then she saw him swallow hard and he took hold of her again. "I'm afraid Katie . . . I'm afraid."

She felt a questioning frown pass across her face. "What . . .?"

"No, it's nothing. I'll walk back to your house with you."

Katie went to visit Suu Meh almost every day, sometimes at lunchtime, sometimes in the evening. "I like to hear the children sing," she would say, but Rosa could see that it was her genuine concern for Suu Meh that brought her there so regularly. She would sit beside her on the bench while the children played around them. Sometimes when Suu Meh wasn't to be seen Katie would seek her out in the lean-to which served as a kitchen, at the back of the building, or in the yard behind.

"What can we do to help Suu Meh?" she had asked Rosa in desperation one day.

"It's upsetting you, isn't it? Sometimes, it just takes time. When my husband and son were killed I never thought I would recover from the shock, but I did. Now, although I am sad, I can live my life and it's all right."

"Well, I was very unhappy, too, after my Mum died. That was eight years ago. I never spoke about it to anyone. It was Sarah who helped me: Sarah Cassidy. She encouraged me to talk about it, and she cared enough to listen. Now I wish I could get Suu Meh to talk about what's happened to her. But I can't even speak her language. It's so difficult."

"Suu Meh might have been very badly abused, Katie." Rosa's words were a warning. "It's not just rape that's the problem. It's the things that women do - have to do - to help themselves. At the time they have no choice. Then later they feel the shame of what they have done and they can't find any peace of mind. There could be things that she will never speak of . . . to anyone."

"Can't someone . . . can't you just ask her? If she sees that you don't condemn her for it then that should help."

Rosa looked tired. "I'll try. I can ask her, at least. And Katie . . . thank you for all your kindness."

The more Katie thought about it, the more Suu Meh's problems disturbed her. She knew she was breaking one of the unwritten rules: she had become involved, much too involved.

And she knew she had reached the end of her own resources as far as Suu Meh was concerned. She had wanted to listen to her, just as Sarah had done when she had talked about her problems. But no, not only was the language a real problem, so they could not even talk to one another without La Meh as an interpreter, Katie also knew that she had already plumbed the depths of her own understanding and capabilities. She couldn't even begin to imagine how it must feel to have gone through what Suu Meh had apparently had to endure. What ever could she say or do that would mean anything to her? Oh, she had prayed for Suu Meh; simple cries of desperation when she hadn't known what else to do, but something more was needed. She felt sure that Sarah would know what to do. She would pray a prayer of real faith. She would know what to say. Sarah would love her, touch and embrace her and Suu Meh would respond and get better, Katie was sure of that. Sarah was coming back in October, then she, Katie, would join the group for their journey home. There were less than three months to go and she would be leaving. She didn't want to think about that, but she did want to think about Sarah. She wanted to know how Sarah worked; she wanted to know what she would do when faced with Suu Meh.

"You're quiet today, Katie," Thaw Reh observed. He had soon settled back into his pattern of regular English lessons with Katie and she reflected on how different he was to Declan. She remembered how he often wouldn't even think about how she was feeling, and yet here, in a few short months, Thaw Reh had come to know her so well that he immediately tried to read her moods.

"I was thinking about the things that have happened to some of the refugees before they come into the camps."

"Anyone in particular?"

"There's a girl staying with Rosa. Her baby was born dead and some terrible things have happened to her. It must be so hard. It upsets me a bit."

"Is this the girl you told me about in Camp Duwa?"

"Yes. It's the same one. We brought her to Rosa's, we couldn't think what else to do with her. I went to see her today. I go most days."

"You're fond of her aren't you?"

"Yes. She's about my age and her story seems so sad. I guess I've got a bit too involved but I can't help it."

"Well, I've some things to show you," he said, pulling children's exercise books out of his bag. "It's the children's story books. Some of them are pretty bad, some of the boys can hardly write, but some are good and some are funny. I'll read some to you. But lets get some coffee first." He made his way to the fire in the adjoining house and sought out the necessary items, returning with mugs of sweet coffee. Katie was glad to see him happy again and her mood began to lift.

"What about you? You must have a story to tell. I've never heard much of what happened to you."

"My story isn't so special. Nothing happened to me that hasn't happened to lots of people."

"But it happened to you and that makes it important."

"Well, there are things I'm sorry about. I'm sometimes sorry I joined the army at all. I never wanted to be a soldier until my father was killed. It was my brother Sah Reh who always talked about going away to fight. And then I wasn't always such a good boy. I remember I drank so much one day that I couldn't get up for roll call. They had me in the guardroom for four days. I soon cooled off after that. It wasn't nice being shackled to the wall for all that time with only a bucket for company." He laughed ruefully. "I didn't do that again." Katie looked at him in horror. That didn't sound so funny. She didn't know such things as shackles still existed. It sounded to her like something out of the middle ages. "Then I shot a boy. He must have been younger than both of my brothers. I saw his face. I looked right at him. Then I killed him. I wish I hadn't done, it but I had to. I think about that a lot. Sometimes when I go to sleep at night I see his face and I just can't get it out of my mind . . . there were others, but it's always him I see."

As she sipped her coffee she couldn't think what to say to him. What did she know of war and hardship? She wanted to change the subject and talk about something else, but she had started it. She had asked him to tell his story and had wanted to know everything about him. He looked across at her. "That's my story Katie. It's not a very good one."

"But it's part of you and I want to hear it."

"I'll tell you more some other time. Now let's look at what the children have written."

'On Saturday I must look after my little sister' he translated *'my mother does weaving all day she is very busy. I want to play football. I want my sister to stay in the house, but she wants to play football with me. I don't want to play with her. She cannot play football. She cries and my father tells me I am naughty. He beats me. Then I have to let her play with me and the other boys. Then she sees her friend and they go and play five stones on the ground. Five stones is a girls game.'*

Katie laughed. "I like this boy."

"Yes. I think he's one of the brightest ones." He rifled through the books for a minute. "Look, here's a story my grandmother used to tell me. He must have had this story when he was little, too. I'll read it to you.

'Once there were two brothers, they were a Karenni brother and a white brother. God gave the

Karenni brother a book. The Karenni brother didn't want to look at his book, so the white brother took it away. The white brother took the book to another country. Then the Karenni brother had no book, so he couldn't read. Then the white brother came and brought the book to the Karenni brother, and taught him to read it.'

"That's an interesting one."

"Yes, it's one of the old stories that parents tell their children. I think a lot of people in Thailand and Burma look down upon the hill people . . . perhaps with good reason. The story says a lot about how we feel about ourselves, I think. Lots of people can't read and for a long time we had no written language."

"I think it sounds a bit patronising, that the white people had to come to teach the people to read," ventured Katie

"Patronising?"

"As if they looked down on the Karennis."

"Well that's the way it was for us . . . and still is."

Katie could clearly hear the note of deep sadness in his voice. "I have to go to renew my visa. I'll be away for a couple of days," she broached the subject, as they packed away the books after an enjoyable few minute of Thaw Reh translating. He looked up from his tidying and Katie saw his face cloud over for a moment. "Thaw Reh?" She was mystified. After all, she was only going for a short time.

"I'm afraid when you go away."

"Why? Do you think I won't come back?"

"Well," he said after some hesitation, "one day you'll go home and then you won't come back. And I don't want that day to come . . . but it will. I know it will."

She didn't know what to say to him.

"And it's not just that. I'm not free to go anywhere. And when I see you and the others coming and going whenever you want to it makes me feel bad . . .jealous maybe . . . or is it angry? I don't know. "

"But I have to go Thaw Reh. If I don't then they might catch me with an out of date visa and I could end up in jail."

"Yes, Katie, I know that. I know you have to go, but I don't find it easy." He took hold of her hand and rested his lips on her fingers. "One day, Katie, I'm going to get out of this camp. I'm going to walk free. I don't know how yet, but I shall find a way. I want to get away from all the terrible things that have happened"

"Kaw La Htoo knows how it can be done, I'm sure he does." Katie suggested.

"Oh yes . . . and he's helped others. He'll help me if I ask him. But the first thing I have to do is get better at my English."

"But you're already very good at that."

"But I must get even better. That's the first step for me, anyway." And Katie watched him as for the next few weeks he redoubled his efforts to improve his English, waking early each morning to read and study. She sometimes worried about him, so hard did he work, but deep down inside her she knew that it was his way of somehow burying all the unhappiness in his life. She recognised the symptoms all too well.

Because there was so much domestic work to do in the orphanage Rosa was often beside Suu Meh and the two worked together. It was on one such occasion when they were preparing vegetables together that Rosa decided to speak out. "I have heard many bad stories," she began. "One of the nurses was telling me that some girls have been raped by the *Tatmadaw* soldiers and many of them are afraid to talk about it." There was a pause in the vegetable cutting as Suu Meh took in what was being said. "I know that if that happened to me I would feel very bad inside. I would think about it all the time but I would be afraid to talk too." Still Suu Meh said nothing. "When we talk about things with someone it helps us to feel better. It would help you to talk. My husband and my son were both killed and it was only when I talked to my friends that I began to feel better," Rosa added.

Suu Meh put her knife down and went through to the front of the orphanage where she could get away from Rosa. It was true, she did think about what had happened to her when she had been with the Tatmadaw almost all of the time. Her days were filled with the shame of what she had done. The only times that her mind rested were those when she was busy with the children; but at night she always had plenty of time to think, especially if the sound of a cock crowing or a dog barking disturbed her sleep. Being a victim of the

Tatmadaw soldiers was bad enough in itself, but what had she done? Sometimes she had gone to Thun Oo almost willingly, not knowing what else to do. Then at other times she had hated him . . . and herself. Now she was so confused. Then she had done the worst thing of all; she had tried to kill her child. The guilt of that weighed on her mind more than anything; surely even Rosa, good and kind as she was, wouldn't understand why she had done that.

Then one day she could bear it no longer. She and Rosa were alone in the house and the children were all at school. She took a deep breath, "Aunty Rosa, when I was with the *Tatmadaw* there was a soldier, Thun Oo, who made me go with him. I couldn't stop him. He was too strong for me."

Rosa's hand came across the table to rest on hers. "Many times?"

"Yes. Many times." The girl's voice was hardly audible, her eyes never left the ground where she sat.

"Was it always the same soldier?" There was an almost imperceptible movement of Suu Meh's head.

This was something Rosa had heard of many times before. Girls allowed themselves to be attached to one soldier as a way to protect themselves. At least they found some sort of safety that way. For many of them it was desperate attempt to retain some sort of dignity. "Did he ever hurt you?" Rosa watched as Suu Meh's pale face contorted with the pain of relived memories.

"He hit my arms and my chest . . . . He banged my head on the post. . . . I thought he was going to kill me. I had to do what he said; it was the only way to stop him." Rosa wanted to reach out and hold the girl in her arms, the girl who could have been her own daughter, but some instinct told her to wait and keep still. Suu Meh paused for a long time, as if gathering strength, then began again." I was pregnant by him. . . . .At first I hated the child inside me . . . Then, when she was born I loved her." Suu Meh's voice almost disappeared. "She was born dead. . . I think she died because I hated her: perhaps she knew that nobody loved her. But I did love her then. When she was born I loved her, but she was dead."

"Were you alone when you had the baby?" Rosa heard her own voice break into the stillness.

Suu Meh shook her head. "I escaped from the soldiers. They didn't want me because I couldn't carry the baskets any more. The guard kicked me and left me by the path. Then some women in the forest helped me."

"Did you say that the soldier kicked you?" Suu Meh nodded.

"Where did he kick you?"

"Here . . . in my belly." She indicated her lower abdomen.

"Well I think that was what killed your baby. That must have been why she died."

The girl's eyes seemed to look far away.

After a long silence Rosa spoke again.

"Suu Meh . . . losing a child is one of the hardest things in the world but talking about it helps, believe me. I'm here, whenever you need me . . . and I'll listen to you whenever you need me to, I promise."

Suu Meh made no movement but then Rosa saw her eyes light up for the briefest of moments and was quietly contented.

23

Suu Meh wasn't with the children. Katie guessed that she would be in the yard so she went through and found her preparing vegetables for supper. There were garlic, onions, chillies and even some potatoes, while a small pile of greens stood ready for attention. She sat down on the step and silently watched Suu Meh work. A large pot of rice stood to the side of the fire where it received some of the heat, but didn't boil over. A large pan simmered on the coals and Suu Meh put in the chopped onions. She peeled several garlic cloves, and using a heavy pestle and mortar she crushed them and added them to the pot, doing the same with the chillies. She then turned her attention to the greens and potatoes. Katie went over to help her and the two girls worked in companiable silence, washing and peeling and chopping until all was ready to go into the pot.

Suu Meh stood up from her squatting position and dried her hands on the cloth that she had tied round her waist. Katie did the same and then on an impulse, took Suu Meh's hand in hers. Then without knowing why or how, her arms were round her. She felt a gentle shaking, Suu Meh's body seemed to stiffen a little and then she heard the stifled sound of quiet sobbing. The shaking grew stronger, Katie's arms instinctively tightened around her and Suu Meh cried for the first time since she had been in the camps.

The man looked tired and ill. The faded *longyi* that was tied around his waist emphasised how thin he was. His lank, black hair was flecked with grey and he looked worried. Rosa wondered if he perhaps wasn't as old as he looked as he stood at the threshold of the orphanage. By contrast, the child he carried looked well. He said her name was Paw Nee.

"My niece has died," he said, "and there's no one to care for the child. They tell me you look after children in your home." Rosa nodded gently in quiet agreement. "Please can you help us? I cannot manage such a young child." His voice fell to a whisper, as if he didn't want to ask such a thing. Rosa was slow to answer. All her children were older and she had never had to take in a baby like this. She guessed she was not yet walking. Aaron came up behind her. His wide smile brought a response from the infant Paw Nee and she stretched out her hand to the teenage boy. He took the child in his arms and began to talk to her.

"Please," said the old man, "I have nowhere else to go." His words dissolved into a fit of coughing. He rattled and wheezed and spat and held onto the post until he recovered his breath. Rosa motioned him to sit down on one of the benches where some of the children were sitting doing their homework. She wondered what disease the old man was suffering from. He was patently incapable of looking after a lively young child when he had such a bad chest. "I will try to visit her when I can," he went on, but Rosa was looking at Suu Meh who had been helping one of the children with her writing.

The girl had glanced up and caught sight of the baby playing in the arms of Aaron; her gaze fixed on the infant, as she moved across to sit beside the boy. Aaron seemed to understand what was happening, and as Suu Meh's hands went out to take the child he lifted her over to her. The eyes of the infant Paw Nee locked with those of Suu Meh and she rested in her embrace. Rosa and the old man stood transfixed by the intensity of what they could see before them.

At last she broke the silence. "I will take your child," she told him.

If there was one subject that Katie couldn't talk about with Thaw Reh, it was the question of her leaving the camp for whatever reason. Most months since she had arrived in April she had visited the town, about half an hours drive away, and each time Thaw Reh had expressed his unhappiness in some way. She comforted herself with the thought that at least he was open about it, which had pleasantly surprised her after her experience with Declan. He had only imposed his will on her without ever expressing anything much in the form of words.

"I have to buy more materials and Kaw La Htoo wants us to pick up things for the school. I shall only be away for one, or maybe two nights." She hesitated for a few moments as she watched his face cloud over. "I

249

know how you feel about it, Thaw Reh, but I have to go."

"I'm going to get out of here one day. I have to. I don't want to live like this. I think if I can just get away, then I'll forget about all that's happened, and start afresh somewhere else."

Katie had noticed a change in him over the weeks. He had intensified his efforts to improve his English, knowing that therein lay the key to his escape and a new life. He had become less interested in the story of Tess that they had been following so closely and had become more frenetic in his efforts to become more fluent at the language itself. He had practised writing and had, with the help of a dictionary, turned out pieces about his work, his home, his family, almost any subject had sufficed. Then he had pressed them onto Katie and persuaded her to correct them. He had asked her about her life, and had written everything down to get the feel of more of the language, and to try to understand more of a way of life of which he knew virtually nothing.

Sometimes Katie felt nothing but admiration for him. It became clear that such was Thaw Reh's determination that he seemed capable of overcoming almost any difficulty and that, true to what he said, he would one day make a new life for himself away from all the unhappiness that clouded his life. He would forget everything and start again. But there were other times when his intensity disturbed her. She longed for the simplicity of the early days of their friendship and wished she could put the clock back to the times when they had enjoyed the easy company of each other and their books.

She knew what the problem was, of course. The day when Sarah and the others would come to visit again was little more than a month away, and Thaw Reh knew that the time that Katie would have to spend with him now was very limited. He didn't know how carefully Katie was considering whether she should stay for longer, and, indeed had almost come to a decision to extend her time in Camp Tewa for another six months.

But it wasn't just that. At an almost intuitive level Katie was beginning to recognise something all too well from her own experience: a deep, unexpressed, unresolved, grief. Where he had once been so content in his work and his determination to make the best of things, he was now so dissatisfied that he could only talk of wanting to get away. And there was anger too. As she had watched him over recent weeks it had slowly become clear to her that he was being eaten away, in a similar way to that in which she and her father had been consumed by pain, disbelief and yes, anger. Suddenly Katie remembered what Sarah had done for her.

"What about the girl?" the words were out of her mouth before she knew they were there. "What about the girl who . . .? Do you think about her sometimes?"

He turned away from her and once again she almost wished she hadn't said anything. "I don't want to talk about her with you."

"But perhaps you need to. I think it would help you. If you could just picture her, you could try and talk with her. I did that with my mother and it really helped me," she stopped, realising that she was talking too much.

"I used to think about her, Katie, but I don't now. I used to have her picture in my mind. Do you understand what I'm saying?" She nodded. She knew exactly what he meant. "Then Sah Reh, my brother, came and told me that she was pregnant when she died, she wasn't mine anymore, she belonged to someone else. Now when I think of her I feel only hate. How could she do that?" Katie could hear the anger rising in his voice and watched as his hands clenched tight. "She was so beautiful once . . .but she changed."

"But perhaps she . . ." Katie started and then thought better of it. She tried again. "Can you think of her the way she was?"

"I can't even see her in my mind now. I can't remember her face. I wish I could. The only thing I can think of is that she had two tiny scars above her eye . . here," and he pointed with his finger to a spot just above his right eyebrow. "I could only see them when I was close to her. And now that's the only thing I can remember."

When Katie had first visited the camp at the beginning of the year, everything had been much more open and the truck had driven right into the camp. Now she always had to remember that she was in the camp without police knowledge, and therefore had to be very careful whenever she travelled anywhere. However there were plenty of westerners in the town, and there were even some who came to see the *Padaung* women, with their brass-coiled necks, who lived just outside the camp. It was an easy matter for the girls to walk out of the back of the camp; they would then be indistinguishable from the tourists travelling back to town.

On the morning of her departure Katie packed a small rucksack; a change of clothes and some toiletries were all she really needed. She had a list of things to buy for the students. There were shops in the camp, but the range of goods on sale was tiny, so many of them craved the things available in the town. They also cultivated any contacts they might have with people in the outside world so she had a pile of mail that needed to be dealt with.

"Aung Gyi is coming with us, and Kaw La Htoo's son is going to meet us outside the camp and take us to town," she told Thaw Reh as he helped her.

Thaw Reh had spoken with Aung Gyi a few weeks ago. "I think I want to move on," he had said. "I want some money and people tell me there are lots of building-sites in Thailand. I should do all right there."

"But if you stay in the school and get a bit of education, you can get a better job."

"That's what the monk said when I went to talk to him. He said I should get an education first, but I'm bored with school. All the students are very good to me and I love your people, but I've had enough."

"Well, what about coming along and helping me with the boys' football? I could always do with someone else to keep an eye on them all."

And sure enough, Aung Gyi had joined Thaw Reh for a while. The closeness that they had experienced in those lonely days in the jungle after their escape from the Burmese Army camp had never left them. Aung Gyi enjoyed the time that he had spent helping Thaw Reh with the football but he had still resolved to leave.

"You'll always have to be very careful," Thaw Reh had reminded him. "If they arrest you, you could get deported straight back to Burma. Remember you're a deserter."

"Oh, I shall be careful," Aung Gyi had assured him.

So he was still determined to leave them. Thaw Reh felt a twinge of disappointment. Someone else that he had grown to love and care for was leaving.

Katie looked forward to her visit to the town. Although she loved the people in the camp, the students and her close friends in particular, she still found the heavy, damp, heat exhausting. To make things worse the camp was in a narrow valley where the heat seemed to collect and there was no fresh breeze to cool the air. In the last few months she had got used to it, and she worked happily now, whatever the temperature, but to tell the truth, she was looking forward to going to stay in a cheap guesthouse for the night. There would be a proper shower, a fan to move the air a little and real shops; Mae Hong Son was a beautiful little town. And her relationship with Caroline was now on a better footing. It had seemed to Katie as if she had had to pass some sort of initiation test before Caroline would accept her. However, whatever the problem was, it seemed to have melted away with time.

Thaw Reh walked through the camp with them in the early morning before school started. They went down to the main street, along it's length, then, at the far end, they turned off and walked between the houses. After they had passed the last one they reached the river. For an instant Katie could not recognise the place. When she had crossed it in April there had been the tiniest trickle of water in the bed of the stream. In July, when she had left the camp for her visa re-application, there had still only been a fairly shallow flow of water, but now the river was wide and the water was high: the rain had been heavy yesterday. As she looked across to the other side she could see all the paddy fields were full of water, with just the narrowest earth barrier surrounding each one.

Aung Gyi was already beginning to splash through the water. As he reached the centre of the river she could see that the water went as high as mid thigh level. He reached the other side without any problem so Caroline, Katie and Thaw Reh followed him, confident that they were quite safe. The water had not reached a dangerous level.

Then they began to traverse the paddy fields, which was more difficult than it looked. Each levee was extremely narrow and slippery in places. At one point, to Katie's horror, they came across a mass of red ants. She negotiated them as quickly as she could, splashing through the water rather than risking a fall from the slippery levee. As they approached the road where they were to meet the truck Thaw Reh left them.

He clasped hands with Aung Gyi, "Thank you. You saved our lives. I'll never forget you."

"Nor I you. You've always been good to me, Thaw Reh. Thank you and good bye." Katie waited as they said their goodbyes. Then Thaw Reh was beside her reaching for her hand. "Come back to us Katie." He whispered in her ear.

"Of course. I should be back tomorrow night." She had never known what it was not to be free.

As the truck approached the town even small contrasts were stark and immediately noticeable. A white painted house struck the eye with it's clear clean lines after the muted tones of brown and green which were the only colours Katie had seen for many weeks. A metalled road contrasted sharply with the mud of the camp and, in spite of the rain, seemed clean and bright. The bright colours of the shops were like an assault to the eyes; the only bright colours in the camp were in the woven clothes worn by the refugees on special occasions.

They checked into the small hotel and began to deal with the necessary chores. By the late afternoon they had finished and began to think about how they would spend the evening. The hotel was idyllically situated beside a small lake and a short distance along the shore was a bar where they decided to take their evening meal. As they sat down Katie was pleased to see a musician preparing to entertain them.

"This reminds me of a place we used to go to in England."

"We?"

"Oh, Declan and I; we used to go to Mac's and listen to the live music every Friday evening. That's all well in the past now."

"Ex- boyfriend huh?"

"Yes. Very ex boyfriend." There was a pause.

Caroline watched as Katie's face took on a warm glow. "And now its him."

"Yes. We get on so well, but there's so much I still don't know about him. He's had such a hard time. I guess lots of them have. I don't think I shall ever really understand what he's been through." She looked across the lake as the singer went through some gentle easy listening numbers. "I've been thinking. I'd been planning to go back home when Sarah and the others come in October. But now I've decided to ask if there's funding for me to stay another six months."

"It kinda gets under your skin, this place, doesn't it? . . Or is it just one person in particular?"

"It's both. I've surprised myself. I never thought I could do something like this, but I can and I'm loving it."

"And they like you too. I think it's the art that's really come up trumps. It's done the students so much good."

"If only Declan could see me now!" Katie laughed. "He wouldn't believe it. I was so quiet, such a nonentity. I've changed so much I can hardly believe it myself."

The next day was spent meeting with other aid workers in the town, discussing needs and generally bringing themselves up to date with what was happening in the outside world. In between the heavy showers of rain they helped load up the truck with all the supplies, ready to drive back to the camp. They collected Saw Thay, Kaw La Htoo's son and began the return journey. It had been a good couple of days but Katie was glad to be going. The camp felt like home to her now.

They left the truck at the bend in the road. The driver took the vehicle and its contents on through the checkpoint at the entrance to the camp while the girls and Saw Thay began their walk across the fields.

It had been raining heavily on and off for most of the afternoon. The water was still high in the paddy fields. As they came nearer to the river, the water seemed higher than ever in the fields. Katie was concentrating so hard on keeping her feet on the levees that she didn't see what was happening. It was only when Saw Thay, who was walking in front, stopped suddenly that she noticed anything untoward. They were still a long way from the river but the water was now flowing fast through the fields. She looked up in alarm. In places the brown water was washing over the levees taking away everything in its path.

"The river's broken the banks." Saw Thay shouted back over his shoulder. "The water's too high. We can't cross."

"How deep is it?" Caroline asked.

"Too deep, and dangerous. There's a strong current now. We must go back, and quickly, before we're caught in the flood. Then we'll have to find someone to drive us back to town. But let's get out of here."

24

The rain had been heavy now for the last two days but that didn't worry Suu Meh; she could do much of her work in the shelter of the lean-to. When the rain cleared she used the respite to see to the garden and when it poured she stayed under the roof and talked to Paw Nee while the water collected in the buckets.

Rosa had given her another *sarong* and with it she tied the baby to her back whenever she had work to do. Paw Nee was a healthy baby and getting heavy, but Suu Meh didn't mind the weight. She liked the feel of the child's warm little body against hers, sometimes kicking her, sometimes touching her neck, sometimes trying to talk. Suu Meh often sang to her. Now she remembered some of the songs she used to sing to her niece and nephew.

A woman from a country far away sent parcels to Rosa. There were clothes and gifts for the children. Rosa let her look through the parcels to find dresses and napkins for Paw Nee, and she found small pieces of soap and washed the clothes to perfection. They were hung out to dry in a corner of the kitchen where Suu Meh would try to press out the creases with her fingers so that Paw Nee was the best dressed of all the children in the orphanage.

When it was quiet Suu Meh stood the child on her feet and helped her to walk. She would hold on tight to the walls of the house and walk around it until one day she took her first steps on her own. Then Suu Meh caught her up in her arms and wept tears of joy. As she held her, she thought about the man who had brought Paw Nee to her; perhaps he was an angel too. At night the two lay down together on the mat and Suu Meh wrapped her arm round Paw Nee and kissed her and gazed at her face until both fell into a dreamy sleep.

But she found the rest of the children hard work when the rain was heavy. They were noisy and picked fights with each other. They would find a game to play but it would often end in disagreement. They wanted to run in the yard and climb in the trees, but the heavy rain meant that the ground had turned to thick mud, and play was impossible.

Today was Wednesday. They had had games at the school, which had been cut short by another downpour so they had all come home early. In their disappointment they had scrapped and picked and Suu Meh hadn't know what to do with them. She was relieved when the time for choir practice came round and Rosa took them all along to the church and left her and Paw Nee in peace. She was glad of the quiet and the chance to cook the meal without interruption.

She busied herself around the lean-to. The air was thick with moisture, the humidity possibly heralding even more rain before long. She looked down at the channel that carried the water past the house and thought how high it was. In the weeks since she had been in the orphanage, she had never seen so much water in the ditch and it was brown too, thick with silt from higher up the slope.

Tying Paw Nee to her back she went out to the vegetable garden and picked what she needed for supper, and then bent her head to go under the house to measure out the rice from the large barrel. Even Paw Nee was restless, kicking her legs against her side.

"You want to walk do you?" she laughed. "Well how about you helping me to collect the eggs?"

She untied the infant and let her walk. Holding her hand tightly she led her to all the nesting places that she knew, under the boy's house, at the end of the lean-to, and in the corner by the new dormitory. She showed Paw Nee how to hold the precious eggs in her hands and then put them carefully in a dish. But she was disappointed; the hens were not laying well, they too were unhappy with the wet weather so there were very few eggs to collect today.

She heard a roaring noise as it started to rain again. But this time there was a new note in the sound and instinctively she glanced up to see where it came from. The earth behind the girl's dormitory had been slipping down the hill. It had been checked in its flow by the building but now the pressure had built up so much that the mud was beginning to pour down towards her.

Dropping the dish where she stood she scooped up the child and ran towards the kitchen with the mud already flowing round her ankles and restricting her movement. She reached the back of the house and lifted the child up unto the main level but her feet were already under the mud. She tried to lift them so that she could climb up the steps herself, but the mud was moving too fast. It was bringing debris from the building with it. A stray timber hit her full in the back and knocked the breath out of her. She stumbled and fell helplessly into the mud.

The children worked, but restlessly. They wouldn't settle and a constant stream of irritations harassed Thaw Reh. Pencils broke, books were finished and there were no replacements. The boys forgot how to spell, they found their neighbours too close and elbows had to poke into ribs. Their feet found legs in front of them, which then of course had to be kicked out of the way.

He prayed in desperation that the rain would hold off for long enough for them to have their football lesson this afternoon. He needed to get outside as much as they did, so it was a relief to him that by the time school reassembled in the afternoon there had been no rain for a few hours and the ground was just about dry enough to play on.

He grouped the boys into two circles and they practiced some of their skills. They worked hard and he could see that many of them seemed to really want to please him. Some of them were learning to control the ball very well and when they played against other classes he could see how disciplined they had become. He was secretly very proud of them. After their skills session had finished he organised them into two teams and they started a game.

"Think of your team," he shouted at them. "Trap the ball, control it and then aim ahead of one of your team members." As the play progressed his mind turned to David for a minute. 'I hope you come here again and see the boys play,' he thought. He wanted him to see how well they were doing.

Then the rain came down. The deluge turned the playground into a quagmire almost immediately, and the boys ran for cover in the classroom. School time was almost over, so abandoning play for the day he dismissed the class early, allowing them to stay in the shelter of the classroom until the rain eased off again. As they loitered outside, Pee Reh passed them.

"Hello brother," he called out to Thaw Reh.

"Hello! Look, I'm just walking down with some of these boys and then I thought I'd go down to the shop. Do you want to come down with us and I'll buy a bottle of beer for us to share?"

"Sounds a good idea."

They made their way across the playground and down the slippery path, then descended one of the alleyways that took them into the main street. Water poured down all the channels but it was the channel that ran down from the orphanage that really caught their attention. The brown water swirled and eddied. At one point the current was so strong that it was cutting away the side of the path so that the water became even thicker with debris.

Thaw Reh glanced up the hill and his eyes widened in horror. He saw immediately that something was very wrong; it was as if the whole configuration of the new orphanage building had changed. It took a moment for him to register what had happened. Then his mind cleared and he grabbed two of the boys.

"Oo Reh, Law Reh, I want you to run back to the students' houses. You are to find some of the big boys. I want them to bring some spades and the timber that's standing by the dormitory. Then I want them to go straight to the orphanage. Have you got that?"

"Yes *thra*, spades and timber."

"And some of the big boys from the Post Ten class. Now go straight away. And remember the message."

"Yes *thra.*"

The two boys sped away. Thaw Reh instructed the rest of the boys to go straight home and then he turned to Pee Reh.

"Let's go!"

The two ran up the muddy path as fast as they could. As they neared the orphanage, their feet began to splash through some of the muddy water that was flowing even faster now the rain had begun to fall again. Thaw Reh ran into the front of the building closely followed by Pee Reh. Apart from the sound of rushing water all seemed quiet. There seemed to be nobody there. Then he spotted a tiny infant apparently alone. He gathered her up in his arms while Pee Reh pushed past him and out to the back where he could see mud sliding towards the house. Above the commotion he had heard a small cry and was concerned to find out who or what had made the sound.

As he reached the lean-to he saw Suu Meh slowly being engulfed by mud. Jumping down to ground level he reached down under her shoulders and pulled her head up and out of the mud and debris. He held her tight but could do no more without help; her legs were too tightly bound in the mud.

"Thaw Reh!" he shouted, but Thaw Reh was already out of earshot. He was carrying the child out of the orphanage, in search of Rosa. Not far along the path he saw a woman sheltering in her own house along the path between the orphanage and the church.

"Aunty!" He called out over the sound of the rain, "Aunty, can you help me? Do you know where Rosa is?"

"Rosa is in the church. The children are practising their singing today. All the children are there."

Thaw Reh breathed a sigh of relief. At least the children were all safe. "Please, Aunty, can you take this child for me? Take her to Rosa. I must go back to the orphanage."

"Yes, I'll do that for you."

He turned and stopped for a moment to recover his breath, as the rain washed down his face and through his clothes. Then a thought struck him. 'The child had nobody with her. But Rosa would never leave a child alone. There must have been someone else there.' He quickly retraced his steps. As he came through the front of the orphanage again his ears picked up Pee Reh's frantic cries.

Reaching the back of the house he looked out and was aghast at what he saw. The water and mud washed across the yard. Beyond, a wall of earth and vegetation was crushing the new building from behind. For the time being the building acted as a kind of dam, holding back the worst of the mud from the yard. Pee Reh, already almost waist deep in mud, was holding up what looked like the lifeless body of a woman.

"I can't move her she's stuck. And I can't move my legs either."

"Is she still breathing?"

"Yes, she's all right and I've got a good grip on her."

Thaw Reh began to pull away at the mud with his bare hands. As he did so he glanced at the woman. There was something familiar about her. For just an instant he wondered if he had seen her before. Then the first of the students arrived with a spade.

"Good. Now carefully, we'll start to dig them out. Where's that timber? We need it to stop any more mud coming in here."

He took hold of a loose plank to use as a spade and together the two of them began to move some of the mud away. They worked feverishly, all the time their movements being hampered by the heavy mud that washed between their legs. Within a very short space of time, they were plastered with dirt and Thaw Reh, in what was little short of panic began to fear that they had an impossible task on their hands. He uttered a brief prayer of thanks as at last he saw more students arriving and digging began in earnest. As the timber began to accumulate Thaw Reh turned his attention to trying to protect Pee Reh and the woman from further mudslides.

He took the timbers and piled them between the posts of the lean-to. In the heat of the moment he had forgotten to ask the boys to bring a hammer and nails, but in the event the pressure of the mud was enough to hold the wood in place at least for some time. They worked frantically, rain soaking clothes through and mud streaking faces.

At last they managed to take mud out of the lean-to faster than it was pouring in. Thaw Reh cast anxious glances at the posts of the structure. Would they hold now they had the added pressure of the earth against them? "We must be as quick as we can. These posts aren't too strong," he urged them all on.

One of the students was studying the ground. "I think that if we dig another channel across here," he indicated a line with his spade, "we could divert some of the water down the main channel and away from the house."

"Good idea. Lets make a start on that."

Meanwhile the students had freed the woman and two of them lifted her gently up onto the floor of the house. Pee Reh flexed his arms. They were stiff from holding her for so long. Once she was out of the mud it took only moments for him to work himself free. One of the students took the woman and carried her to safety at the front of the house. He lay her down on the floor and began to try to rouse her. Wiping her face with a corner of his *longyi* he shook her gently by the shoulder. Her face creased into a grimace of pain.

Thaw Reh was so engrossed in digging the new channel and trying to make the yard safe that he hardly noticed that Pee Reh and the woman were both out of the mud. When he at last turned round, Pee Reh was sitting exhausted on the floor of the house. There was no sign of the woman.

"Is she all right now?"

"One of them took her inside."

The student who had taken care of the woman came out to the back of the house again. "She's not well *thra*. I think we should take her to the clinic."

"Yes, you do that." He replied. "And will one of you go along to the church and tell Rosa what's happened? And tell her that one of the women is in the clinic. She can go along and take care of her. How are you Pee Reh?" He tried to wipe the sweat from his face as he spoke but only succeeded in smearing more mud on it.

"I shall recover. I don't know about her though. She must have taken quite a knock when she fell. I found her unconscious."

"Do you want to go and get cleaned up? The rest of us will try and get the rest of the mud out of here. I think we may save this building if we can stop any more mud pouring in."

25

Katie and Caroline spent two more nights in the town. Saw Thay didn't want to risk trying to cross the river again until they could be sure the water was down to its normal level. He guessed it would take a couple of days, assuming that the rain stopped.

He was right. They arranged to hire another truck to take them back and by the time they reached the river it was down to a manageable level and they could cross over into the camp. Katie had enjoyed herself in the town; there had been plenty of westerners there to talk to and compare notes with, but she was glad to be back. She had also phoned her father and was pleased to hear his news.

"Theresa and I are planning to marry," he had told her. She had felt a slight pang of sadness at hearing this. If only her mother hadn't died, they would still be happy together, a real family. But she knew that her father and Theresa were well suited, and she liked Theresa in spite of the shaky start that they had had. "But we won't do anything 'til you're home," he assured her.

"Well, I'm thinking that I might stay here for longer." She had wondered how to break the news to him gently. "I tell you what, Dad. Why don't you think about coming to visit me out here? Sarah can help you, and I can come and meet you at the airport. It'd be great to see you."

She sensed the hesitation at the other end of the line. "Well, we'll have to think about that, but we just might."

"Oh, please, . . I'd love you to come here. I'll write to you with Sarah's address and you can ask her about things." Katie caught a glimpse of what life would be like if she did stay for longer.

The attractions of life in the town soon palled, and she longed to get back to the friends she had made in the camp. To Katie it seemed as if these feelings were a further confirmation that her decision to stay on for another six months, was the right one. So she was relieved that they found the river quite fordable again, although there were obvious signs of the recent flood and the river water was still thick with brown sediment.

As they walked through the camp Katie recognised several people; some of them were the women who had been in her classes and their greetings made her feel as if she belonged here now. Even the privations of life in the camp, the cold showers, the impossible climate, and the monotonous food, were nothing against the acceptance that she felt. This was like coming home.

And then there were her real friends, the people she really looked forward to spending time with, La Meh, Suu Meh, Rosa and of course Thaw Reh. She had brought presents for them all. For the women she had decided on scented soap with some matching body lotion; these were the sorts of thing that all women loved and would never be able to buy in a place such as this. It had been surprisingly hard to buy things for people who have so little. She didn't want to patronise them with expensive gifts and besides, she didn't have much money herself.

For Thaw Reh she had bought a watch and a large box of crayons for his class. She couldn't wait to see his face when she gave him the watch, knowing he would love it.

She had wanted to buy a doll for Paw Nee, "But won't the other girls be jealous if you buy a toy just for her?" Caroline had suggested. And Katie had to agree; none of the children had toys. But she could hardly bear to put the doll back onto the market stall. She had already pictured Paw Nee's face at the sight of the doll and she knew that it would give Suu Meh such pleasure. She had sadly deferred to Caroline.

Katie heard the creak of the wooden steps and looked up to see Thaw Reh already on the veranda. It struck her that she could predict who was coming to the house by the sound that the steps made and, when the visitor was Thaw Reh, she could know his mood before he even reached the top of them. It was interesting because Caroline had assured her that the Karenni people were reticent about saying what they really felt about something. Well, Katie had found, in some cases, that she was able to make a sort of diagnosis just by listening to the creaking of the steps; words were superfluous.

There was the shyness of some of the women she taught that manifested itself as a very quiet, slow sound.

There were the children, from whom she had heard no sound at all at first, since they had been afraid of her, but now there was a noisy clattering as they had decided that there was safety in numbers, so several of them climbed the steps at the same time. La Meh's lightness, and Caroline's steady plod, could all be easily distinguished, as could the sound of Thaw Reh for the last several weeks as grief had sapped his strength and added a sort of heaviness to his tread. But now there was a new sound, or rather the old sound again. Katie could hear immediately that he had regained some his enthusiasm for life that she had first encountered on her arrival in the camp some five months ago.

Before she knew it he took her hand, led her into the house where there would be no prying eyes to watch, and then surrounded her with his arms in an embrace that spoke both of relief and welcome.

"I'm glad to see you again Katie," and he kissed her with a warmth and tenderness that was reminiscent of their time together in camp Duwa.

"It's good to be back. Did you hear what happened to us?"

"They told me about the river. I came to see you twice and when you weren't back I knew why. But did you hear what happened here?"

"No. What?"

And he told her the story of the mudslide and how it had engulfed the new building. "The worst thing for me was that I built that dormitory. I knew at the time that it might cause a problem in the future. We dug away too much of the hillside, you see, but Kaw La Htoo said it had to be there, and so that's what we did. It would have been all right by next year. The trees would have grown back. But this year it was all too fresh and the earth was still too loose."

"What happened to the children? Were they all right?"

"Yes. They were all in the church at the time so they knew nothing about it until we had cleared most of the mud out."

Katie felt the air that she was holding in her chest suddenly release itself as relief washed over her. At least they were all safe, that was all that mattered to her. She knew that Rosa had a wide network of friends and helpers in the camp and they would have all rallied around to help her with the care of the children who had lost their dormitory.

"I'll go and see them all tomorrow. I've got some presents for them anyway. And I've got a present for you," and she delved into her rucksack and pulled out the box that contained the watch.

"Here . ." and she kissed him as she gave it to him then watched as he gently took off the wrapping, scarcely believing that anyone should want to give him a gift. And for a few moments Katie wondered if she had overdone it. Then she saw his eyes widen as he pulled the watch out of its wrappings.

"Katie . . .is this really for me?"

She nodded her head. "And I've decided to stay. As long as Sarah says I can then I'm going to stay for another six months."

He embraced her again, this time with happy abandon. "Katie, Katie. I love you Katie."

The morning dawned clear and bright. The heavy rain of recent days had at last stopped and it had been dry for a whole day. The sound of running water that had formed an incessant backdrop to every other sound had at last quietened, the large patches of mud were shrinking away and the air felt considerably fresher. There was every hope that the monsoon was almost over for the year.

Pee Reh had risen as soon as he heard the snapping of the kindling being gathered for the fire and had gone to sit outside to smoke one of his homespun cigarettes while he waited for the water to boil. As he watched the fire take hold of the twigs and then the larger logs he thought back to the day of the disaster at the orphanage and the woman they had found there. While Thaw Reh and the other students had desperately fought to keep back the terrifying tide of mud that had filled the little yard, he had held onto her, an act that had taken all the strength he could muster. From time to time he had tried to speak to her, with the intention of reassuring her that she was safe and that they would get her out of what would have been an early grave, but she hadn't responded. It was as if her body had shut down temporarily in an attempt to conserve what strength it had, which at that time had seemed to be precious little. It had been a struggle for him to hold her as the mud continually dragged her down, but he also had a clear impression in his mind that she was of a very light build. He had not even been able to see her face, so disfigured was it by the filth that she had fallen into. He had heard Thaw Reh's voice telling one of the students to take her to the clinic, and that they were to tell Rosa about her, and he remembered the relief he had felt that the woman would now be well looked after. Everyone knew Rosa to be one of the most competent women in the camp, and all the sad and lost children that came under her ministrations seemed to flourish in her hands. But he was still curious to know how the woman had fared since then.

Something like depression had descended on everyone who had been involved with the mudslide, but he could feel the clear morning air lifting his spirits, and so as he made his coffee he began to plan the day in his mind. He had classes all morning and then he had promised to help Thaw Reh with his football class in the afternoon now that Aung Gyi had left; but there was still a space in the middle of the day. He decided there and then that he would go and see how the woman was. She had been on his mind since he had first found her and he hoped that she had recovered from her ordeal.

That decision made, he finished his coffee and began to tackle the business of the day. He tidied his corner of the dormitory, rolling up his mat and blanket and hitching up his net so that it was well out of the way. He then made his way back to the yard, took hold of a broom and began to sweep away some of the debris that had been brought in by the storms and that was now dry enough to be cleaned up properly. Meanwhile the students around him roused themselves until it was time to assemble for drill in the school-yard.

After the anthem and flag break classes began, which this morning included Rachel's English conversation. She always found some new way of taxing their abilities to speak the language. It seemed to Pee Reh that they just mastered one of her teaching methods and she introduced another. No doubt it was good for them but it was also very hard work. This was followed by a lecture, one of a series by a visitor from a foreign university, on political theory that lots of the students attended. Coming from a place that offered them almost no political representation they were curious to know how other countries managed their affairs. The teacher allowed them plenty of time to discuss issues and many of the students stayed behind after classes to ask the man questions about things that concerned them.

Pee Reh saw this as his chance to get away and go down to the clinic, so absenting himself as soon as he could, he made his way down into the valley and along to the long wooden building at the bottom. The clinic was manned by nurses and medics who had been taught to diagnose and treat many of the ailments that afflicted the refugees. Apart from some minor recurrences of the malaria that had troubled him when he had been on the run from the Tatmadaw he had never had occasion to visit the clinic and certainly he had never been into the inner recesses of the building where there was an area set aside for inpatients.

All was quiet as he approached. He guessed that the morning session was over and the nurses were at lunch, so he turned away again, not wanting to disturb anyone, when he heard a quiet voice calling to him.

"Do you want to see one of the medics?"

"No . . . no, I wanted to visit someone . . . a patient," he said while hurrying back into the clinic.

"Yes . . .who is it?"

He realised he didn't even know the woman's name. "There was a woman. She was hurt in the mudslide. I helped to rescue her . . .with some of the students."

"You mean Suu Meh."

"Uh . . .yes. Can I see her or . . .?"

"She's gone home. She's gone back to the orphanage. She was well enough to go."

"Ah . . .yes. I can see her there then."

"I think so. Rosa took her yesterday. She's getting better."

"Good . . .Thank you then." And he turned back up the hill again with a lighter step, relieved that the woman was well enough to have left the clinic, but at the same time aware of a vague anxiety that he couldn't quite understand. Perhaps, he thought, I shall feel better when I actually see her face, then I shall know that she really is safe. He quickly covered the ground that led up to the orphanage and hesitated for a moment outside the front when he was startled by a woman's voice.

"Come in *powquoi.* What can I do for you?"

He climbed the few steps and peering into the gloom inside saw Rosa and a younger woman sitting at a table with a small child.

"Er . . . I 've come to see the woman who was hurt in the mudslide. I wanted to see how she is now."

"She's well, this is her sitting here," Rosa said with a laugh in her voice, while the younger woman smiled at him.

"I er . . .it was me that found you. I held onto you while the others dug you out. But . . .er . . but you seemed so ill. I was worried for you . . . I . . .My name's Pee Reh," he added as an afterthought.

"So it was you. I'm sorry I can't shake your hand . . . it hurts me to move."

"No, . . .please don't do anything. I'm so sorry that you're hurt; . . .but I'm glad to see you're getting better. Is this your child?" He bent down as the child returned his smile.

The woman hesitated for a moment. "This is one of the orphans," Rosa broke in, "but Suu Meh looks after her. It's hard work caring for such a young child. Can I get you something . . . tea or water?"

"No, I won't stay. I have to help my friend. He's a teacher and we have a football class. I don't want to be late. I just wanted to know that you're well."

"Thank you for coming Pee Reh," Rosa said, "and please come and visit us again. You can have supper with us . . and come and hear the children sing."

"Yes, thank you, I will do that, but I must go now."

And with that he left the orphanage with a glow of satisfaction that the woman was recovering well but at the same time with a strangely unformed question in his mind. He was so distracted that he almost bumped into

La Meh and Katie in the doorway. Then after stopping to say a few words to La Meh he began his walk along the path towards the playground. It was as his mind drifted over some of the people in his life that the question suddenly crystallised. The woman they had rescued now had a name . . . and he knew what it was, but where had he heard that name before? The train of thought was in motion now and the sight of Katie had started it, because he always associated Katie with Thaw Reh, and it was Thaw Reh who used to speak of . . . But that's impossible. She had died. This must be someone else with the same name.

"Pee Reh, I'm glad you're here . . . what kept you?" Thaw Reh's voice broke into his concentration.

His mind was so full of what he had just been thinking about that he had reached the playground without even noticing.

"I'm going to divide the boys into two groups and I want you to take one of them. We practise out skills before we play a game . . . are you all right? You look just like a *kolah wah.*"

Pee Reh laughed. He was glad Thaw Reh had lightened the moment.

"Don't worry about me. Just tell me what to do and I'll do it."

"Well, I want them to practise passing. No hands. Only knees, feet or heads remember. And I want them to learn to be more accurate."

For the next hour they were busy watching and encouraging the boys, Pee Reh could see why Thaw Reh was so proud of them and it was obvious to him that the boys liked him and wanted to please him. Sometimes he caught a glimpse of the pleasure on his friend's face and then he agonised for him, as he thought about what he should tell him, or whether he should tell him anything at all. Supposing he told him that he had met Suu Meh and it turned out that this was a completely different woman? What would that do to Thaw Reh? But supposing he said nothing and then the two met and she really was the one he had spoken of so tenderly all those months ago in the forest? He was grateful that the children kept him so busy for the next hour, it meant that he had something to distract him from the concern that was suddenly so pressing.

"It's time we got a new ball. This one's getting a bit rough," said Thaw Reh as they left the playground.

"Maybe you could ask one of the visitors when they come in a few weeks time?" Pee Reh suggested vaguely. "Look, can we go for a walk? We haven't talked much for a while."

"But I have to go to see Katie. I'm a bit late already. I'll see you later brother. We can talk then."

"Yes . . .but. . ."

"Later, Pee Reh, I promise. Tonight . . I'll call tonight." For a moment Thaw Reh wanted to stay and spend a few more minutes with his closest friend. He was obviously disturbed about something. Then quickly brushing that thought away he hurried back to the teacher's house to have a quick wash before seeing Katie.

26

Katie decided that it was time she took up sketching again, so having arranged to visit the orphanage with La Meh that afternoon in order to give the gifts she had brought for them, she spent some time assembling her new drawing supplies. It was so simple, no colours or paints were needed, just soft pencils and paper, and when some of the students saw what could be done she was sure that they would produce some decent work. Some of them were very artistic and drawings would complement the posters that were gradually adorning more and more of the walls in the school, the clinic, and now even the orphanage. Perhaps she could cheer up Rosa and the children after the disaster of the mudslide, and produce some pictures for the walls.

As they reached the orphanage they saw Pee Reh, and La Meh spoke to him for a few minutes while Katie went inside. Suu Meh was sitting at one of the tables with Paw Nee on her lap enjoying the quiet of the early afternoon before the children came home from school. Katie sat down opposite her and watched as she opened her gift of simple toiletries. Suu Meh had barely looked at them when she pushed the package across the table towards Katie again. Katie wondered if the girl didn't understand what the gift was for.

"La Meh," she said as she saw her friend approaching. "I don't think Suu Meh knows that this is for her. Please can you tell her it's for her to keep . . .to use for herself and for Paw Nee?"

"Suu Meh thinks she shouldn't have a gift from you," La Meh explained after a minute.

"But I want her to have it. Why does she think that?" Katie was mystified.

"She can't explain to you," came the reply.

"Please tell her that I am giving her the gift because I love her and . . ." Katie found it so hard to explain. She waited and then saw with relief, Suu Meh smile in gratitude. She watched as La Meh sat down beside her and the two fell into a conversation that clearly didn't need any input from her.

Before sitting down with them Katie walked out to the front of the orphanage again and along the path to where she had seen a white flower beginning to bloom. Frangipani is its name in English, Rosa had told her. Picking a few of the small flowers she made her way back into the house and sat down at the table. Dividing the flowers she picked up a tiny bunch and hooked it into Suu Meh's upswept hair. As she did so Suu Meh looked up at her for a moment, her eyes speaking a silent gratitude. There were enough flowers for La Meh's hair too so she did the same for her and the scent of the bruised flowers filled the air. Then she took out her paper and pencils. It occurred to her that what Rosa, she and Monique, had all hoped for was gradually happening. Suu Meh was opening up and as far as she could see, was talking animatedly. Katie had to admit that there were many times when she felt excluded by conversations that were in a language that was still almost completely unknown to her, but on this occasion she was so grateful that Suu Meh was talking to someone at last that it was no problem to her. As she began to draw, the world contracted and nothing else seemed to matter except the little group bathed in a circle of domestic warmth while the rest of the world carried on with its business outside.

As the picture took shape, Katie moved herself along the bench closer to her subjects. She wanted to catch all the features of their faces. She had always thought that La Meh and Suu Meh were very attractive with their high cheekbones and almond eyes and she knew she could never reproduce the full depth of their beauty on a mere piece of paper. Then there was the light of love that shone each time Suu Meh glanced at Paw Nee. The girl was obviously in pain when she moved, everyone could see that, but here in the stillness the pain had melted away.

The conversation floated around her. All her friends were helping her to learn the language and she made some small attempts to understand and speak it on occasions but it was always a great effort requiring considerable concentration. Here and now she was thinking about the sketch so she took little notice of what the girls were saying.

She leant back slightly to assess the effect of the whole drawing and as she did so the sound of Thaw

Reh's name pierced through into her consciousness and immediately she glanced up. In that split second she had imagined that La Meh was telling Suu Meh about him, but no. That had been Suu Meh's voice. Suu Meh was talking about Thaw Reh. In an instant her eyes returned to the picture and she saw that in her faithful reproduction of Suu Meh's face she had drawn two tiny scars just above her right eyebrow. She glanced up again, La Meh's eyes met hers across the table and in that instant of recognition it was as if all the facts slid together in Katie's brain.

"Thaw Reh?" exclaimed La Meh. Katie shifted her glanced between two of them, her drawing temporarily forgotten.

She could understand little of what was being said and in spite of her determination to try to follow the conversation she was soon lost. "Tell me what you're saying, La Meh, please?" she could hear the desperation in her own voice.

"Suu Meh is telling me that she was to be married to someone called Thaw Reh, but she was taken away by the soldiers and she has never seen him since that day.

Katie felt the blood drain from her face and then it was Suu Meh's turn to shift her glance between Katie and La Meh in her bid to understand what was going on. The cosy circle of friends had become covered with a web of confusion and Katie suddenly had a desperate urge to get away. She had to find a place to think. She quickly stood up and for a few moments had to steady herself against the table while she struggled to overcome the cold faint that threatened to overwhelm her. She massaged her hands together quickly to try to warm them, then filling her lungs with air she went outside and almost ran along the pathway towards her own house.

There was a soft tap on the door and she looked up to see La Meh entering.

"Is Suu Meh all right?"

"Yes, but she may be talking about another Thaw Reh. It's quite a common name." La Meh was reading all of Katie's anxiety.

"No she isn't. I know because he told me that she had been pregnant and that the women with her had to leave her, believing that she had died. That fits exactly with her story. She was pregnant, but she didn't die, she survived. The baby died but the KNPP soldiers brought her to us and you know the rest. But the most important thing happened as I was drawing the picture. I drew the two scars on her forehead and Thaw Reh had already told me about them. He pointed here," and she indicated the point above her right eyebrow, "and then I knew. There can't be another Suu Meh with the same scars in the same place, can there?"

La Meh gently nodded her agreement, her face covered with perplexity.

"Does she know about Thaw Reh and me?" Katie asked the question before she really had time to think about what she was saying.

"No. She doesn't. And she doesn't know that he's here either."

"Well, I don't want you to tell her, La Meh. I don't want her to know."

"But Katie. . . ."

"And I don't want him to know she's here."

"Katie . . . we saw Pee Reh there . . . at the orphanage. He saw her, he'll tell him. You can be sure of that."

"Yes, of course . . . but he doesn't know for sure that it's her, does he? Anyway, we don't know if he knew about her at all. Perhaps he won't say anything."

"Katie . . . how can you keep such a thing from him?"

"I have to . . . if I can. He's only just started to feel better again after hearing that she was dead. What will it do to him? And he's . . . he's with me now. I know he loves me."

"Katie . . ."

And Katie heard an edge to La Meh's voice that she had never heard before as her most precious companion turned, climbed back down the steps, and ran through the alleys into the fastness of the camp.

She felt her face grow hot as her stomach churned. Holding her head in her hands she groped her way into her own room and sat for a long time. 'It's not as if I'm only thinking about myself,' she said to herself as she tried to think her way out of the fog and rationalise what was happening. 'What about him? I don't want him to go through anymore. I can't watch that again. He won't cope with it. I know he won't.' She walked around the room adjusting her clothes on their hangers, picking up the small, domestic ephemera that had accumulated during the last 5 months, and moving each piece to another place. 'He'll be here soon,' she thought, glancing at her watch. 'No, it's Wednesday. It's football day. He's always late when he plays football.'

She took some deep breaths, then stumbling out to the wash house she splashed her face with some of the water. As she did so an idea began to form in her mind. 'We could go away. That's what he wants isn't it? He wants to go away. We needn't go far. Just to a place where nobody knows us.'

"Katie. . .Katie. Where are you?"

He was here already. She felt her hands form themselves into fists with the tension. Quickly she shook them and wiped them on her cotton trousers, took some deep breaths and emerged from the wash house to see Thaw Reh coming round the side of the house.

"Thaw Reh. How are you?" she asked breathlessly, still struggling to bring herself under some semblance of control.

"I'm well, Katie. What about you? Are you all right?"

She could see by the very normality of his demeanour that nobody had told him anything. She almost collapsed into his arms with relief. "I'm fine. It's just the heat: it gets to me sometimes. Lets go inside, it's cooler there."

"Katie. What is it? You seem so upset."

"I told you. It's the heat," and walking with him up the steps she took him by the hand and led him across the veranda, up the small step into the sitting area and into her own room. "I'm so glad to see you." And with that she put her arms round his neck and kissed him hungrily on the mouth. In no time at all he had responded to her and as she opened her mouth to him she could feel her lips softening. She suddenly wanted him with an intensity that she had never known before. He moved away from her. "No, Thaw Reh,"

"It's all right. I'm closing the door," he laughed. And as she reached for him again she felt his arms tighten around her.

"Let's go away together," she whispered as they lay together in the stillness.

" Katie, you know I want to . . . but how?"

"I mean it. We could leave here and be together. I want to, Thaw Reh, I want to so much."

"But I thought you wanted to stay here. I thought you were happy."

"And I thought you wanted to leave. Don't you?"

"Yes, Katie," his face turned serious again. "But you know I can't just walk out of here like you. I have to make plans and prepare things properly. It's too dangerous for me if I don't."

"But if you left with me? We could find you some smart trousers . . . you could be a tourist. You could be my husband. If you were with me you'd be safe."

"Katie. What's happened to you suddenly? Why?"

"Why do you ask? Don't you like it?"

"Oh, I like it," and he kissed her again, "but it's so sudden."

"Well I realise that what I really want is to be with you. I don't mind where I am. We could even go to Camp Duwa if you don't want to go too far."

"Katie . . . Katie," he whispered into her ear. "All in good time I promise you. We'll find a way."

And she turned to face him with a look that she knew was full of desperation, but she had no idea what to say to him any more.

27

Thaw Reh rounded the corner of the last of the boarding houses. This was where he always knew he would find Pee Reh and sure enough there he was, sitting hunched over his cigarette. "You're smoking a lot now, Pee Reh. Don't you know it's bad for you?" He tempered his short lecture with a mild laugh.

"I don't smoke much. It helps me to think, that's all. Anyway, what about you? You smoke too."

"But not as many as you. Now I'm busy with my job I never seem to have much time."

"Well, you're late," Pee Reh said after a pause. "And I was worried about you. I can't help it when I'm worried."

"I went to see Katie, that's all. Then I was late for supper. You don't have to worry about me,"

"Sit down, Thaw Reh."

"What is it? What's the problem?"

"Thaw Reh, I have something to tell you. And I don't know how to say it. I don't know what to do."

"Can't you just say it? You have to, now you've made me curious, wondering what it is," he wanted to lighten the atmosphere a little. He could see the lines of tension on Pee Reh's face

"Have a cigarette, Thaw Reh."

"No, I don't want one. I want you to tell me what your problem is."

There was a long pause. "I don't know how."

"You've already said that."

"Thaw Reh . . . Do you remember . . .you once told me that you loved a girl called Suu Meh . . . and your brother came to tell you that she had died?" Thaw Reh said nothing. "The woman we dug out of the mud."

"Yes?"

"Her name is Suu Meh."

Thaw Reh was very still. It was as if he had forgotten to breathe. "What is she like, this Suu Meh?"

"She's the same age as us. Very nice. I went to see her today. She has a child with her . . . but it's not her child, it's one of the orphans that Rosa has taken in." Thaw Reh's mouth seemed to dry out. He licked his lips to moisten them. "You could go and see her. Then . . .then . . ."

"No . . .

"But you can't be sure . . ."

"No . . . I don't want to . . . No."

"You see, I can't be sure whether this is the same Suu Meh. Until you go and see her we don't . . ."

But Thaw Reh had already walked away and was staring into the thick darkness at the edge of the camp. The sound of the cicadas, a constant backdrop to every other sound and therefore normally hardly noticed, seemed now to be clearly defined; now it was as if Pee Reh heard them for the first time. He stayed still and quiet, watching his friend who now stood within sight a few yards away at the edge of the trees. A long time passed. Pee Reh knew instinctively that his purpose for that moment was to maintain a silent vigil over Thaw Reh for as long as was necessary. He didn't have to do anything else for him, just watch.

The lights went out and then all that could be seen were the candles that had been lit by those who were still up and about. Pee Reh lost sight of Thaw Reh but he knew he was still there. At last after everything but the cicadas had fallen silent Thaw Reh came back to his friend's side.

"She's still dead for me Pee Reh. I don't need to go and see her."

"But . . ."

"She's dead, Pee Reh. She died months ago." And he walked away into the darkness towards his own bed.

Pee Reh couldn't let the matter rest, even as he readied himself for sleep and lay down. He tried to think of something else and would begin to doze then he would find the woman entering his thoughts once more. This Suu Meh, whoever she was, had somehow touched him with her good and gentle nature and he couldn't bear to think that she should be the victim of any wrongdoing.

Sleep overtook him at last, until suddenly, from the deep recesses of his mind, a new thought came into his consciousness and he woke with a start. Thaw Reh had regularly gone to visit a woman who had been the mother of his Suu Meh; he had said her name was Maw Meh. If he could find this woman and bring her to the orphanage then at least he would have the answer to one of his questions. If the woman at Rosa's couldn't be identified by anyone else she would be by her own mother, there was no doubt of that. At last he was able to find some rest for what was left of the night.

As he sat over his morning coffee he began to put together a plan. The person he would see first was old *Phu Kwe Htoo*, the grandfather who had been elected commandant of the camp. Once he had been a general in the KNPP, now he devoted his time to managing the civilian affairs of the refugees. He was a heavy, irascible-looking man who did much to try to sustain a good relationship with the local Thai Border Police, a duty to which he gave more time and energy than most of the people ever realised. In spite of his gruff exterior he was known to care deeply for his people and was always willing to help everyone who needed him. One of the duties he took on was that of helping families to become reunited with those who had become lost in the recent fighting. So it was for this reason that Pee Reh determined to visit him. If he hurried he could even get there before morning parade.

"Yes, *powquoi*." The old man came to the front of his house, his heavy face set into a frown.

"*Thra,*" Pee Reh began, "I want to find someone."

"Yes?"

"Her name is Maw Meh. I want to know where she lives."

"And why do you want to know that?"

"Uh. . ."

"Speak up, *powquoi"*

"*Thra*, there is a young woman in the orphanage. Her Name is Suu Meh. I think she may be the daughter of Maw Meh. But I cannot be sure. I want them to meet." Pee Reh explained but Kwe Htoo had already disappeared in order to look for one of the many people that shared his house with him. A young man of about Pee Reh's age appeared with sheets of well worn paper covered with lists of names and began to search through them for the relevant ones. One of the reasons for Phu Kwe Htoo's sometimes-bad temper was his inability to read due to deteriorating sight.

"No Suu Meh *thra.* She isn't here," the young man announced after a search that lasted several minutes.

"But you don't understand. I know where Suu Meh is. I want to find her mother, Maw Meh. Then I can bring the two together." Pee Reh was beginning to feel exasperated.

"Maw Meh. Find Maw Meh," the old man barked, and the young man began his search through the old sheets again.

"Here, *thra.* There's a Maw Meh living with the *Bwe* in section 3," the young man pointed out somewhat nervously.

"Well, now you take him. You take him to see the woman," Kwe Htoo commanded with such a loud voice that Pee Reh wondered if the old man was also going deaf. Meanwhile the nervous young man put the papers away again in the back room and returned to Pee

Reh's side, seeming grateful for the opportunity of escaping for a short while.

He led Pee Reh out of the commandant's house and the two set off across the camp to the place where Maw Meh lived. This was strange territory to Pee Reh. In the several months since he had lived in the camp he had very rarely crossed to this side. Still, the young man seemed confident that he knew the way and it was only as he reached section three that he had to ask directions of the people that he found hanging about with nothing much to do. In the event it was a simple matter to find the house that Maw Meh lived in. They reached the front and were directed round the back where they found her bent over the fire. It was only at that point that Pee Reh began to wonder how he was going to tell the woman.

Approaching gently, for he didn't want to alarm her, he spoke softly to her. "Maw Meh . . . Aunty." She looked up from her work.

"Yes?" her weary eyes rested on the two visitors. The young man began to talk before Pee Reh had the chance to compose himself.

"Aunty, I am from the commandants office and we have news for . . . "

"There's a woman in the orphanage that they call Suu Meh," Pee Reh interrupted him. "We want you to come to see her. She may be . . ." The woman's face dissolved in a flood of emotion.

"Our brother here isn't sure," the young man tried again. "That's why we need you to come and see her. You can come with us. We will take you there."

But the woman needed no further prompting; already her face was flushed with anxiety as she hurriedly explained where she was going to one of her relatives. Then she followed the two young men along the path, stumbling with the haste of one being drawn with the cord that forever binds a parent to their child, especially if they have been in any sort of danger.

Suu Meh was her youngest child, borne of her middle years when Ku Shwe's health was already deteriorating, and she held a special place in her mother's affections. She had been the one who had brought light into their lives at a time when light was badly needed. Both parents had doted on her as a little girl and she had rewarded them with a sunny personality that had warmed them when life had seemed cold and hard. Not a day had passed for the last year and a half without Maw Meh thinking about her youngest daughter. She could hardly bear to speculate what might have happened to her all those long months. She had prayed every day but had found it difficult to keep her faith in the face of such hopelessness. Now she was almost afraid to hope.

Pee Reh and the young man glanced at each other as they walked along with the woman, each aware of the unspoken prayers of the other, that somehow this woman would gain some respite from the grief that had almost driven her insane. Once they had crossed the main street it was a short walk up to the orphanage. In her anxious haste the woman seemed not to notice the steepness of the path and they were soon entering the front of the building. To his relief Suu Meh looked up from her work and immediately her face registered its recognition of the older woman. Then she winced as her mother's arms reached round her shoulders, and he turned away from their reunion and made his way home again feeling a hard lump settle in his own chest.

28

Katie woke from a fitful sleep with a vague feeling of depression. For the first time in over five months she felt she no longer understood herself and instead was oppressed by a bewildering sense of uncertainty. It was as if she had nothing to hold onto any more.

Yesterday evening's supper had been a miserable affair. La Meh had been nowhere to be seen, the other girls hadn't seemed that inclined to be with her and she hadn't particularly wanted to talk to Caroline, so having collected her food from the kitchen she had taken it back into the privacy of her own room and eaten there. The brief moments of physical pleasure she had experienced with Thaw Reh now embarrassed her as she reflected on them. She had flung herself at him knowing that he would respond, he hadn't had much choice. It had been the act of someone who was desperate and out of control and she felt shame as she thought about it. What ever must he think of her? Would he ever want to see her again?

She decided that the only way to deal with her own feeling of stupidity was to concentrate hard on what she had to do for the day, and give her all to the people she met in her classes, then perhaps she would get through the day with something intact. She began to gather her things together, hoping La Meh would call, then, deciding that she could wait no longer, went in search of her.

"La Meh," she called as she climbed up the steps, "Are you there?" Katie went right through the house before she found her sitting in the yard at the back. "La Meh," she smiled." I'm going to the classroom. Are you coming?"

The girl seemed unsure of what to say.

"I need you La Meh. I can't do the class without you. I can't explain things and they won't understand me."

"All right Katie, I'll come." Katie heard the unsaid 'but' at the end of her words and knew instinctively that La Meh's only motivation for accompanying her that day was her strong sense of duty and her desire to see the students learn.

By the afternoon her head was aching. She felt as if a heavy weight was pressing down on a point somewhere between her shoulders and her neck felt stiff with tension. It was as if a thick wall had appeared between her and La Meh, so that she wished she hadn't even tried to talk her into working with her for the day. Katie decided that she probably could have managed without her now she had become so used to working with the women.

She dragged herself back to the house alone, all the while longing for cool water to somehow wash away everything that had happened since coming back to the camp. Could it only be three days? It didn't seem possible that such a short time had elapsed, the time was going by so slowly and painfully.

"Katie," his voice startled her. The vague feeling of nausea that often associates itself with a headache was replaced by a rush of excitement; the air crackled with tension.

"What is it, Thaw Reh?" She could hear her voice sounding at a higher note than usual as she walked on and up the steps of the house.

"I want to talk to you, that's all. Are you all right?"

"Yes, of course. I'm just tired . . . and hot," she laughed to try to make light of her inability to get through the day without complaining about the heat, but it was a tight, brittle laugh.

"You sit down then and I'll get a drink for us."

"No, I'll go out and have a wash first." Dropping her papers and bag onto the floor she escaped out to the wash-house where she pulled off her clothes and poured the lukewarm water over her face. As she dried herself with the small towel that had grown permanently grubby after months of mud and dust, she took some deep breaths in an attempt to compose herself. She pulled on the same clothes, cross with herself for not picking up some clean ones before she came out to the wash house, and momentarily cross with Thaw Reh for taking her by surprise so that she had no time to get ready at her leisure.

"I've been thinking about what you were saying yesterday," he said as he poured some boiled water out of a battered metal jug.

"Yesterday?"

"Yes, Katie. We could get away from here. Go somewhere else." She could hear the agitation in his voice.

"But, I thought . . ."

"Katie, there is a way, but I need money. I can get a card if I have money. I can become a Thai citizen, then I can get out of here."

"How much does this cost?"

"I don't know exactly, Katie. Perhaps thirty thousand baht . . .perhaps sixty thousand."

Katie made a quick calculation in her head. He was talking of between five hundred and a thousand pounds. "But how can you find that amount of money?"

"You must have money, Katie."

"I have a little . . . but not that much."

"You must have. All westerners have money. Don't you have a bank account?"

Katie gulped, alarmed at the turn of events. "I do, but I don't have much in it. And I need that to last me until I get home."

"Can't you ask your father? Couldn't he give you some?"

"Thaw Reh?" Suddenly she wanted to cry.

"I want to get away from here, Katie. I though you felt the same." The agitation was quickly turning to anger.

"I did, but . . . I don't know. I don't know." She fought to hold back tears that she could feel beginning to form themselves.

"What's happened, Thaw Reh? Why do you want. . .?"

Then, in an instant her mind cleared. "You've heard haven't you? You've seen her."

His glance shifted quickly away from her, over the side of the veranda to the other houses crowded into the valley. She watched intently as he turned back to her. "Yes, Pee Reh told me. But I haven't seen her. I'm not even sure it's her. But I think . . . "

"It's her, Thaw Reh, I've seen her. She has scars here," and she pointed to the place over her eyebrow. "She survived; she didn't die. She's alive. She's been in the camp for over two months now. That's why you want to go isn't it?"

The mounting anger had suddenly dispelled and he sat slumped against the wall, the shock freezing his face into a mask. She couldn't think what to say. It was as if there were no words in the whole world to fit such an occasion.

"Don't you want to see her?" she ventured after what seemed an endless silence.

Then he woke from his stupor. "No Katie. I can't . . .I can't." His voice disappeared and Katie realised that he was crying, or was closer to it than any man she had ever seen.

"So that's why you want to go away," Katie broke the silence at last.

And then there were no more words to be said. Thaw Reh dragged himself to his feet. "I'm sorry, Katie," he said as she watched him stumble back down the steps, her own thoughts in complete turmoil.

She refused supper; there was no possibility of even putting the most attractively presented food into her mouth, let alone the unpalatable rice that was the usual daily fare in the camp. Already the smell of cooking, mingled with the scent of wood smoke had drifted into the house and was sharpening her vague queasiness into an acute nausea. She shut herself inside her room, then immediately wished she hadn't, realising that meeting up with some of the other girls would have distracted her and somehow eased her mind. After a few minutes she came out of the room to escape from her own company and immediately Caroline began fussing around her.

"Why aren't you eating? You've lost enough weight as it is, you can't afford to lose any more."

That was true, the small amount of padding that Katie had wanted to shed last year had completely disappeared and her clothes were hanging more loosely around her than she had ever remembered. "I can't today. My stomach's not too good . . . and my head aches."

"Perhaps we ought to get you tested for malaria. It's around at the moment, and some are coming out positive for *falciparum*. That's very dangerous. Some of the kids have had it."

"No. I'm so careful. I always sleep inside my net."

"Well it wouldn't do you any harm to have a test."

"Leave it, Caroline. It's just the heat. And I've got things on my mind." She could hear herself snapping.

"What sort of things? Anything I can help with?"

Katie found Caroline was kind enough, but her efforts were clumsy after the gentle, yet penetrating accuracy of Sarah. Sarah. She was coming back in less than three weeks. What would she make of the confusion that seemed to have permeated every pore of her being. Would she have an answer? Suddenly Katie longed for her friends . . . and her father . . . and Theresa. Thoughts of home seemed sweet beyond words.

"You wouldn't understand," she said impatiently. It seemed a cruel thing to say but she was beyond trying to be nice to Caroline.

"Try me." Caroline was clearly unfazed by the remark.

"I have to go back to town. There's something I have to deal with."

"Back to town? But you've only just been there."

"I need some more money. That's all."

"More money? What do you need more money for?"

"Look, it's a personal matter. I can't discuss it at the moment."

"It's for Thaw Reh, isn't it? Be careful, Katie."

"It's none of your business, so leave me alone," she could hear her voice rising to a shout but could no longer control it. "Go and have your supper . . . get out and leave me alone," and with those last words she slammed the flimsy door of her room and flung herself onto her sleeping bag.

Katie lay for a long time shaking with anger, frustration and disappointment, too angry to cry. She clenched her fists into tight balls and banged them into her pillow until she collapsed exhausted with tension. Everything had gone so wrong. The irritation she had often felt around the plodding Caroline had almost turned into hate. Kind, loyal La Meh was pointedly maintaining a distance between the two of them and Suu Meh . . . in spite of the difficulties with language they had become friends. But that could no longer be, since circumstances had ripped them apart.

Then there was poor Thaw Reh, tormented by what had happened to Suu Meh. As her thoughts turned back to him, which they inevitably did every few minutes, hot, painful tears began to flow which seemed to dissipate some of the tension, for which she was grateful. Rosa. She would go and talk to Rosa. Of all the people in the camp she had almost the best English and Katie found her to be an easy going and understanding woman, used to dealing with all the waifs and strays that came her way. Thoughts of Rosa made her feel better and by degrees Katie began to regain control over her wild emotions.

She sat up and rubbed her face with her hand then began to burrow into her bag for the wipes she had bought from one of the shops in the town. She would do the job properly and pull herself together. It was as she was looking into her mirror that a new thought struck her. Rosa was a very good woman, she had something about her that Katie had seen in lots of people in the camp, a sort of selflessness, an inner strength borne out of pure motives and what Katie could only describe as love, but real love, not the sort that grasps things to itself but the kind that gives generously and freely.

She stopped short. So what would Rosa think of her? She squirmed inwardly as she thought of her sordid efforts to keep Thaw Reh for herself and prevent Suu Meh from knowing that he was so close to her and she knew that it would not be possible to confide in her either.

And Sarah too. Sarah would ask for honesty. No, she would demand it. There would be no gentle sympathy while she was practising such deception. Sarah would have no truck with anyone who wanted to run away and hide from problems. They had to be faced fairly and squarely and dealt with. Any illusion that she might have been nursing about Sarah's ability to help her to find the answer to the way she was feeling instantly melted away with the harsh realisation of her own utter loneliness.

There was one other person she could talk to.

She sat down on the floor and tried to breath slowly and deeply. She wanted to be ready for him, so she closed her eyes and imagined the easel into existence. Her mother was there but she could only see her back; today of all days she needed to see her mother; she wanted to talk to her, but try as she might she couldn't get far enough round to see her face. At every point she could see nothing more than the side of her head. Katie felt the pain of deep disappointment but had to go on regardless. She imagined herself into the picture and hurried towards the house. She wanted to go inside this time; she knew she would be safe and secure there. As she came close she looked expectantly at the old man but as she did so she knew she would again be disappointed. The hoped-for smile of welcome had been replaced by an expression that confused her at first. She stood for some time and realised that in fact he did want to invite her in but it was she, Katie, who was holding back. She knew she couldn't go in because of what she was doing and that hurt the old man because he wanted her, he wanted to love her as his own. At that moment he wanted to be her mother and her father and everything she ever needed but he couldn't because of the shame that stood between them. And then for just a moment the old mans face looked a little like Suu Meh's. Katie tried to move forward but still she couldn't; then she caught a small glimpse of how it must feel to be lost and unloved.

Now she wept. She started to cry tears of real sorrow for her own selfishness. She reached across to pull her own sketch out of her bag to look at it once again through her tears. She realised that she loved Suu Meh; she had helped to save her life, had nursed her back to health and had watched her slowly recover from her ordeal, mentally as well as physically. If she was to continue to recover she had to at least have the opportunity to be reunited with Thaw Reh. And at that moment Katie came to the painful realisation that that would be unlikely as long as she stood between them. If only she could get out of the way, then they would at least have a chance. It was true, that in spite of the love that had grown between her and Thaw Reh, she knew she could live without him, however painful it might be at first. She had a home, a family and friends to help her. But Suu Meh had nothing, and nobody to call her own except little Paw Nee and for her Thaw Reh would be everything.

She looked for the old man again, "Help me . . .please help me," she heard the desperation in her own voice and she knew he would answer her.

Then she was back on her own sleeping bag, surrounded by four bamboo walls, the soft, warm, darkness enfolding her and she knew she could do it. She could stand back and allow events to take their course, with honesty. There would be no running away and no hiding.

29

Katie slept soundly and woke early. There was no doubt in her mind what she had to do and she knew that now was the time to start. The fire was already alight and the water had boiled, so taking one of the tea bags that she had bought in the town she made her way to the kitchen and brewed up. There was no such thing as milk in the camp except the canned, sweetened variety, but still, a real cup of tea felt like a luxury after several weeks of concoctions very kindly served by the students, but still of indeterminate origin.

Wrapping her hands round the mug, she walked carefully across to where La Meh lived and quietly asked after her. Before she had spoken a few words, La Meh appeared at the top of the steps. "Can we talk La Meh?" Katie could hear the quiet determination in her own voice.

"Yes, Katie, sit down here," a look of perplexity passed briefly across La Meh's face. "What is it?"

"I want to say sorry . . .to you . . . and I have to talk to Suu Meh. I want to tell her about Thaw Reh. I'm not going to stand between them any more. I want them to meet again. Do you understand me, La Meh? She needs him. She needs him so much and . . . I need you to help me."

"Katie, . . .you're right, I know you are but . . ."

"But . .but what?"

"She's ashamed, Katie, she's ashamed of . . ."

"But why should she be ashamed? She couldn't help what happened. And anyway, hasn't she suffered enough?"

"I think she has Katie, but there's a problem." Katie could see La Meh struggling to explain.

"How do you mean, a problem?"

"It's this. Some of the Burmese soldiers take Karenni women and make them stay with them. They want them to have children and then those children will be Burmese. They want to stop us being Karenni, so they make us become Burmese."

Katie stared at La Meh in disbelief. "So did this happen to Suu Meh?"

"Yes. He didn't really marry her, but I think he thought of her as his wife. And he made her think that way too, even though she hated him."

"How do you know this?"

"Rosa told me. It happens Katie . . . it happens," said La Meh in answer to the baffled expression she could see on Katie's face.

"And does that mean she believes that no other man will ever want her?"

"I think perhaps she does."

"So what ever we say to her may make no difference."

"I don't know. But I still think we should tell her about Thaw Reh."

"I want to tell her now, La Meh. I must tell her. I feel so sorry that I didn't tell her two days ago, but I was so shocked, I didn't know what to do. Now I can see things more clearly."

"What about you . . .and . .?"

"La Meh, I've been thinking . . I like him a lot . . . But, I won't take a man from another woman. Someone once did that to me, and I promised myself I would never do it to anyone. And I could never be happy with him knowing I had kept the truth from him. Anyway, he knows about her now."

"He knows?"

"Yes, Pee Reh told him. Do you remember? We saw Pee Reh at the orphanage when we went to visit and I drew the picture. He told Thaw Reh, of course he did. They are the best of friends."

"Katie. There's just one problem. What if he doesn't want to see her? What would happen if we told her about him and then he doesn't want to see her?"

Yesterday's horrid scene with Thaw Reh came flooding back into Katie's mind. "He told me yesterday that he didn't want to see her . . . but I think he's in shock. It's so difficult to understand him. I think he's still angry . . . deep down he's so angry. He's angry because his father was killed, he's angry about Suu Meh, he's angry because he's a refugee. The more I think about it, the more I realise that I would have found that very difficult to live with, because I would never really have understood. But she'll understand. And I still think we should tell her. How can we keep the truth from her now?"

"All right Katie. We'll go together and talk to her. When?"

313

"Can we go now? We can see her before school."

La Meh nodded her assent, "Katie, I think you're doing the right thing." And Katie felt the warmth of the old man's smile.

Katie had been pleased with her day's work. Her classes had distracted her, as they always did, and she felt better, freer somehow, now the things that had tormented her were out in the open. She still had to speak to Thaw Reh of course, and she guessed that that would be the hardest task of all, but still she felt empowered by her new-found strength and knew that whatever happened she would be able to cope. The time that they had spent with Suu Meh in the early morning had had the effect of clearing the air, if nothing else, and at least she knew now that she was at one with her and Rosa once again. In the end the difficult telling of the story had been taken out of her hands because of the obvious language difficulty and because of what had preceded it. The first revelation of the day had been that Suu Meh had at last been reunited with her mother and, of course, Maw Meh herself had told her daughter about Thaw Reh's presence in the camp. There had remained nothing more to do than to renew their friendship.

With the day's work over, Katie washed and dressed herself carefully. She had decided to visit Thaw Reh herself, she wasn't going to wait in, wondering if he would call. Be proactive, she had heard people say when she had been working in England. Well, that was what she was going to be now. She was going to act and take control of the situation if she possibly could.

Shouldering her bag, she set off along the short path towards the lower school. She reached the playground and walked along the side of it until she reached the alleyway that led to his house. From there it was just a short walk and then she turned into the yard. As she turned the corner towards the front she saw him standing outside the wash-house with his *longyi* tied around his waist, obviously unaware of her presence. His naked chest was wet from his wash and as he rubbed his hair with another *longyi* she saw the sunlight reflected on his lean body. Her stomach lurched and she realised that any sense of her being in control was only an illusion and that this was going to be far from easy. He started towards the house, his head still swathed in the fabric of the *longyi*, so she moved to reach him.

"Thaw Reh . . .Thaw Reh," she called softly and he wheeled round, his face registering his amazement.

"Thaw Reh, I have to speak to you."

"Katie . . ." she felt rather than heard the slight embarrassment in his voice. He obviously hadn't been expecting her to call.

"Come round to the front," he said gently while motioning with his hand for her to walk round to the other side of the building. "We can't talk here. I'll get my clothes and we can go for a walk."

She waited on the veranda, acutely aware that this house that he shared with some of the other teachers was an exclusively male preserve, and was grateful that he soon appeared fully dressed and freshly scrubbed.

They walked together along the alleys that led to the main street and then turned towards the forested hills at one end. Children were playing in the street and he stopped to speak to them. They, in return, called after him, and a brief exchange of laughter followed. Katie caught a glimpse of the man she had come to know and admire so much, at home with his own people, good at his job and loved and respected by everyone he knew.

"Thaw Reh," she began as soon as she knew that they were clear of the houses, "I need to talk to you."

"Yes?" she saw him swallow nervously.

The words that she had been rehearsing for half of the night and for every free moment of the day left her completely. "It's about Suu Meh." It was as if she plunged head first into water with no thought of its depth. "I went to see her again today and . . ."

"Was she the girl you told me about when you were working in Camp Duwa?" She quietly nodded her affirmation. "So you saved her life, you and Baw Gyi?"

"Well, we operated on her to stop the bleeding. She was very ill and . . . .she needs you Thaw Reh. She needs you so much. You must go and see her."

"But what about you, Katie, you and me? What about our plans?"

"That was crazy talk. It would never work. It would be running away . . . and I couldn't do that. It would be dishonest, for one thing. I've been thinking about nothing else for two days and I know I can't. Then when I saw you just now with those children I knew that your place is here. You're happy here. I know you are. You can't leave them . . .and you can't leave Suu Meh.

You'd never be happy if you did that. I know you wouldn't."

They were nearing the top of the path and Katie was beginning to be short of breath. Suddenly Thaw Reh, who was walking ahead of her so that she couldn't see his face, stopped and turned to look at her. "Katie. You don't understand."

"What do you mean, I don't understand?"

She watched as he struggled to put his thoughts into words. "She was with those soldiers. She was with them for a year. She had a child. I can't forget that. Every time I think of her, I think of that."

"But they forced her. It was rape, Thaw Reh. It's a horrible crime. Can't you even try to imagine how terrible it was for her? You can't blame her." Katie watched as his face hardened so that she almost didn't recognise him anymore.

"But for me she's not the same girl. She's not the girl I used to know."

"She can't help that. And she is the same girl. She's good and kind and sweet. What happened to her wasn't her fault."

"She won't be the same for me Katie."

Katie could feel herself almost exploding with indignation. "So you want a girl to be a pure virgin do you? It's just like in the book that we read," she found herself almost spitting the words out at him. "It's the old, old story. Angel Clare could do what he wanted, but the minute Tess tells him what happened to her he hates her for it, even though it wasn't her fault. It's just like that here isn't it?" She could hear her voice rising in disbelief. She paused for a few moments in an attempt to gauge his reaction but was left wondering if she had ever known him. "What about me? At home in England I used to live with a boy until he left me for another girl. You didn't seem to worry about my past."

"But my people, they're ..."

But ignoring his struggles with the language, she impatiently interrupted him. "But you said you loved her. Yet you turn your back on her when she needs you. You don't care at all, do you? You just think it was all her fault" In her rage she could hear her own voice turning into a scream. Then she stopped. Tears of frustration and anger stung her eyes as she wrenched herself away from him and started off down the steep hill.

30

His encounter with Katie had left Thaw Reh hurt and bewildered. In it's early stages his relationship with her had made him feel as if he was venturing into a territory that was completely strange to him. He had been an alien in a country where everything was new, with anxieties at every turn and the ever-present danger of finding himself lost and alone, but the place had been an exciting one, with the thrill of new experiences and wonderful sights and sounds to tempt the senses.

After a time he had relaxed and felt quite at home; the anxieties had slowly melted away and he rejoiced in the good and bountiful land. But now it was as if the sense of being at home had been an illusion and he had been quite right to be anxious. He had always been afraid that Katie would leave him one day, indeed that very fear had only fully left him since her most recent return from the town just a few days ago. Now he saw that he should have nursed that fear and reminded himself of it daily. Instead he had allowed himself to believe the impossible, that a girl like her should want to be with him, a refugee, homeless and stateless, with no money and nothing to offer a woman. As he stared bleakly across the camp he caught sight of the watch that she had bought him, and was reminded that he had not even been able to buy her any sort of present in return for the generous gift that she had given him and the shame of that thought sickened him.

There was only one place he could go, one person he could talk to, who would give him a clear, honest answer. He would go and see Peter. Everyone else seemed to be saying only one thing to him, and that was that he should see Suu Meh again. They all seemed to assume that it would be easy for him, but the truth was that he couldn't: not yet anyway. It wasn't a case of not wanting to although nobody seemed to understand that. But Peter would understand, he would know what to say.

In order to meet with him he had to walk back to his side of the camp, right up the side of the valley beyond the school, and then to climb the hill up to the chapel. He didn't want to meet anyone that he knew, and that would be difficult if he crossed the main street where children played, their parents walked, and the other teachers and students would, no doubt, be milling around the way they always did. Instead, he decided to go right round the outside of the camp. It would mean a longer walk, but he knew somehow that solitude suited him at the moment; it would give him a rare opportunity to think without interruption.

Pee Reh had given him some of his cigarettes, so he offered one to Peter and the two of them sat for a time quietly, knowing that there was no need for words. The catechist was the first to speak.

"I remember when you first came to see me. You were looking for a girl."

"You're right, I was. And I remember what you said to me. You said I should have faith . . . faith and patience . . and hope."

"What's happened since then brother? Things not so good?"

"I don't know what to say."

Peter sat watching. He gave the impression that his whole being at that moment was intent upon Thaw Reh and his unspoken grief.

"I lost hope . . . there was no hope. They told me she was dead."

"Who told you?"

"My brother . . . and he said some women had told him." Thaw Reh outlined the whole painful story to Peter. "And Sah Reh believed that what the women said was true. But now I find that she isn't dead, she's alive and I don't know what to do."

"It's the shock," Peter said into the silence that followed these last words.

"But there's something else. I met an English girl."

"And you fell in love with her?" Thaw Reh briefly nodded his head. "And you want me to tell you what to do? I can't be much help, I know nothing about women," he laughed mildly.

"Everyone seems to want to tell me what to do. Even Katie, the English girl, says I should go and see Suu Meh. But I . . . I just can't, not yet anyway. I don't want to see her."

"Forgive her, Thaw Reh. Before you do any thing else you have to forgive her."

"Is that your favourite word?" Thaw Reh could hear the bitterness in his own voice. "I remember you telling me once before that I had to forgive. You wanted me to forgive the soldiers who killed my father. You make it sound so easy."

"It isn't easy, I know that. But we have to do it. That's why Our Lord made such a point of telling us. It's because he knew we would find it so difficult."

"Impossible you mean.'

"No, not impossible, just very difficult sometimes. But it's essential. We can't move forward without it. And I think you need to forgive Suu Meh in your heart before you see her." He watched while Thaw Reh stared at the ground for what seemed like an age and the remains of his cigarette burnt down. "What about the English girl, this Katie?"

"It's over. She hates me."

"What makes you think that?"

"She was angry with me . . .very angry. She shouted and screamed. I didn't know what to do."

"She made you lose face, did she?"

"Huh. Yes she did."

"What was it all about?"

"She wants me to see Suu Meh too . . . but it was as if she went mad when I said I found it difficult to think about her."

Peter stared at the ground for what seemed like a long time. "Thaw Reh, I've worked with a few westerners now, and I think they do things a little differently from us. I've heard them get angry, sometimes they 'lose their temper,' as they say, then they seem to get over it and go back to the way they were before. It doesn't seem to matter so much to them. It seems that when they're angry it doesn't mean they hate you, although it sounds like it at the time. They are just saying what they feel. I suppose they are being honest. Perhaps we cover up our feelings too much."

"She got so angry because she thinks I don't care about Suu Meh."

"Is that true?"

"No it isn't. She made me realise how much I do care."

"Then perhaps she just wants to give you both a chance. And if that's the case, she is a very good woman and she doesn't hate you at all." Peter watched as Thaw Reh got to his feet, as if he was considering leaving, then turn back to face him. "You're a good man Thaw Reh. I've heard some of the mothers . . . and fathers, talk about you. They think you're the best teacher in the school . . . and the children like you. You've got so much to give to them."

"Yet I feel so bad inside."

"The way you feel isn't everything, you know that. What if you had been married to Suu Meh? Would you have taken her back, or are you one of those men who would turn his wife out of the house because she had been raped by a soldier?"

"I don't think I am. I hope not anyway."

"So what's the problem? Is it this English girl, this Katie?"

Thaw Reh took a deep breath before he spoke. "I'm with Katie now. In my heart I want to be with her, or I did until this afternoon. And it's all because I thought Suu Meh was dead." He stared at the dusty ground while he thought further about what he had just said. "No, that's not true. I was with Katie before I knew Suu Meh was dead. It's me that's wrong. I can't face Suu Meh because of Katie."

"So the first person you need to forgive is yourself."

"Yes," he whispered.

"Forgive, Thaw Reh. Forgive yourself, forgive Suu Meh, and pray for her, pray for her every day."

By the time Thaw Reh reached home it was almost dark and his housemates were all eating. He helped himself to some rice and chilli from the communal kitchen and joined them at the low table that was placed in the middle of the floor, finding their company somewhat restorative after the tensions of the day. When he had finished he took his plate to the water bowl, cleaned it meticulously and placed it in the wooden rack with the others. Then he went back inside to the room where he slept and looked at the untidy pile of clothes that he had left unkempt in the box. He pulled them out one by one, sorted them and put the ones that needed a wash to one side. As he reached further into the box, folding and making things presentable again his hand came across the smooth texture of a book, which he then pulled out. The sight of it caused a choking sensation in his throat as he thought again of his early days with Katie: lazy afternoons of reading and talking that seemed to last for ever, the memory of which now felt infinitely precious. That was how he had got to know her so well, that was how he had come to love her, that was how she had brought so much light into his life. But he hadn't read like that for almost two months now. They had left the story after the wedding of Angel Clare and Tess, the terrible wedding night with such tragic consequences. Tess had confessed her past and Angel had left her alone the next day, she to return to her old life as a farm labourer and he away to some unknown destination.

He left the pile of clothes in the box, spent some time looking for the place where he had left the story and then began to read by the light in the centre of the house that enabled him to just see the writing on the page.

31

"I wonder if he's been to see Suu Meh yet?" Katie asked of La Meh as the two of them had settled down together on the veranda. They had been over the same ground so many times in the last few days that Katie imagined her friend must be thoroughly bored by the subject.

"I don't know. Have you seen him?"

"No. I know he hadn't been to see her by yesterday and I haven't seen him."

"How do you feel about it now, Katie?"

"I thought I was doing the right thing. I said I would stand back and let them meet again. I thought it would all be clear from then on, even though I knew it would be very hard. But now I'm having doubts. He really doesn't seem to want to see her. Perhaps it will never work out for them."

"Maybe it will take a long time."

"Mmm . . . but I just wish I knew what was happening. I'm due to go home soon. Part of me wants to go home and part of me wants to stay for always. I've been so happy here. But there are some sad things too. And I just don't know what to do about Thaw Reh. I wish . . ."

"What is it, Katie?"

"I don't know. Whatever I decide to do, I wish I had done the other thing. At first I wanted him for myself, but I realised that I was being selfish. Then I decided I wouldn't stand in the way of them being reunited, but that doesn't seem to have worked. Now I sometimes find myself wishing we could go away and be together somewhere else. I can't stop myself loving him just like that. It's not so easy. But then I love Suu Meh too. I want her to be happy. It's as if I love both of them."

"Katie?"

"Crazy, isn't it?"

"Crazy?"

"Yes, that means mad, stupid, I'm an idiot. He was almost the best thing that ever happened to me, but if I knew he was going to be happy with her I think I could cope . . but it's not knowing that's so difficult."

"You said almost the best thing that happened to you. What's the best thing?"

"It was coming here in the first place. I wouldn't have changed that for the world. I'm going to come back one day, I know I am." For a moment, both of their thoughts turned to the date that seemed to be accelerating towards them.

"And think what we've done since you came here Katie," La Meh added.

It was true. The women and the students had designed posters and they had both been preparing them for printing so that they could be distributed to other camps. They had put some material into books, with La Meh refining the text. What was being achieved was beyond anything either of them had ever dreamt about.

"La Meh, there's something I've never told you about. It's something you said to me that I've never forgotten."

"What's that?"

"You said you would pray for me."

"Yes, Katie. "My Aunty taught me to pray, and I always do, every day. I didn't know you found my prayers helped you."

"I think they did. And I need you to pray for me now too. "

Kaw La Htoo came to sit in on one of her classes as he sometimes did. He congratulated her as always. "You are teaching them to think. That's what they need. When they were younger they always learnt only what the teacher taught them. Your lessons are different. And once the posters and books are printed they will be so pleased with what they've achieved."

Katie swelled with pride. It was true, she could see how they were progressing and she could go home satisfied that she had done a good job. Did he know what was happening between her and Thaw Reh, she wondered? Did it matter to him? She had the impression that not much happened in the school without his knowledge so she decided she should assume that he probably knew.

"I have a letter from Sarah here. She tells me she is arriving next week. The local police are letting us travel at the moment, so I will go and meet them at the airport. Do you want to come with me?" Kaw La Htoo asked her knowing what the answer would be.

"Yes, of course. I'm so looking forward to seeing them again."

For the last couple of weeks she had been counting the days until Sarah and the others arrived. She had received a letter telling her that Sarah was bringing someone else, but there was no clue as to who this was in the letter. Katie had been intrigued, so much so, that she could hardly wait until the day came. Some of the visitors were planning to stay in Tewa, while others would visits other camps for the next three weeks until they all went home together.

She needed the certainties that Sarah's presence would impose upon her. As far as her work was concerned she was enormously fulfilled and almost everything that she had done was leading towards a happy conclusion. But, as far as her dealings with Thaw Reh were concerned, she realised that she was reaching the point of exhaustion and she almost buried herself in her work, as this seemed to be the best way of handling the situation. And she was grateful that the weather was slowly becoming cooler and drier again so that the physical business of getting through each day was becoming easier.

32

"Dad!" She heard her voice rise almost to a scream as he rounded the corner of the arrivals lounge of the tiny airport. Then the two of them were lost in an embrace, the like of which Katie had never known from him before.

"I never dreamed it would be you!" She exclaimed as she stepped back to glance around to see who else was in the party, "is Theresa here?"

"No, she couldn't get the time off but I decided to come with Sarah and the others anyway."

Katie saw Sarah and David with a small cluster of people standing around them and with a slight twinge of disappointment realised that none of her friends that had travelled with her last time were in the group. As she did so, Sarah's eyes met hers and quickly traversing the few feet of floor that separated them she found herself in Sarah's arms.

"It's been so good," she whispered in answer to Sarah's unspoken question. "The best thing that's ever happened to me."

"You must tell me all about it."

"There's lots to tell . . . and I have some things to ask you, but they'll keep. Who else is here?" And she began to turn her attention to the rest of the group.

"We'll find a time very soon, Katie." Sarah responded.

"Sometimes I think this the most beautiful place in the world," she was telling her father as she held onto the side of the truck while it slid down the steep road and into the river, "with all these rivers and the forest and the flowers. And there are all the people I've got to know, especially the students and La Meh and the other teachers. I can't wait for you to meet them all." She was both nervous and excited; afraid that her father would be appalled at the simplicity of the life she had been living and at the same time thrilled that she could show him what she had achieved.

"I can see you're happy here," he laughed, "you haven't stopped talking since I arrived." In return she laughed at her own transparency. Never had she known such lightness when talking with her father before. "But I was worried for you. When you said you wanted to stay here I had to come and find out what was going on."

"I did want to. I was so happy that I got carried away. But I'm going to come back with you. I have to be at home for the wedding haven't I?" The truck rattled as it rocked violently from side to side and Katie watched the faces of the newcomers as they looked around them in wonder at the sights of the forest. "There's about another half an hour of this before we get to the camp," she announced to them all with laughter, tinged with a trace of irony, but her father had seen the cloud that passed across his daughters face.

"Mum would have been so proud of you." Since arriving at the camp Philip Britton had changed into his thinnest trousers and shirt and had put on his oldest sandals, as instructed by his daughter. He had been taken to the school and had watched some of the classes at work. From there, he had been taken to one of Katie's classes and had seen the posters they had been making, where he had felt a glow of pride at the sight of what his own daughter had been doing. At last he had protested his own exhaustion, and she had taken him to the house where she had been staying to wait until suppertime. There he had watched as Katie's frenetic activity died down and unpeeled to show the confusion that lay beneath it.

"Proud?"

"All the work you've been doing with these people. Some of it is amazing."

"It's all been done by the students themselves, and by young girls already with babies and young children. Some of them can't even read or write. They've never even been to school, but they can paint pictures. Once they got the idea they were great."

"And that's just what Mum would have been so pleased to see." He stopped for a moment. "What is it Katie? What's happened to you? You seem so happy but . . ."

"There has to be a but does there?"

"Well, I can see it."

She gave a deep sigh. "I hardly know where to start, Dad."

"Have they been kind to you?"

"Yes, very. They're the kindest people in the world."

"What's the problem, then?"

"It's one of the other teachers. He and I . . . well we spent a lot of time together. I gave him English lessons."

"Where is he from?"

"He is one of the refugees," then seeing the look of consternation on her father's face she hastened to reassure him. "He was so good to me. And very intelligent. He teaches a class of younger boys. You'd like him, Dad, I know you would."

"And you wanted to stay here because of him?"

"Yes, I did . . . and because I was happy here. You can see that, can't you?"

"Oh, I can see it, but you're my only child. That's hard to take, Katie."

"It's not going to happen now, anyway. You see there was someone else."

She watched him take a very deep breath. "It's not like that Dad, don't misjudge him. The girl, Suu Meh is her name, had been taken away by the Burmese soldiers, and his brother told him she was dead. Then it got very complicated. I met her in one of the clinics; the Karenni soldiers had brought her in. She was only just alive. It's horrible when you find out what happens to some of the women here. Anyway, I've got to know her quite well, in fact I am very fond of her, and I want them to be reunited for both of their sakes. I've decided I must be prepared to stand aside and give them a chance."

"Katie?"

"It's so hard, Dad. And I don't know what's happening between them, or even if anything is. If I knew I think it would be easier. As it is I feel as if I'm in some sort of limbo, not knowing which way to go."

"Are you still hoping that he might choose you above her?"

"No, I don't think I am. The strange thing is, I want them to be happy. And I don't think I could ever be happy knowing I had taken him away from her."

"So drop him, Katie, that's the best thing."

"I think I have, deep down inside me . . .but I just wish things had been different."

"Regrets?"

"I don't know. I'm a bit sore at the moment."

That evening the school put on a party, as they always did when visitors came to stay. Such was the appetite for contacts with the outside world that all the students and young teachers of the camp hungrily took advantage of the opportunity to meet different people. They had killed one of the young pigs and had made pot after pot of spicy stewed pork. Sarah and David had bought several bags of vegetables from the market in the town and quantities of home brewed rice beer were brought out to help the celebration along. Katie and her father walked along to the largest of the students' dormitories to join the assembled and growing crowd where they were each handed part of a banana leaf, which was to serve as a plate for the occasion.

"All this food?" He exclaimed, as he looked at the array of dishes laid out on the low round tables. Then he whispered to Katie, "I thought they would all be going hungry."

"It's because of the visitors, Dad. They've done all this because of what Sarah's done for the school; and because they want to welcome you. We had a meal for us all when we came last time. They don't eat like this most of the time, I can assure you."

"What is it like most of the time?" he asked while beginning to carefully negotiate his way through the dishes spread out on the tables.

"Rice, rice and more rice, rice for breakfast and rice for supper."

"What, nothing else but rice? Make sure I don't take anything that is likely to set my mouth on fire, won't you?"

"Just be careful of these," she indicated two of the dishes with her hand, "and that's fish paste which can taste a bit nasty if you're not used to it . . . and the chilli of course, watch that. It all depends who you eat with. Some people try to grow their own vegetables and keep chickens. Then you get quite a nice meal. But sometimes there isn't much more than rice . . . and a bit of chilli sauce, and that's for weeks on end."

They looked up from their deliberations and found a place on the floor next to a couple of the visitors from England. It was the first time that Katie had really had the chance to speak to any of them. "This is Jonathan," her father introduced a young man of about Katie's age, "and this is Anna."

"And you're Katie. We've heard all about you," Jonathan was saying, but Katie's attention had already begun to wander. Thaw Reh had come into the room, and suddenly it was as if nobody else was there. She watched him while he went across to speak to some of his friends from the highest classes of the school, then followed him with her eyes while he went to the food tables. With a supreme effort she pulled her eyes back to the group that she was sitting with.

"Jonathan's going to visit some of the other camps with Sarah," her father was saying. "He's a politics student and he wants to study some of the things that are going on here."

"Oh yes?" Katie tried to sound interested.

"I'm starting work on my PhD soon and I'm looking for suitable subject matter. Sarah's my aunt and she suggested there might be something here."

"And Anna's a lawyer."

Katie watched as Thaw Reh left the food table and joined his friends again.

"She thinks there are some human rights abuses that need looking into. Sarah invited her because she thought she might be able to do some good . . . Katie . . . you're not listening."

"Sorry, Dad, sorry . . .I was thinking about something else. It all sounds very interesting . . . what you're doing." She smiled at Anna, as if inviting her to begin again which she did.

"As Sarah's gone on with the projects here she's realised more and more that it's no use just helping the refugees, you have to look at the reasons why they are here in the first place, and then try to do something about it if you possibly can."

"I quite agree," Katie found herself wanting to talk with Anna and Jonathan after all. "Once you come to a place like this it makes you want to ask questions. It has me, anyway. Once, I thought that we just had to give people things, or money, and everything would be all right. It sounds naïve, I know. But I now see that these people have a lot to give us . . . and to teach us. It's not as simple as I once thought. There are a lot of issues to look at."

"And it would be great to hear all about what you've been doing." Anna said encouragingly. "Now tell us what some of these dishes are, will you?"

As they talked, Katie settled down. In all the months in the camp she had never realised how much she missed home, but she found her father's company and that of Jonathan and Anna enormously comforting. Others joined them and some drifted away. The conversation flagged as the visitors began to show obvious signs of exhaustion after their long journey, while Katie sat easily, forgetting her own concerns as she learnt of what had been going on at home.

Suddenly there was a familiar warmth close to her and she turned instinctively to find Thaw Reh at her elbow. "I haven't seen you for ages,"

"I didn't think you wanted to see me."

She felt herself swallowing hard. "It's not that simple."

She saw him take a deep breath. "Katie, I finished the book."

For a moment she couldn't think which book he meant. "You . . ."

"I finished reading Tess of the D'Urbevilles."

"That must have been hard work," she couldn't think what else to say.

"And I went to see Suu Meh . . . "

"Ah . . ." Katie made as if begin another statement of no real consequence and then stopped short.

"It was the book, Katie. It was the book that made me realise what I had to do. I went to the church and spoke to Peter. He said a lot about forgiveness. He said I had to forgive Suu Meh. I didn't think that was necessary at first. But then I read to the end of the book." Katie was speechless with amazement. "Angel Clare wouldn't forgive Tess, that was what was so tragic about the story. He went to see her in the end, but he had left it too late. That made me see what I had to do."

Katie found her voice. "What happened?"

"I didn't go in. Rosa told me that Suu Meh didn't want to see me."

"Will you try again? Perhaps you should write to her. Let her know that you really want to see her."

"Do you think so, Katie?"

"I don't really know, but I don't think you should give up too easily." She turned round to see who was still sitting nearby and as her father caught her eye she saw the understanding on his face.

As they walked back to the house together through the balmy tropical night he brought up the subject again. "That was him, wasn't it?"

"Yes, it was. How did you guess?"

"By the way you looked at him."

"Ah. Am I that obvious?"

He stopped and looked up at the stars. "If we're going to live life to the full, Katie, we have to take risks. That's what I didn't do for a long time. After Mum died I was afraid to step out and do anything. I didn't want to get involved with anything or anybody. I suppose I didn't want to get hurt, or I didn't want to depend on them and then lose them. I thought it would be easier if I kept myself to myself. But I missed out on life because of the way I was." He turned to face her in order to see whether she understood. "What I'm trying to say is, I'm glad you took the risk and got to know him and the others. Think how sterile and miserable you would have been if you hadn't got involved with any of them. I guess you're feeling a bit sore and confused at the moment but you'll come through this, I know you will. And think how rich you'll be then . . with all the things you achieved here, all these friends, the classes and so on."

"So you don't disapprove of him then."

"No, of course not. I'm past worrying about that sort of thing. Theresa's taught me a lot. I just wish I'd done something like this when I was younger."

"It's not too late, Dad. After all, Sarah and David are your age and that hasn't stopped them."

"No . . . and it's not going to stop me either."

"Dad?"

"I'm not really making any promises yet, but lets say I've been learning some important lessons in the last couple of days. Some of them from my own daughter."

33

"It sounds as if it's been a very good six months, Katie"

They had found the time to meet at last. Sarah had been busy. Her work had grown and developed in just a few months. Now there were other camps to visit, more teachers to be sponsored, new buildings to be designed and paid for and more projects needing attention. What she had once considered to be a relaxing break and part of her holiday had now become real work. Several days had passed before they had the chance to find any time, but now Katie was able to tell her story. She went through the whole stay beginning with her experiences in the classrooms, explaining how she had branched out more and more into artwork and painting, and including what had happened between her and Thaw Reh, wading through her current confusion as best she could. "And what upsets me most now is Suu Meh. I can't believe that so much can have happened to one person."

"You first met her in the clinic in Camp Duwa?"

"Yes, that's how I know so much about her. The sad thing is that there are lots of people wanting to help her to feel better, but nobody seems able to get far with her. She talks a little and then clams up."

She stopped for a moment, then looked up at Sarah, "I guess I've broken some rules here."

"What rules are they?"

"I've become too involved, so I can't see clearly."

"And who says you shouldn't get involved?"

"I don't know. That's one of the unwritten rules isn't it?"

"Well, it's not one I necessarily adhere to. It's all very well hearing about people who've suffered all these things. Lots of people do that and then they give a little money to salve their consciences; and that's as far as it goes. The problem comes when you meet just one person who's been imprisoned, or raped, or worked on forced labour, and you begin to see things differently. You begin to hurt for them and you want to shout for justice for them. Then you're involved. I think you're doing the right thing, Katie; however hard it may seem at the moment, you haven't been afraid to get involved and that's very important. I think that's the secret to living life to the full."

"That's what my Dad said. But what about Suu Meh, what can we do for her? I've been looking forward to talking with you about her for weeks now."

"I don't know, Katie, there's no easy answer to that question. I think she needs to talk about her experiences and it sounds as if she has begun to do that."

"Yes, she has, but I thought that perhaps if you talked with her you could help more."

"I think you are making more of my ability than is really the case. Anyway I doubt she would say any more to me than she would to any of her own people, probably less in fact."

"But we can't just do nothing."

"No, we won't do nothing, and I do have one idea. You know that I've brought Anna with me and she's a solicitor who wants to do some work on human rights abuses? We could set it up for Suu Meh to talk with her. Part of the problem is that these women who've been abused have no power to help themselves. If she was to realise that her testimony could be used in the future, then she might feel better about herself. After all, that's what it's all about. She feels worthless and unimportant at the moment."

"Do you mean she could get some sort of justice?"

"Not immediately, but I've been talking with some concerned people in the last few months who are gathering evidence for the future. There are cases that the regime needs to answer, the forced labour for one thing. It is considered to be a crime against humanity. And the targeting of civilians by soldiers is a war crime."

"And it's going on all the time in Karenni State from what we hear."

"Yes, that's right. And it's important that material is gathered now, so that in the event of a possible future war crimes trial, there is sufficient reliable documentary evidence."

"I hadn't realised any of that was possible."

"It's only recently that any of us have. And, of course, for someone like Suu Meh it may be very important. If she can be made to feel that what she has to say really counts and may even help other women in the future, she might start to feel better about herself.

Anyway, it's certainly worth a try. We could ask Anna to talk to her. What do you think?"

"That sounds great. There's only one problem, it would have to be through an interpreter. She doesn't speak any English."

"That's all right. As long as she trusts the interpreter, she should be fine. It will probably take some time, but Anna won't mind. She realises it is a slow business getting these women to talk. Nobody has ever asked them what they think before."

There was a pause in the conversation as Katie assimilated what had been said. Then she spoke again.

"Sarah."

"Yes."

"There's something else I wanted to talk about with you. But it's not that easy to explain."

"Try me."

Katie took a deep breath. "Remember you said I should talk to my mother."

"Well, it was just an idea. I thought it might make you feel better."

"And it did. Mum showed me one of the pictures she was painting. She had never painted a picture like that, and yet every time I close my eyes to think about her, there it is. It's as if she is speaking though it. It's beautiful. It's of a house in a field of wild flowers, especially poppies. I really saw those very clearly. I imagined myself into the picture. I was walking along the path that led to the front door and there I met an old man. I could see past him to the house but I didn't go in. But it was the old man's face that was the most amazing thing. He made me feel that he really cared for me and wanted me . . . he wanted the best for me." Katie paused to gauge a reaction from Sarah but she simply nodded her head as if she wanted her to go on with the story.

"And then," she paused again. "You see I felt he guided me. When I wanted to know what to do I would conjure up the picture again and then I would have the strength, no, the confidence to go on. Then one day when I felt so alone, and in such a mess he made me see how wrong I was. He wanted to welcome me but he couldn't. It seemed to make him sad, almost heartbroken and I realised that I could no longer go to him if I continued with what I was doing. He made me see. It was so clear. There was no doubting what I had to do and I knew I would feel right when I had done it."

"What do you think about it all now, in the cold light of day, so to speak?" Sarah said after a long pause.

"Well, it was real, very real and I know I've done the right thing. I knew it wouldn't be easy, but I couldn't live any other way. It's as if that old man's face is more important to me than almost anything else. I've never had what you might call 'a religious experience', but that's what it was, definitely."

"Yes, I believe it was. I think the spirit of God came to you in picture form. I know some people see pictures in that way and you could be one of them. It's a gift, Katie. God is a God of love and a God of perfection too. He loves us and wants us to be with him, but if we are wilfully doing wrong then he cannot welcome us. I think you are very fortunate to have been shown that so clearly. Hold onto it Katie. Whatever else happens you can hold onto that. It's a very precious thing."

Katie nodded as the tears began to flow.

Eth Yu was a quiet, serious child. Suu Meh had drawn closer to her than she had to all the other children, apart from Paw Nee, of course. All of them would play with Paw Nee but Eth Yu was the one who would sit quietly and sing to her and tell her stories when they were all out in the street.

The child would often talk to Suu Meh and through the childish chatter she found some respite from the terrible feeling of self-loathing that often engulfed her. She found simple acceptance, when she could hardly believe herself worthy of good human company.

"What is it Eth Yu?" she asked as she watched the child listlessly rolling up her bed in the early morning.

"My head hurts . . . and I feel sleepy,"

Suu Meh instinctively put her hand on the child's forehead. It felt warm but not excessively so. She had heard about the malaria that was affecting some of the school children and didn't want to take any chances. "Do you feel bad enough to stay in bed today, Eth Yu?"

"No, I must go to school. *Thra* Jonathan came yesterday and said he wanted us to write a story for him and *thramu* Wah Paw said she will read the best ones to him. I wrote my story and I want him to hear it."

"How will Jonathan understand it if *thramu* reads it out, he is a *kolah wah?*"

"*Thramu* Wah Paw speaks English, I heard her talking to him yesterday." And the sparkle in Eth Yu's eyes was enough to banish all thoughts of headaches and sleepiness for the moment.

"And is *thra* Jonathan coming to school today?"

"Yes . . . and I want him to hear my story."

"What's your story about?"

"It's a secret."

"Will you tell me after school?" Suu Meh smiled as she saw the little girl's face brighten further.

Suu Meh sometimes had to bring herself up short when she realised how much time she spent with Eth Yu. She often caught herself gazing at the girl as she worked intently at her homework and went quietly about her childish business in the orphanage. Many of the girls had been found temporary homes after the damage to their dormitory but Eth Yu had stayed behind and Suu Meh had been glad. When the child brought a book home from school, Suu Meh would spend many minutes looking at it, helping with the homework, Eth Yu believed, but for Suu Meh it was the other way around. She wanted to learn. Having left school soon after she had learnt the rudiments of reading and writing, she was teaching herself through the books that Eth Yu had. But, in spite of her enthusiasm for her story, Eth Yu was far from her usual contented self. Suu Meh was anxious for her as she carefully packed her bag and set off along the dirt path with the other children to the school playground ready for early morning drill.

Thaw Reh watched as David came along the path towards his classroom with a new football under his arm. He momentarily reflected on how simple and satisfying life was when he concentrated on his class and what they could achieve. Now his happiness reached new heights as he anticipated the looks on all the boy's faces when they saw the new ball and got ready to show David how they had improved in the months since he had last been with them. The children were at their lunch break so Thaw Reh ushered his friend inside with him.

"How are you, Thaw Reh?" the older man asked. "I didn't expect to see you teaching your own class when I was here last."

"School's going well. Kaw La Htoo asked me to take a class just after you left last time and I'm enjoying it more than I thought I would. Some other things aren't so simple, though. Have you heard?"

"Mmm . . . yes, a little. Katie told Sarah, and Sarah told me."

Thaw Reh stared bitterly at a colony of highly industrious ants intent on devouring one of the posts at the corner of the classroom. "I'm thinking of going back into the KNPP."

"I thought you said that you regretted ever going into the army . . . and why do that if you're so happy teaching the children? Think what you'd miss if you left them."

"But it sometimes feels as if there's nothing here for me. And if I went into the army I could get back inside again. I still have my mother, my grandmother and two brothers and a sister there. I would more easily see them again if I was with the KNPP."

"This is to do with Katie, is it?"

"If it was just Katie it would be easy to think about. Did she tell Sarah about Suu Meh?"

"I don't know. Who is Suu Meh?"

"The girl I was once to marry. They told me she was dead. Then she came to the camp. Katie met her before I did. I have been to see her but she wouldn't see me. She told the woman Rosa to send me away. Now I don't know what to do. That's why the army seems the best idea for me. Then I could get away from all the problems." Thaw Reh caught David's quizzical expression. "You see she was taken away by soldiers. She had a baby by one of them. They say that when that happens, the women feel so much shame that they won't ever come back to their families."

"What about you? Do you want her back?"

"At first I didn't think I did. I shouldn't have thought that way, I know. But I feel different now. And the strange thing is it was Katie who made me see that I must accept Suu Meh. Katie and the book."

"The book?"

"Yes, the book she gave me. We used to read it together."

"And reading the book made you realise that you should see Suu Meh again?"

"Yes, but what am I to do if she won't see me?"

"You have to keep trying."

"Katie said that, too."

"What about writing to her. You could explain everything in a letter."

"That's what Katie said I should do. And that's what they did in the book too."

"This book . . . it seems to have had quite an influence on you."

"It was how I got to know Katie. It was reading that made my English so much better."

"And what the book said seems to have been pretty important too."

"Let's say I leant some important lessons from it."

David stared at Thaw Reh for a moment then knew it was time to move the conversation on. "Football?"

"Yes . . . we always start with a skills session, the way you taught us. And I think we could do with a bit of help with some of the rules."

34

Suu Meh sat in the house with Paw Nee on her lap. As her cheek rested on the child's silky soft head she could smell the sweet perfume of the soap that Katie had given her. She and Paw Nee had just had their wash and they were enjoying the quiet time before the children came home from school, so breaking the peace for the rest of the day. Together they took one day at a time; the future was something that could not yet be contemplated.

Rosa had come to her one day and asked her to tell her story. At first she had been so afraid of what the older woman would think of her that she had taken hold of Paw Nee's hand and run to the back of the house. But after that she had been unable to look her in the face. Then at last, when she could bear the burden no longer, she had found the courage to tell her some of her experiences at the hands of the Tatmadaw. And she was glad she had done so. She realised how much Rosa cared for her when she listened without turning away, and then spoke calmly and kindly to her.

But it seemed that nothing could erase the memory of the raw terror that she had felt as the two young soldiers had held her down while Thun Oo raped her. Sometimes in the small hours of the night, when she had been woken by a sound, or some discomfort, she would lie in the darkness and the same image of screaming, and pain, and his hated face close to hers, would come back to her.

When she had found out that Thaw Reh was also in the camp a part of her had been glad, especially to know that he was safe too. Before that she had imagined that he had forgotten all about her. But now she was afraid, afraid that he would come close and touch her, good and gentle as he was. He would ask questions, too, and she didn't want him ever to know what had happened to her.

In truth there were things she didn't know. She knew nothing of the young men who had saved her life when the mud had poured into the orphanage almost burying her. She had never been told that one of them had been Thaw Reh. She hadn't known how close to death she had been when Katie and Baw Gyi had operated on her in Camp Duwa. She didn't know how many people cared, and wanted to see her well and happy once again. All she knew was loneliness, fear and shame. How could she have been so wicked as to have tried to kill her own child? What was going to happen to her?

Thaw Reh and David ushered the excited and contented class of boys back towards their classroom in order to dismiss them from their day's schooling. The classrooms were built in a long row of six along one side of the playground and a matching class of girls was situated next door to Thaw Reh's class of boys.

"Goodbye, Thaw Reh, I'm going to meet Sarah now. I'll see you at supper," David called out, turning to leave. As he did so he caught sight of the anxious face of Wah Paw in the doorway of her classroom at just the same moment as Thaw Reh saw the same thing.

"It's Eth Yu," Wah Paw said, her alarm registering itself in the pitch of her voice. Having attracted the attention of the two men she hurried back to the child who was slumped over a desk at the back of the classroom. "She fell asleep. She's always so quiet and good, so I let her stay there. Now I can't wake her."

"And she's burning," Thaw Reh said as he felt the child's forehead. "Eth Yu . . . Eth Yu, wake up," he said quietly, as he shook her by the shoulder. There was no reply, instead he felt some strange, jerky movements under his hand as she lay otherwise motionless across the desk.

"Where does she live, Thaw Reh?" asked David.

"She's one of the orphanage children. I'll take her there myself. Wah Paw, will you dismiss my class for me?"

Saying this he carefully disentangled the child from her school desk, took her in his arms and, picking his way through the throng of children still hanging about the playground, made his way to the orphanage. As he went he called over his shoulder to David who was just considering whether he should involve his wife.

"Go down to the clinic for me, will you, and ask one of the medics to come up to the orphanage? I'll meet him there." Then he continued along the well-trodden path, talking to the child all the way but still receiving no response from her.

The woman sat at the rough-hewn table, her head bent over a young child. He hadn't expected to see her; last time he had called it had been Rosa who had welcomed him and then sent him away. She looked up as his shadow fell across the doorway and her eyes locked with his for a moment. Then a small gasp came from her lips and grasping the infant to her, she hurriedly ushered Thaw Reh to one side and unrolled one of the sleeping mats

"I shouldn't have let her go. She didn't feel well but she wanted to go . . . I shouldn't have let her . . . I . . " she muttered continually while he gently lay Eth Yu down on the mat.

"Suu Meh, get some water . . . and a rag, quickly, she 's burning with fever. Look at her."

She stood for a moment transfixed by the sight of the twitching child and almost paralysed with fright.

"Suu Meh . . water . . . please. Get some water," his voice was rising almost to a shout.

She quickly put the toddler down and ran to the kitchen to find some water; then returning to the child began to bathe her face and body with it. She was so intent on her task that she was quite unaware of Thaw Reh's eyes which moved from it's close scrutiny of her face to a look of concern for the sick child and back again.

"I shouldn't have let her go," she continued to repeat in what had become a sad whimper of distress, which was added to by the equally unhappy Paw Nee, who was now clinging to her as if she understood the anxiety of the one she now knew as her mother.

"Don't be afraid, Suu Meh, please don't be afraid." He tried to reassure her. "You can't always stop a child wanting to do things, you know that. And the medic will be here soon. David went to fetch him."

As he bent close to her, the two scars above her right eyebrow came into focus and in that moment he knew his place was here beside the girl he had once adored and would have given the world for. It had all been so simple then, the pure love of a village boy for a village girl. Now, for him, everything had changed. The door to a new life had opened and then it had shut again, abruptly and without warning. But in that instant there was no doubt in his mind where he belonged.

"Where is she?" the voice of the medic rang through the front of the building.

Thaw Reh leapt to his feet and ran to the doorway. "In here. She's unconscious. . we're trying to bring her temperature down."

"It could be *falciparum* - there've been a few cases recently," and marching on into the house he glanced quickly at the girl, who had become calmer and stiller under the ministrations of Suu Meh.

"Can you wake her?" he asked briskly and taking Suu Meh's distraught face for a negative, continued with his diagnosis.

"It could be Cerebral. I've been dreading a case like this since the outbreak began."

"She had a headache this morning but went to school. She fell asleep on the desk in the classroom and . . ." Thaw Reh put in helpfully.

"Yes, it comes on very quickly especially in a child, and especially a severe form like this." The medic set to work. Having placed a thermometer under Eth Yu's arm he then felt for her pulse and watched the rise and fall of her chest. While he waited for the thermometer to register he took a syringe and needle and some glass slides and tying a strap round the child's upper arm he found a vein and took a sample of blood. This he spread on the slides, carefully secured them in one of the boxes that the visiting doctor had provided, and placed the box in his bag. He talked continually while he worked. "Its almost certainly *falciparum,* but I will need to check. I'll need to put a line in too, don't stop bathing her while I'm doing this, she's still very hot, but I won't put it in the elbow, it doesn't last long there. I'll try the hand instead," and so saying he moved the strap to the lower part of the girls arm and carefully inserted a cannula.

"Where's Rosa?' he asked as he secured the cannula with strapping and a bandage, then not waiting for an answer he continued, "you can't be too careful with these. She'll need some I/V, I'm going to assume it's falciparum, and we haven't got much medicine. I wonder if we should try to get her to hospital in town. We took one of the women last week with a case like this . . . she did OK and she's already back." His verbal flow, which did little more than wash over them as they tended to Eth Yu, was briefly interrupted by the arrival of David, with Sarah and Katie following closely behind. "Oh, hello Sarah," the medic turned round briefly to acknowledge the presence of the westerners by speaking to them in English, then continued with his monologue.

"We need to get her down to the clinic now so that we can get going with the I/V, Chloroquine and Proguanil, and I can check on this," and he patted his bag which contained the blood specimens. "Do you want to carry her?" He nodded briskly to Thaw Reh as he closed up his bag.

Thaw Reh did the medic's bidding and bent down in order to take Eth Yu in his arms again. As he did so, he spoke quietly to Suu Meh. "You come with us . . . please . . you know her better than anyone. When she wakes up you should be there." For a moment it looked as if she was going to say no. "Please Suu Meh . . . we need you," and his steady gaze into her eyes reinforced his plea.

She hesitated briefly, then picking up Paw Nee she looked around for Aaron. "Tell Rosa I've gone to the clinic won't you?" She asked him and made to walk with the rest of the group down the hill.

"And you, sir," said the medic, quickly switching to English and addressing David. "You might be able to help us."

"Of course, what can I do?"

"If we need to take her into the town we will need a car. Last week the police let us borrow theirs. One of the boys can go and talk to them, but if you go too it will help," the medic laughed briefly. "And take the other gentleman with you too. What's his name?"

"Philip."

"Yes, Philip, take him. That'll help even more."

"Katie," said David, turning around to address her, hovering as she was at the back of the small procession, seeming unsure whether to join it or not. "Go and find your Dad, will you? I've got a little job for us both. Ask him to come down to the clinic. Thanks," then turning back to the medic, he spoke to him again. "What do I have to do, will I need to bribe them?"

"No," replied the medic, "when they see you're white they'll say a price. You can beat them down a little, but we must have a car. Take some money with you, but not too much, OK?"

"OK," repeated David, inwardly laughing gently at the medic's tone, but admiring him for his skills and grasp of the situation at the same time. He could imagine such a character running a corporation in London and behaving in exactly the same way.

Thaw Reh reached the main street, crossed it and soon reached the entrance to the clinic. The medic hurried forward and ushered him into one of the side cubicles.

"Heh Reh," he called out in the same efficient tone. "Find Heh Reh will you," he said briskly to one of the nurses as he marched through the clinic, "and I want to start an infusion straight away. Chloroquine with Proguanil to follow."

In almost no time the infusion had been run through the tubing and was beginning to drip into the child's hand through the cannula. The anxiety that had surrounded her had settled into a quiet vigil with Thaw Reh, Suu Meh and Sarah watching intently over her. Meanwhile Heh Reh took David and Philip, with Katie in tow, to negotiate the loan of the car.

Now the child was still, Sarah's concern was growing. "It's her breathing," she said quietly, "it's getting shallower. I've been watching her closely."

The medic took a small pen torch from his pocket, snapped on the light and shone it into each of Eth Yu's eyes, one at a time. "You're right. I think it must be Cerebral Malaria. We need that car. We haven't got enough I/V for one thing. It's been a bad few weeks."

"Have you got an Ambu bag?" asked Sarah, already thinking ahead to the possibility that the child might stop breathing altogether.

"Yes, I have."

"Oxygen?"

"Just one cylinder. It won't last too long. If we have to use it we must be very careful."

Sarah was suddenly afraid at the thought of being isolated with a sick child and having almost nothing with which to treat her. She looked around her at the little group, Suu Meh never taking her eyes away from Eth Yu except to occasionally comfort the younger child that sat quietly on her lap, Thaw Reh looking intently at Suu

Meh for long moments, shifting his gaze to the child only to shift it back again to Suu Meh. Sarah could feel her anxiety rising, and in an attempt to steady her nerves she thought about the young couple, for indeed, she thought, they did look like a couple, and prayed silently for them with all her heart, until her own thoughts returned to the child once again.

Katie hovered around the edge of the vortex that had centred itself on Eth Yu. She had hurried across with Sarah as soon as David had come to find them, thinking she would have something to contribute, but instead she had felt quite useless and surplus to requirements. Then there was the whole collection of emotions that was almost impossible to untangle as she saw both Thaw Reh and Suu Meh bending over the child. There was hurt at the sight of them together, then shame at the unworthiness of such feelings. Of course he would be there, David had already told them that he had brought the child home. Most important of all, he was where he was happiest, with his own people, with one of the children that loved him so much, and he was with Suu Meh. That was what she had wanted wasn't it?

As she looked at the two of them with the child she knew that they belonged together and she was the outsider. The door finally closed and she knew she would have to accept it however hard it was going to be.

When David asked her to go and find her father she was grateful for something to do, and now she had returned with him to the clinic she decided to stay with him and David to try to get the help they so badly needed from the police. It seemed strange to her that for several months she had had to avoid meeting the police that occasionally came into the camp, and now she was openly going to ask them a favour.

In the event there were no problems at all. The policemen, seeing the opportunity of doing something that would break the monotony of guarding refugees, who in the main, could hardly be described as troublesome, were only too pleased to help and volunteered to drive them back to the clinic and then on to the hospital.

Katie settled down in the back of the pick up with her father. "I love you Dad." The words came from nowhere, at one and the same time a small gesture of affection and a cry for help.

"Katie," his arm came round her shoulders.

"That's her. That's the girl he . . I just don't know where to . . . " Her words disappeared in the struggle to keep back the tears.

"And he thought he'd landed on his feet with the best girl in the world."

"Dad," and her tears disappeared in laughter.

"I mean it, Katie, and the best thing you can do now is stand aside."

"I know . . . don't I know it . . . but it isn't coming easy."

"Of course it won't, but you're going to be fine, I know you will."

Outside the clinic the pick up was made ready for the comatose Eth Yu. Blankets were packed into the back to make the journey as comfortable as possible before Thaw Reh picked her up again and lifted her in to the vehicle. Suu Meh joined them, and the medic climbed into the front with the driver. Everyone stood for a moment looking at the three heads bent over the child, Thaw Reh's, Suu Meh's and that of the infant Paw Nee.

Suddenly Katie stepped forward. "I'll go too, they need someone on the back with them."

"No, Katie, no," her father spoke firmly and authoritatively and she quietly returned to his side. "They'll be all right now."

Then Sarah spoke. "I'll go with them," she said and climbed up into the back of the truck before the policeman secured the tail.

Katie's father stepped forward, then reaching for his wallet he took out a number of bank notes and gave them to Sarah. "Make sure they're all right won't you?"

"Thank you, Philip," she smiled her appreciation. Then the engine leapt into life and the truck moved away in a cloud of dust.

35

Once EthYu was successfully installed in the little hospital in the town the medic returned to the camp, taking the fresh supplies that he had bought in the local pharmacy with him. Underneath his bluff exterior he was deeply worried about the possibility of further serious cases and Sarah, instinctively reading the frown that had set itself on his face, had provided money from her funds.

Suu Meh remained by the bedside day and night, only sleeping when exhaustion overcame her. Meanwhile, Sarah and Thaw Reh stayed in one of the safe houses in the town, and took it in turns to keep her company.

It was during the second evening that Suu Meh spread a blanket on the hard floor and lay down beside the already sleeping Paw Nee. Even though Eth Yu was encased in a net Suu Meh was aware of every tiny sound and movement of her frail body and now the child's quiet, shallow breathing had lulled her into such a state of drowsiness that she could no longer help herself; she fell into an exhausted sleep.

She had no idea how long she had been sleeping but she woke just as quickly and lay staring into the darkness for a few moments with the growing awareness that something had changed, perhaps the very sound or

363

movement that had sent her to sleep in the first place. She sat up with a start with the sense that Eth Yu was pulling at her very soul.

In the orphanage Rosa had taught the children to sing together. They were ordinary children and the songs were simple, yet when the harmonies had woven together they had an outstanding beauty about them. They had sung of a father who would one day take them home, and Suu Meh knew in the strangeness of the hospital room, that the father of whom they had sung was with her now. He had come for Eth Yu, and the child was already slipping silently into his arms. With all her heart Suu Meh wanted to go with her. She reached across to the small lifeless body on the bed and clung to it. For just an instant her heart caught a glimpse of him, and then she knew that it didn't matter what she had done, he would come for her one day, but it was not to be today.

For a moment she was overwhelmed by an intense happiness that seemed to fill her whole being. Then everything broke apart. Her mind seemed to slide away as if she had no control over it any more. She tried to think of Thaw Reh, the one who had sat beside her for hours, never speaking, yet somehow giving her the strength to keep going when she had been so afraid for Eth Yu. She had cruelly ignored him but now she wished he were here with her. She knew that if he had been he would have held her together and tried to protect her from the darkness that was engulfing her. She heard the sound of a woman wailing, almost screaming, somewhere far away and a small child began to cry.

Then came arms that encircled her and held her tight and voices that spoke to her in a strange tongue.

The truck that Sarah had hired drove into the camp just after dawn. The family who lived in the safe house had been woken by the messenger from the hospital and had quickly swung into action. Sarah had paid the hospital bill and they had gathered up the little body that had been carefully washed and wrapped and placed it in the back of the truck with Thaw Reh to watch over it. Then she secured Suu Meh and Paw Nee in the front with her. By mid morning the funeral was underway.

The western visitors stood on the fringe of the proceedings, but the outpouring of grief for the motherless child from the orphanage touched all of them. The whole school, all the teachers, the clinic staff, in fact everyone who had ever known the child was there to take part in a ceremony that lasted all day. Then, in the evening the body was carried up to the graveyard on the hill. There she was buried facing the homeland that she would now never see. Suu Meh looked on, and in spite of the pain of her own grief, knew that the child was in a far better place, her real homeland, with the father who loved her and had taken her to himself.

The truck stood waiting as the group began to load up their bags and cases. Katie had more than any of them, the accumulation of nearly seven months of living in the camp. The students and teachers had thrown a goodbye party for her although everything that had happened in the last few days had been tinged with the sadness of Eth Yu's death. Now was the time for those final embraces and promises. She knew now that she had received far more than she had ever given to these people. She had already said goodbye to Suu Meh in the quiet of the kitchen yard where she spent so many of her waking hours and now, as she prepared to climb into the front seat, she saw Rosa was there, most of her students and most important of all La Meh.

"I'm going to carry on with the classes," La Meh said as she embraced Katie, " But please come back to us one day."

And Katie promised that, yes, she would come back, but there was a hint of sadness as she took her seat. The one other person she really wanted to say goodbye to wasn't there. Thaw Reh hadn't been at last night's party, and he hadn't come to say goodbye here either. A painful disappointment settled over her as she sat waiting for the others to say their farewells.

And then a hand appeared on the frame of the open car window. Her heart leapt as he bent his head down to look into where she was sitting. She would be strong. She would say the right thing in spite of the turmoil churning its way through her stomach.

"Don't forget us Katie, please. And come back one day . . . and thank you for everything."

"And thank you, Thaw Reh . . . and love her . . . love her, and look after her. Please."

"Goodbye Katie" The truck started down the rutted road towards home while the combined emotions of all the months she had spent in Tewa welled up inside her and hot tears began to fill her eyes.

Sarah had slipped into the seat beside her, and through her own tears Katie caught the look of sadness on her friend's face; good, kind Sarah, the one who was always so strong. In a sudden flash of insight Katie saw how self-indulgent her own tears were and quickly blinked them away as hard as she could.

"Sarah?" she said, with as much kindness as she could muster.

"I'm sorry, Katie, don't take any notice of me."

"What is it?"

"I'm disappointed about this trip. I had such high hopes of what I was going to get done and I didn't do half of it."

"Because of Eth Yu?"

"Yes."

Katie fought to push her own pain to the back of her consciousness.

"I was there and we couldn't do anything to prevent her death. And I feel so bad about that."

"What was it like in that hospital? Did they have everything they needed?" Katie seized the opportunity to give her attention to something practical.

"Yes. Oh, there was nothing wrong with her care. They know all about malaria in this part of the world and the treatment was good. It's just that I felt so helpless.

She must have had a very severe strain of the disease to die like that."

"I've been reading up about it. Cerebral malaria is always serious, with quite a high death rate. There was nothing anyone could have done."

"And I guess that's how it is in this part of the world. Tragedy like that is unavoidable. But, do you know, I don't think I had ever faced up to it before? It sounds incredible, but in all the times I've been here I've never seen anyone die like that. It put a damper on everything didn't it?"

"I'm not so sure. Perhaps you're feeling bad because you were so closely involved with her. For the rest of us I think it was really moving."

"Do you think so?"

"Yes. My Dad for one. I think Eth Yu's death made him decide to get more involved with what you're doing. I think he wants to see if he can help with fund raising . . . or writing. Perhaps he could do some of that for you?"

"Really? You Brittons do come up and surprise everyone don't you?"

"How do you mean?" Katie laughed.

"Well, I have to confess that of all the people I took on the last trip, you were the one I thought would find it the most difficult, and look at you now. And your Dad, well I didn't know how he'd fit in, and now you tell me he wants to do more."

"And there's Jonathan and Anna. You probably haven't talked to them much recently. Anna is really keen to get going on gathering evidence now, I don't think you'll be able to stop her, and Jonathan can't wait to get back next year and start his research. He's decided on a topic, and he knows where he's going to base his work too. He's been telling us all about it."

"And this has all happened since the funeral?"

"Yes. And since Jon came back from the other camp that he visited."

"I don't think I'd realised. I must be losing touch a bit."

"No you're not. But you can't be everywhere at once. I was just trying to say how everyone was very moved by what happened. It was as if they were all standing on the sidelines a bit until that point, and then after her death I think they really saw that underneath the surface there are a lot of tragic stories."

"And you, what about you?"

"Me? Oh I shall be back. Some day soon, I shall come back. I'm going back home for a few months, maybe a year, then I shall come out and do some more work. I don't think I can ever let it go now."

"So it was a good time after all?"

"Yes, I've had the best seven months of my life."

"And you can say that even after all that's happened with Thaw Reh?" Sarah turned to look at Katie. "I'm sorry, I shouldn't have said that."

"Its all right. Not your fault. I was doing such a great job of thinking about other things then."

"Do you want to talk about it?" Now it was Sarah's turn to fight back the tears.

"Not yet. Its all too raw . . . but the strange thing is, I want him and Suu Meh to be happy too. They deserve that more than anything else in the world."

The truck driver turned on his cassette player and as the sound of children's voices filled the cab Katie caught Sarah's eye and through the tears saw a quiet smile of recognition, which only those who have been there can know.

36

Thaw Reh walked round the house towards the kitchen yard; he had been a regular visitor of late. At last the plans for the reconstruction of the orphanage building were going ahead and the wreckage of the ruined one was being cleared away. He hoped he would meet Suu Meh as she cleared up after the children's supper so he lingered for a few minutes outside. She wasn't in the lean-to and he didn't want to go inside the house, not today. Now they were well into the dry season and the light always faded quickly, but still he could see enough from the strip light that was just visible from inside the house. He was happy to wait for her; he didn't mind how long it took.

"I've heard some of her story," Sarah had told him. "It won't be easy for her . . . or you."

He hadn't known what to say to her.

"Don't be afraid to ask for help will you?"

Then he had wondered what could ever be done to erase the memories that Suu Meh must have locked away inside her mind.

The flimsy back door was thrown open and she appeared carrying dishes. He waited until she had put them down before stepping forward and into the lean-to.

"Suu Meh," he called out to her.

She stopped momentarily and then continued with her tidying up. He came and stood behind her. "Suu Meh," he said more quietly, and gently took hold of one arm. Then when she made no move, he moved closer and took hold of the other one. He was almost afraid to breath, so anxious was he that she would pull away from him. As it was, her body was rigid with tension. When she didn't move he stepped closer and brought his head close to hers. The recent weeks and days had brought about a resurgence of the longing for her that for months had just been a distant memory. Now that longing reached a new height as he waited for some sign that she wanted him as much as he wanted her.

Then he felt it, she let the air out of her lungs and her body softened in response. It was a tiny movement, almost imperceptible, but it was there. And a flood of happiness washed through him.

Seven thousand miles away a new mobile phone rang. A few moments passed before Katie reached for it, she still hadn't become accustomed to the sound. Her father had bought the phone for her. "I'm so fed up with trying to get anyone to answer that bloody phone in the flat," he had joked. But the truth was that the phone signalled for her how much better everything was now. He and Theresa could talk to her when they wanted and there was nothing standing in the way anymore.

"Hello. Katie speaking."

"Hello, it's Richard."

"Richard. It's so good to hear you. Where are you now?"

"Oh, still around. Sarah told me you were home. How was it?"

"Incredible. I had the most amazing time."

"And how do you feel about coming home?"

"Well, it's good to see everyone again, all my friends . . . and Dad . . . and Theresa now. But I'm finding it hard to adjust to this run up to Christmas. Everyone seems to have so much money and there's so much greed. I hate to say it, but it sickens me."

"I quite agree Katie. I know just what you mean."

"It's just that over there nobody had anything, but they still had so much fun and I learnt so much from them all. I shall never be the same again."

There was a few moments pause.

"Katie, there's a half marathon coming up in the spring. I'm going to enter, and I wonder if you would like to train with me. That is, if you aren't too busy."

"I would love to Richard. But isn't it a bit dark in the evenings at the moment?"

"Ah, I've been asking around and I'm told that there's a track in Buckwood Park that's floodlit every Thursday evening. We could train there. And then there are the weekends. How about it?"

"Mmm, I'm a bit out of condition."

"You're not trying to wriggle out of it, are you?"

"Oh no, but you'll just not have to mind if I'm a bit slow at first."

"That's no problem. What about tomorrow night? I could call for you at 7."

"Yes Richard . . . and thanks."

"Thank you. You've just made my day."

'And you've just made mine,' thought Katie as she clicked the 'end' button on the phone.

In February 2001 The International War Crimes Tribunal at The Hague found three Bosnian Serbs guilty of enslaving, torturing and raping Muslim women during the war in Bosnia-Hercegovina, thereby challenging widespread acceptance that the torture of women is an intrinsic part of war. It's the first time the tribunal has judged rape as a crime against humanity although such a crime was recognised by the Rwanda war crimes tribunal in 1998.

(Just Right: The Jubilee Action magazine. Spring 2001)

Notes

Karenni State was never fully part of British Burma. Its own sovereignty was acknowledged in a statement issued in 1875, which declared that it was a separate state with it's own rulers. However, after independence from British Colonial rule in 1948 the state was claimed as part of the new Burma. At that time the right to secede after ten years was promised to the Karenni, but this was never honoured. In common with many of the ethnic minorities of Burma the Karenni have nursed separatist objectives and as a result have been in conflict with the Burmese Military Junta for much of the last fifty years.

'in a strange land' is entirely fictional but I have made every effort to remain faithful to events as they occurred in the years 1997-98. Similarly, all the sufferings of the Karenni people as outlined in the story are well documented by the numerous agencies working in the region.

Karenni names.

The Karenni do not have surnames so people who have similar sounding names are not necessarily related. This is the case with Thaw Reh and Pee Reh. Many males have the suffix –Reh, while females have the suffix –Meh,. The suffix Htoo is also commonly found among the Karen who are a better known tribe occupying neighbouring territory and it's use in the story is indicative of the fact that the tribal groups are not as clearly defined as we may imagine, but are often mixed as a result of migration, intermarrying etc.

People are also known by their position in the family or their age so all old men would be known as 'grandfather' and middle aged women would be known as 'aunty' even to those who are not related to them.

I have found the following texts helpful during the preparation of 'in a strange land'.

Mary Bolster 2005

Burma Ethnic Research Group (BERG) Conflict and Displacement in Karenni: The need for considered responses. Chiang Mai Thailand 2000

Dudley Sandra Displacement and Identity: Karenni Refugees in Thailand
D Phil Thesis Oxford 2000

Burma: Human Rights Year Book Human Rights Documentation Unit (National Coalition Government of the Union of Burma) 1995

Hardy Thomas Tess of the D'Urbevilles. First published 1891

Smith Martin Burma: Insurgency and the Politics of Ethnicity Zed Books London and New York 1999

Glossary

Karen State The Karen are the largest ethnic minority in Burma, with their own state to the south of Kayah State. The Karen and Karenni are related linguistically and culturally.

Kayah State A small part of Eastern Burma. The area is inhabited by the Karenni people who themselves are subdivided into numerous smaller sub groups, including the Padaung, who are known for the gold rings that some of the women traditionally wear round their necks, earning them the name ' long necked people'.
At the time of the independence agreement in 1948, Kayah State was promised political autonomy after ten years. This was never honoured.

KNPP The Karenni National Progressive Party. The largest of the local armies of the Karenni people. There are several other smaller groups operating in the area.

LORC Law and Order Restoration Council. After the student uprisings of 1988, the State Law and Order Restoration Council (SLORC) was set up, in order to impose martial law on the people of Burma. Each district would have it's own LORC. Since 1996, this has changed to the State Peace and Development Council (SPDC).

corvee labour a feudal system in which chiefs and local warlords would extract a certain number of days of unpaid labour from the people living in a village or district.

Dicu and ka thow bow Karenni festivals held each year.

falciparum *plasmodium falciparum*. A particularly virulent strain of malaria

longyi a sarong worn by males

mahout elephant handler, one of the traditional skills of the Karen and Karenni people.

Padaung, Yinbae, Bwe Sub-groups of the Karenni.

Phi (Phi phi) grandmother

poquow son

Salween The major river running north / south through Eastern Burma.

Tatmadaw The Army of the Burmese Military Junta.

thanaka White paste, made out of ground bark, and worn by Burmese women and children on their faces.

Thra, tharamu: teacher or leader

About the Author

Mary Bolster works in the Operating Theatre of a North London Hospital.

in a strange land is her first novel. As well as having recently taken up writing she enjoys gardening and being in the 'great outdoors'.

She first visited the Thai Burma Border in 1993 and since that time has sought to understand the background to the situation there. Currently around 140,000 refugees from Burma live on or close to that border. Mary is a trustee of Karenaid, a small charity that gives some support to them.

For further information and links to other charities active in the area visit the website:

www.karenaid.org.